GENTLE COURAGE

CONNIE JOHNSON

ISBN: 9-781-0724-0085-1

"Cast your burdens on the Lord and

He shall sustain you."

Psalm 55:22

Other books by Connie Johnson

The Tales of Hackett County Series

The Journal

The Letter

The Diary

The Signature

PREFACE

Between the years 1841 and 1869, the largest immigration of this continent opened a path to the Pacific coast of America, known as the "great migration." Among the Oregon, California, Mormon, and Santa Fe trails, an estimated 500,000 people packed their earthly belongings and walked across the nation.

The endurance and faith within the hearts of these people changed the face and the future of America. This is the story of Rebecca Quaid and the Oregon Trail.

CHAPTER ONE

Kansas-Nebraska Territory—1857

"Lord, help us. Hank's not back and a storm's brewing." Rebecca Quaid peered out of their covered wagon. Lightning lit the sky and a clap of thunder filled the air.

Since making camp, dark clouds continued to build over the prairie.

Hannah, her five-year-old daughter, wedged closer. "Mamma, can Jesus hear us over the noise?"

"Yes, honey." Rebecca hugged her. Their wagon rocked back and forth from the approaching wind and storm. Ben scooted over by his big brother, Jace.

"Get the buckets," Rebecca said to Jace, "and set them where we can catch some water. We'll need all we can get."

Jace jumped from the back of the wagon and hurried before more lightning streaked the sky.

"Ben, you and Hannah stay right here. I need to check on the horses and oxen."

"Yes, Mamma," said Ben. Rebecca climbed from the front of the wagon and peered at the dark sky. *Hank, where are you? You've been gone too long. I'm scared, and I can't let the children see it.*

After placing several buckets around the wagon, Jace ran to the stake line where the animals were tethered.

Rebecca pulled on the ropes making certain they were secure.

"Mamma, you think Pa's getting close by now?"

"He should be back soon," said Rebecca hoping her answer would ease the worried look on his face. Jace was fifteen and old enough to know something was wrong.

Ben yelled, "Mamma. Hannah's crying, and she won't quit."

"Tell her I'm coming." Rebecca held on to her bonnet and fought the wind. She scanned the prairie. Her eyes longed to see a rider coming their way.

This wasn't the first time Hank rode off to find fresh game or a good water supply, but the first time he didn't return by nightfall. He'd been gone three days now and Rebecca's imagination was her worst enemy.

She and her children huddled in the wagon awaiting the approaching storm. More lightning danced across the sky. The wagon pitched with each gust of wind.

"Mamma, I'm hungry," said Ben.

"I know. We'll have to do with hardtack and jerky for now. I can't start a fire with this storm coming down on us."

They had faced several storms on the trail, but never without Hank. Will they get through this one without him?

Ben asked, "Do we need to pray for Pa?"

She gazed down into his big brown eyes and tried to sound strong for her seven-year-old son. "Pa's fine, but prayer will help him on his way back to us."

Hannah perked up. "Can I pray?"

"Yes, you pray too."

Rebecca glanced at Jace. He didn't say a word, but she knew what he was thinking.

When the storm arrived, rain pelted the wagon. Rebecca and her children gathered closer. The storm persisted into the night. Hannah and Ben finally fell asleep, but for Rebecca and Jace, neither closed an eye until the storm passed.

For the last month, the Quaid family had traveled north from Cutter Springs, on the plains of the Kansas-Nebraska Territory, to meet up with a wagon train headed for Oregon. They sold everything and purchased a covered wagon, a good team of oxen, and enough supplies to get them to Fort Kearney once they joined the wagon train. But with Hank missing, the burden of caring for the wagon and animals lay squarely on Jace's shoulders.

The next morning, Rebecca stepped from the wagon and gazed across the prairie. What was a dry, dusty trail the day before was now a boggy mess. Worse, still no sign of Hank.

"Ben, Hannah," Rebecca said, "you'll have to walk today. It'll be hard enough on the team to pull this wagon through the mud."

"What about breakfast?" asked Ben.

Rebecca reached over the tailgate of the wagon and grabbed a jar. She opened it and doled out a handful of dried apricots to everyone. She studied the morning sky. "This will have to do for now. It won't take long for the hot sun to dry the trail out some. Jace, help me hitch the team, and you children jump out of the wagon."

Jace swallowed his apricots, swung down from the wagon seat, and made his way to the oxen.

Lucy, the milk cow, let out a bawl.

Rebecca glanced back from the wooden yoke while she helped Jace with the oxen. "Ben, get a bucket out of the wagon and milk Lucy. And make sure it's clean. Use some of the rainwater we collected." She cast her eyes at the sky again. "At least we have fresh drinking water for a few days."

While getting the wagon ready for the day, Rebecca periodically stopped and searched the prairie hoping to see Hank coming their way. Fear swelled up inside Rebecca, but she did her best to push it down.

She filled the water barrel with the buckets of rainwater. Then poured what was left of the milk, after washing down the apricots, into the milk can. Lifting her hand to shade her eyes, Rebecca steered the team toward the north hoping to meet up with the wagon train by the end of the day.

Hank had assured Rebecca it would take thirty days to get to the Oregon Trail where they would join the other wagons. She had scratched a mark on the wagon seat for each day and now there were thirty. She prayed this would be the day they would celebrate

Hank's homecoming and become a part of other families making their way across the vast country to begin new lives.

The sun beat down on the crusty ground and constant wind blew across the prairie. Blowing Ben's hat from his head, Rebecca called out, "Hurry Ben and grab your hat." She was unsure of how far they had traveled, but the dread of spending another night without Hank hung over her.

Ben and Hannah ran alongside the wagon. They gathered buffalo chips and anything else they could find to fuel their campfire. Jace rode ahead searching the horizon for a sign of his pa.

Ben hollered and ran to his mother as she walked beside the slow-moving oxen. "Jace won't ride too far from us, will he?"

She started to answer when a shot rang out. She looked in the direction of Jace. He jumped from his horse and picked up something. "Looks like Jace is holding up a rabbit." She smiled down at Ben. "We'll have a good supper tonight."

Ben grinned, revealing a gap where two new teeth pushed through. "I wish I could go with him. I know I could learn to shoot just like him and Pa."

At the mention of Hank, Rebecca's heart trembled. She again looked down at her son. "When your pa gets back, he'll need to teach you how to shoot so we'll have plenty for supper."

Ben ran to Hannah. "Did you hear that, Hannah? When Pa gets back he's going to let me shoot his rifle."

Rebecca prodded the team while her children ran and played along the trail.

Jace rode up with a big smile. He held two good sized rabbits. "I got them both with one shot."

Hannah and Ben jumped up and down.

Rebecca stretched to look at them. "Your pa couldn't have done any better." She pulled on the lead line to halt the oxen. "This looks like a good spot to make camp. Jace, if you'll unhitch the team I'll get started on those rabbits."

The western sky glowed as the sun lowered on the vast plains. Rebecca and the children had fought the wind all day long, and there was still a lot to do before the day ended.

Jace tied his horse up behind the wagon and grabbed the ropes for the stake line. Rebecca was thankful Hank had taught Jace how to tend to the livestock. She was also grateful for the rainwater they caught the previous day, but was concerned how long that water would last. Though, she knew when Hank returned he would know where the next watering hole was.

By the time Jace finished bedding down the livestock, Rebecca managed to turn the rabbits into a pot of savory stew. They ate supper by the campfire and talked about joining Hank's brother and his family in Willamette Valley, Oregon.

Hannah squirmed in Rebecca's lap. "Will Uncle Rob and Aunt Carol be waiting for us when we get there?"

"Your pa wrote and told them we should be in Willamette Valley no later than November."

"Mamma," said Ben, "when Pa gets our house and barns built will there be a place for me to have my own horse?"

"Yes, and a big garden so we'll have fresh vegetables." She lifted Hannah from her lap. "The sun's gone down, so we need to get to bed. We've got a long day tomorrow."

Jace sat by the campfire and worked on a broken lead line. He glanced at his mother. "We should be getting close enough to see the dust stirred up by the wagon train. Do you think we'll meet up with them by tomorrow?"

"I'm praying so."

He stared at the lead line. "And Pa should be back by tomorrow."

She smiled. "I'm praying for that too."

Rebecca stepped from the wagon after getting Hannah and Ben to sleep. She and Jace were putting more twigs on the fire when Rebecca heard a rider approaching the wagon. She whirled to see a man coming from the north. Her heart leaped, but in the next moment she saw it wasn't Hank.

Rebecca climbed up onto the wagon seat. "Jace, get in the wagon." She felt for the loaded musket revolver that lay underneath the seat.

When the rider got close enough, he slowed and said, "Howdy, Missy. I smell somethin' good cookin'. You got anything for a hungry man?"

Rebecca trembled. "Sorry, we didn't have any supper left, but I have some hardtack if you'd like."

He looked around and smiled. "I don't see a man anywhere around. You crossin' this country by yourself?"

Despite being a moonless night, Rebecca made out a jagged scar running from his temple down to his chin.

"My husband should be back any time now." She reached for the canister of hardtack. When she turned back he had dismounted.

"Well, ain't this nice. I got here just in time to make myself at home." He moved toward Rebecca and reached up to grab her arm.

Jace stepped from behind the wagon. "Mister, step away from her or I'll shoot you." He aimed a Colt Ring Lever rifle at the man's head.

The man jerked back then his bravado returned and so did his smile. "Boy, you're just a kid. Put that gun down. You're not gonna shoot anybody."

"Do as I say or I'll pull the trigger." Jace kept his aim and stood firm.

Rebecca held her breath.

The man laughed. "You're not old enough to know what you'd do." He moved closer to Jace. "Now gimme that gun 'fore I have to get a hold a you." He glared at him. "Now, boy." The man reached for the barrel of Jace's gun.

A shot rang out.

He slid to his knees then fell face down to the ground.

Jace stared at his mother. She held the smoking revolver.

"Jace, step away from him."

Rebecca climbed from the wagon. Her hand shook so fiercely she dropped the pistol. Reaching down to pick it up, her head began to swim. She grabbed the wagon wheel to steady herself. Pressing her hand to her head, she closed her eyes thinking she was going to be sick.

Ben hollered from the wagon. "Mamma. What happened?"

"Ben," Jace said, "you and Hannah stay right where you are. Everything's okay."

Rebecca slowly bent and picked up the pistol.

Jace studied the man. "I think he's dead."

Rebecca focused to stay calm, her mind reeling. "You think you can help me roll him up in a blanket? We don't need your brother and sister to see this."

He hurried to the wagon to retrieve something they could use.

Rebecca didn't want to look at him but couldn't divert her eyes. Somehow, they were going to have to bury him before Ben and Hannah realized what had happened.

"Here, Mamma." Jace handed Rebecca an old wool blanket. He carried a shovel in the other hand.

Rebecca's voice quivered. "Help me get him on this blanket. Then we can drag him away from the wagon and bury him."

The stench rising from the man's body was nearly unbearable. He smelled of a year's worth of sweat, whiskey, and filth.

Rebecca and Jace struggled to roll him over onto the blanket. As he rolled, something fell from his shirt pocket. Rebecca scooped it from the ground and threw it into her pocket then continued the job of disposing of the human being she had just shot and killed.

Jace walked a few paces from the wagon and dug a shallow grave. They both worked as fast as they could to end the despicable ordeal. A night owl screeched when Jace shoveled the last bit of dirt onto the mound and patted it down.

Rebecca lowered her head. Her arms hung limp. Jace stepped from the other side of the grave and put his hand on her shoulder. "Mamma, it couldn't be helped. He was going to hurt us. We had no choice. Pa would have done the same thing."

Rebecca squeezed back tears. Hank. If he were only here. She wanted to disappear into the darkness and forget that she just killed a man. But Jace, Ben, and Hannah depended on her.

Rebecca finally spoke. "I know." She stood in silence for a minute, staring at the mound of dirt near her feet. "We need to say some words over him."

Jace darted his eyes at her. "How can we pray over a man like him? He had nothing but hate in his heart."

She sighed. "I know. But he can't hurt us anymore, and I think it's more for us than for him."

"What does that mean?" He frowned. "I don't understand."

"Jace, honey, that man's destiny's been determined. But we have to figure out how God wants us to deal with this. We can be angry about it, or we can ask God to forgive us for taking a life and help us forgive the man who caused it all."

"All right then." He shook his head. "Whatever you say, but I still don't understand."

She gently cradled his face with her hand. "I know, but someday I hope you will."

CHAPTER TWO

The next morning, Rebecca woke and her body ached when she tried to move. The memory of the previous night flooded her mind. She sat up. The children were gone, but she could hear their chatter while they helped Jace hitch the team to the wagon.

Hannah crawled into the back of the wagon and giggled. "Mamma, Ben's already milked Lucy and you slept right through it. And I helped Jace with the team."

"My goodness, you're getting to be a big girl. And I bet you're ready for breakfast."

She giggled again. "We've already eaten our breakfast. We ate leftover biscuits with apricot jam and milk. We fixed it all by ourselves."

Rebecca groaned. "I must have been tired to have slept through that."

"We have everything ready to go," said Hannah. "Jace said we may see the wagon train today."

"I hope so, sweetheart." Rebecca tried to sound optimistic.

She stretched her sore muscles and climbed from the wagon. Rebecca gazed at the blue sky and prayed this would be the day. Checking the wagon, she saw the children had done a good job getting it and the livestock ready for their day's journey. Hank would be proud of them.

Rebecca grabbed her lead staff to start nudging the oxen down the trail. She reached into her skirt pocket for her neckerchief. Touching something solid, she retrieved the object. A chain swung from her hand and from it hung a gold pocket watch.

Rebecca opened the face of the watch and stared at a picture of herself. She covered her mouth and muffled a cry. Turning the watch over, she read the engraving. "Hank Matthew Quaid, September 1852." She caught her breath and gripped the watch so tightly it dug into her palm. How and where did that man get this?

Jace came from around the wagon. Rebecca turned her back to him and quickly slipped it back into her pocket. He can't know about the watch. Not now. She squeezed her eyes shut. Hank, I need you. However, she didn't have time to dwell on it before a lone horse approached the wagon from the west.

Jace hollered. "It's Pa's horse."

The man she killed must have ridden in on Hank's horse and the gunshot spooked it.

She prayed Jace wouldn't figure it out before she could talk to him. It all made sense. The man under the mound of dirt knew where Hank was and why he hadn't returned to his family.

"Jace, hitch him to the back of the wagon."

"But Pa must be out there somewhere. I need to go look for him." He jumped on Hank's horse and took off before Rebecca could say a word.

She started to call out for him to stop but knew there was no use. She took in a breath and slowly exhaled. Her strength seemed to be ebbing away.

Rebecca slapped the back of the ox and yelled. "Giddup." Glancing over at Ben and Hannah, she said, "Help me sing while we walk."

The relentless wind carried fine grains of dirt which managed to find its way into every possible crevice. Rebecca bit down on the grit in her teeth. It had been a long, hot day. The sun was going down, and Jace was still somewhere out there looking for Hank.

Rebecca goaded the oxen to make them move a little faster. Ben came up and took her hand. "Mamma, is Jace coming back? He's been gone all day."

"Don't worry, he'll be riding up before you know it." She turned her face to conceal her concern. "Maybe he'll bring us some more rabbits."

Ben smiled and ran to catch up with Hannah while Rebecca walked alongside the oxen praying for Jace's return.

Hank and Rebecca had spent a year planning this journey. They mapped out exactly where their trail would meet up with the wagon train and how long it would take to get to Oregon. They viewed it as a great adventure and were encouraged by the stories told by fur traders and missionaries who earlier forged a trail to the plush, fertile land of Oregon. However, this was much harder than Rebecca anticipated. With every day that passed, she doubted her fortitude.

She was recalling what they left back in Cutter Springs when she noticed a cloud of dust rising in the north. She shaded her eyes with her hand and squinted.

Ben ran toward the dust storm yelling. "Jace. Jace."

Rebecca's heart raced thanking God all the while.

Jace galloped to the wagon. "I saw them." He waved his hand. "The wagons are just over that ridge."

"How long will it take us to reach them?" said Rebecca.

"I'd say about half a day." He swung the horse around and smiled. "From a distance, there looks to be around thirty wagons."

As the oxen slowly plodded along, Rebecca climbed up on the seat and gathered the lead line. "Whoa, whoa."

By that time Ben and Hannah were jumping up and down they were so happy to see Jace. He dismounted, and his siblings tackled him.

Jace laughed. "Just think, tomorrow you'll see the wagon train for yourselves."

"I'm just happy you're back," said Ben.

Hannah put her arms around Jace's leg. "Me too."

Rebecca stepped from the wagon. "Let's make camp a little early tonight and get some food in you. You must be starved."

"I am."

"Ben can help you unhitch the team while I get supper started." She couldn't help but notice how weary he appeared. He never said a thing about Hank, but Rebecca could sense his restlessness.

Hank's watch came to mind. Eventually, Jace would have to know. But for now, he needed food and rest more than anything. Later there would be time for her to talk to him about what may have happened to his pa.

⚬⚬

The excitement of meeting the wagon train had everyone up early the next morning. Before Rebecca could finish packing the skillets and plates from breakfast, Jace and Ben had hitched the team, greased the axles, and milked Lucy. This was the day they dreamed of from the moment they embarked on the journey. The Oregon Trail would take them to their promised land.

With every step, they longed to see another human being. Jace galloped across the prairie with Ben seated behind him hanging onto his waist.

Ben said, "Are you sure you saw the wagons?"

"Yeah, Ben, I'm sure. We ought to be seeing some sign of them soon."

"You think Pa's with the wagon train?"

"No, Pa would be with us before he would be with the wagon train."

"Oh." Ben was silent for a second, then said, "Then where is he?"

"I don't know." Jace didn't want to say what was going through his mind. He searched for words that could somehow comfort Ben and himself. "We'll find him, though. And maybe when we reach the wagon train there'll be someone to help us search for him."

"Yeah, we'll find him then," said Ben.

They rode in silence until Jace spotted a cloud of dust. When they came upon the ridge, Jace caught sight of the wagons. "Ben. There they are." He reined his horse around and took off. "Let's go tell Mamma." Jace spurred his horse. Ben's grip tightened around his brother's waist as they flew across the gap that stretched between them and Rebecca and Hannah.

When they reached the wagon, Jace yelled. "They're right over that ridge. You'll be able to see them in an hour or so."

Rebecca took Hannah's hand and twirled her around. "Did you hear that, Hannah? By tonight we'll be with families just like us." The boys whooped and hollered. She hollered right along with them then slapped the staff across the oxen and yelled. "Giddup."

Jace and Ben rode beside the wagon alongside Rebecca and Hannah. "While we walk I'll tell you the story of Jesus and all His miracles."

Jace smiled at his mother. "And He still does them today, doesn't He, Mamma?"

Rebecca decided she and Hannah could travel on the wagon as they neared the wagon train. A rider approached, dust kicking up behind him. She reached down for the revolver and slipped it under the folds of her skirt.

When he got closer, he tipped his hat. "Ma'am, are you the Quaid family?" His broad shoulders and direct demeanor gave him a commanding air.

"Yes, we are."

"We've been expecting you. I'm Captain Brenner, ma'am." He looked around. "Where's Mr. Quaid?"

Tears rose in her eyes, but she managed to reply. "I'm not sure. He rode off a few days ago to find a fresh water supply and hasn't returned yet." She tried to keep her voice from breaking.

Captain Brenner furrowed his brow. "Ma'am, the contract says every wagon has to have a man to oversee the day-to-day repairs and such. Unless your husband shows up soon, we'll have to leave you at the next settlement we come to."

Reining his horse closer to the wagon, Jace spoke up. "Until Pa gets back, I can take care of the wagon."

Captain Brenner eyed Jace. "Son, how old are you?"

"I'll be sixteen next month."

The captain turned back to Rebecca. "Mrs. Quaid, unless your husband finds his way to this wagon train, we have no choice but to take you to the nearest fort, which is Fort Kearney. We only have enough men to take care of the wagons we have."

"Mamma, tell him," Jace said. "I can take care of our wagon. Pa'll be back soon, but until then I can handle it. Pa trusts me."

"Captain," said Rebecca, "we'd be obliged if we could ride along with you for now. My husband should return soon."

The captain adjusted his hat and nodded. "Yes, ma'am." He pointed toward the caravan. "Just pull up alongside the wagon on the left. We'll be making camp soon. I'll send Luke Barker to help you get settled."

"Thank you, Captain."

Rebecca watched him ride off. As thrilled as she was to join the wagon train, doing so without Hank was more than she could bear. As time passed, her heart sank even deeper. For the first time, she found herself thinking that there was a strong chance Hank would never be back. Ben and Hannah she could comfort, but Jace was different. He was just a boy but now would have to bear the responsibilities of a grown man.

Jace and Ben dismounted, and Jace tied the horse's reins to the tailgate. Rebecca stepped down from the wagon seat and helped Jace nudge the team of oxen toward the caravan. She brushed tears from her face out of sight of her children.

A few minutes later, a lean cowboy with dark hair and a nice smile rode up to their wagon. "I'm Luke Barker, ma'am. Captain Brenner sent me to help you and your family get situated."

Within a short time, Rebecca's wagon was in position on the outer edge of the caravan. Thirty-one wagons traveled side-by-side across the prairie alongside the North Platte River, followed by fifty head of cattle and fifteen oxen. A couple of milk cows trailed each wagon.

Luke Barker reined his horse closer to Rebecca as she walked beside the oxen. "Mrs. Quaid, just keep beside that wagon and you'll be fine. It belongs to Carl and Sarah Webster. While we're on the prairie, we'll travel alongside each other. That way only the cattle and cowhands have to contend with the cloud of dirt caused by the wagon train. When you hear Pete, the chuck wagon boss, sound the bugle to circle the wagons and set up camp for the night, I'll be back to get you settled."

Rebecca worked the lead lines to keep the wagon in position. "Thank you for your help. Jace and I'll make sure our wagon doesn't fall behind."

"Much obliged, ma'am." He smiled, tipped his hat, and rode up ahead.

Jace moved a few steps closer to his mother. "Captain Brenner doesn't have to worry about us. We'll do fine."

She knew Jace. He would do all he could to keep them with the wagon train, but without Hank she wasn't quite as confident. She reached into her pocket and held tight to her husband's watch. Letting it go, she gripped the lead line and paid attention to the task of keeping the oxen moving. She would think about Hank later.

Rebecca glimpsed to her right at the Webster's wagon, then peered down at Ben and Hannah. "Tonight we'll sleep good knowing we're with the wagon train."

Ben smiled. "Maybe they can help us find Pa."

"Maybe so." She put her hand on his shoulder. "You both are going to have to pay attention now that we're with all the other wagons. Don't get too close to the wagon wheels."

"Yes, ma'am," they said in unison.

As the sun set, Rebecca pulled her bonnet lower to shield her eyes from the glare. She was tired and glad to hear the signal to set up camp for the night.

Mr. Barker rode up and pointed at the wagon to their right. "Mrs. Quaid, you and Jace pull your wagon behind the Webster's. You can lead your animals down to the river and let them drink once we've circle up." He glanced at Jace. "We'll leave an opening in the circle of wagons until the animals are watered. After they've had enough to drink, lead them back to the middle of the formation."

Jace stood tall. "Yes, sir."

Walking alongside the team, Rebecca peered up at Mr. Barker. "Can you tell me what time we'll get started in the morning?"

"You'll hear the bugle at five o'clock sharp. That's the signal to get breakfast and tend to your livestock. Captain Brenner wants everyone ready to go by six. That'll give us plenty of time to make a ten to twelve-mile drive tomorrow."

"We're grateful for your help."

"Anytime, ma'am. And don't worry. A few days on the trail, and you'll get the hang of how everything works."

She nodded. "I'm sure you're right."

He touched the brim of his hat. "I'll check on you and your family when we get the camp set up." He nudged his horse and rode off to another wagon. It appeared to Rebecca that Mr. Barker's job was to make sure everything ran smoothly for the wagon train.

Jace unyoked the animals and led them to the bank of the river while Ben and Hannah searched for firewood and buffalo chips.

Rebecca sighed. Being with other families brought her relief. Her concern over the safety of her children eased. Though, meeting so many new families without Hank saddened her.

CHAPTER THREE

Ben and Hannah came from around the back of the wagon with their arms piled high with firewood. Rebecca pointed from the makeshift table. "Just put it by the fire pit while I slice this bacon. Jace can start the fire when he gets back."

Chatter behind Rebecca pulled her attention in that direction. She turned. Several women approached, their arms filled with cloth covered pans and jars of fruit. A robust woman with a smile as warm as sunshine greeted Rebecca. "We noticed your wagon joining ours earlier. I'm Sarah Webster." She introduced the others. "And this is Mildred Shaw, Millie Johnson, and Penelope Brewer."

A young girl, who appeared the age of Hannah, peeked from behind Sarah's skirts. "Emily, don't be so shy." said Sarah. The little girl smiled at Hannah, and Sarah continued, "Welcome to the wagon train. If we can do anything to help you get settled, let us know. "

The women set the pans on the table beside the bacon. Millie held up a jar. "These are my prize-winning apricot preserves." She set them down. "And I hope you like ham and potato stew. Penelope made her mother's recipe of currant bread."

Rebecca put her hand over her heart. "Oh my, how kind of you." She didn't know if her reactions came from fatigue or that she was around women for the first time in weeks, but her words caught in her throat. She dabbed at her eyes with her apron. "I'm sorry to be so emotional. My children and I thank you."

She gathered Ben and Hannah in front of her and introduced herself and her children to the women. "Jace, my oldest son, is at the river watering the stock. Hannah, say hello to Emily."

Hannah smiled. "Hi, Emily. Do you like to pick wildflowers?"

17

Emily smiled back and nodded.

Sarah grinned. "I can see they're going to be good friends."

Penelope looked around. "Where's your husband?"

Rebecca straightened her shoulders. "He rode off a week ago to find some fresh water and game and hasn't returned yet. He knows we should be with the wagon train by now and should be back any time."

Millie placed her hand on Rebecca's arm. "I'm sure he'll be riding up in no time."

"If you've a mind to," said Penelope, who appeared several months pregnant, "you might want to join us after supper at our wagon. Jim, my husband, plays the guitar, and Millie's husband plays the fiddle. Several families usually join us for a little music if we're not all too tired."

"That sounds wonderful." She gave the ladies a smile. "Thank you again for supper."

"Come to the Brewer's wagon when you can," said Sarah, "and we'll listen to music and get to know each other."

Penelope and Millie's husbands filled the evening with music. Hannah and Ben danced and sang with the children while Rebecca savored the conversation with the women. Rebecca didn't want the evening to end. She enjoyed hearing Millie, Sarah, and Penelope share their experiences of traveling across the country in a covered wagon.

"One thing I'll never get used to," said Millie, "is the wind. I don't know where it comes from, but there's always an ample supply."

Rebecca agreed. "From the first day we left Cutter Springs we met with some awfully strong winds. Hank would always say, tomorrow the wind will blow itself out." She laughed. "He knew better, but it sounded good."

"And I haven't baked a pie yet," said Penelope, "that hasn't had a little grit in it. It's hard to keep the dirt from settling on everything."

"What about Sunday's?" Rebecca said. "Will the captain let us rest rather than travel on?"

"It depends on if we need to make up time or not," replied Millie. "Reverend Jamison holds services for those who want to gather."

For a brief time, they all sat in silence, listened to the music, and enjoyed the night air.

When a lively song ended, Sarah broke the silence. "As difficult as it's been living out of a wagon, you have to admit, the prairie offers the most beautiful sunsets you could ever imagine. And a sky full of stars."

"They are lovely," said Penelope, laughing. "But most evenings I'm too exhausted to enjoy them."

"Well, if we don't turn in soon, we'll be too tired to see the sunrise," said Millie.

The women gathered their children. Rebecca, Ben, and Hannah headed for their wagon with Jace following close behind.

Rebecca was about to put the children to bed when she heard someone whistling. A white-haired man with whiskers strolled up to their wagon. "May I come into your camp?" He approached wearing high-topped boots with silver spurs that jangled with every step. Suspenders stretched over his round belly. He walked with a hitch in his step.

He moved into the light of their campfire and apologized. "I know it's late, but I wanted to meet you folks before we get on the trail in the morning." He raised an eyebrow at Ben and Hannah. "Well, who do we have here?"

The children turned to Rebecca.

"I guess your folks gave you names, didn't they?"

Ben stammered, "I'm...Ben Quaid."

The man smiled at Hannah when she said, "My name's Hannah Quaid."

He took the homemade pipe from his teeth. "Those are fine names." He turned to Rebecca. "And you must be Mrs. Quaid."

"Yes, I am." She pointed. "And this is my oldest son, Jace."

He stepped forward and shook Jace's hand. "Nice meeting you, boy. I'm Zebadiah Calhoun. My wagon's on the other side of the circle, along with my missus. Clara said she's raring to get to know you folks."

"Thank you, Mr. Calhoun." Rebecca sensed he possessed a heart and hospitality as big as the prairie they were crossing.

Zeb stared at Ben. "How old are you, boy?"

"I'm seven. I'll be eight in August."

Zeb slapped his knee. "Why, Ben boy, I was about your age when my pappy and I killed a black bear in the hills back in Tennessee."

Ben's eyes got big. "You killed a bear?"

"Sure did. I'd never seen a bear that big or mean before. I'll have to tell you all about it sometime." He removed his hat. "Ma'am, I was told your husband's not with the wagon train yet. If you or the children need anything at all, you just let me or Clara know. It's just the two of us." A warm smile spread over his face.

"We're much obliged, Mr. Calhoun, and I look forward to meeting your wife."

He grinned at Ben. "Hope to see you again, Ben boy." He waved and walked off with spurs jangling. The tune he whistled drifted through the night air.

The warm welcome she and her family received on their first night with the wagon train lightened some of her burden. But Rebecca knew tomorrow would begin the true test.

The sound of a bugle woke Rebecca from a deep sleep. She peered over at her slumbering children.

"Ben, Hannah." She gently shook them. "Time to get up. We've got a long day ahead of us." She stretched and could hear Jace yoking the oxen. After getting dressed, she stepped down from the wagon. "Jace, how long have you been up?"

"Way before anyone else. I wanted to get a head start this morning. Lucy's been milked, and the wagon is just about ready to go. I have hot coffee on the fire."

She smiled at her son. "I bet you're ready for breakfast."

"I'm starved." He poured himself a cup of coffee. "Did you rest last night?"

"Yes, I did. I think just being with other folks helped."

She understood what was going through her son's mind. He needed to show Captain Brenner he was as capable as any other man of overseeing the responsibilities of their wagon. She admired the way he checked the yokes and could see his pa in him. Jace had Hank's auburn hair and blue eyes, along with his mannerisms. Her heart stirred knowing the burden he carried.

Ben and Hannah jumped from the tailgate of the wagon.

"Mamma, are we going to get to hear the music again tonight?" Ben grabbed his hat and put it on.

"Yeah, that was fun," said Hannah, beaming. "And there're lots of kids to play with. Emily even knows some of the words to the songs."

"I'm sure Mr. Brewer and Mr. Johnson will play and sing for us again."

After breakfast, Rebecca was about finished putting the pans away when Luke Barker rode up. "Morning, Mrs. Quaid." He acknowledged Jace and the children. "Hope you folks rested."

"Thank you. A good night's sleep was just what we needed."

Luke glanced at the wagon. "Jace, you did a good job hitching the animals. I noticed you were up long before anyone else."

"Yes, sir." His chest swelled.

"When we get started, just stay beside the Webster's. I'll check on you again later. We stop around noon for a meal and water the animals at the river before we get back on the trail. I don't have to tell you to be careful. Ben, Hannah, pay attention, and watch where you step."

Rebecca never imagined their first day on the Oregon Trail without Hank. She knew she needed to talk with Jace and tell him about Hank's watch. There seemed to be no other explanation for his disappearance, but that the man she shot and killed was the same man who knew the whereabouts of Hank. As much as she wanted to deny the evidence, Rebecca's hopes dwindled with each passing minute. And their future in Oregon could be in jeopardy, as well.

Prayer, at this point, seemed her best option. Her faith gave her strength and her precious children gave her purpose.

The wagons pulled out on the trail. "Giddup!" Rebecca slapped the staff across the oxen. Ben and Hannah kept pace with the team while Jace walked on the other side of the oxen working to keep up with the other wagons. Rebecca smiled. "Jace, we're on our way to Oregon."

He returned her smile and gave the team another nudge with his staff.

She gazed out across the wagons. Each one held families with dreams and hopes for a place to raise their children, worship, and prosper. Rebecca hoped for the same thing. Only now it took on a different light, without her husband, as she and her three children traveled west.

Since leaving Cutter Springs, Rebecca found traveling across the territory in a covered wagon difficult. Though, the first week with the wagon train proved to be a comfort.

She and Sarah Webster were drawn to each other, as were Hannah and Emily. From the moment the little girls met, they were inseparable. They laughed at the same things, mostly Ben, and found every step of the trail exciting.

With Hank missing, it only took Rebecca a short time to learn how Sarah's gentle manner could soothe her anxious concerns. She was a godsend with her calm and pleasant ways. Her words were strong and comforting. She made a point to never let Rebecca lose hope about Hank.

However, without Hank, Captain Brenner's words kept resounding in Rebecca's mind. She had no idea how she would take care of her family in this wilderness. Rebecca walked alongside the team of oxen and prayed. "What do I do, Lord? Everything we own is in this wagon."

"Mamma, who you talking to?" Ben smiled up at her.

She smiled back at his freckled face. "Just talking to the Lord." Her heart swelled with joy at Ben's sweet innocence.

He took his mother's hand. "You read to us from Pa's Bible that Jesus knows everything."

"That's right, Ben, He does."

"Can you ask Him where Pa is?"

Her breath caught. She worked to hold back tears. "Jesus knows where your pa is. And it's our job to trust Him."

"Yes, Mamma."

Rebecca knew Ben didn't understand, but he accepted her words and ran to catch up with Hannah and Emily. As much as she trusted God, she found it equally as hard to understand her predicament. She couldn't recall a time in her life when she was as unsure of herself and the future of her family as now. But watching Ben and Hannah, she confessed she would have to lean on God's promises with the same assurance as a little child.

Luke Barker rode up beside her. "Ma'am, we're going to stop for the noon meal a little early today. There's a cavalry troop approaching, and Captain Brenner is meeting with their lieutenant. We'll give the signal when we're ready to get back on the trail." He nodded and rode off.

Jace called out from a distance ahead. "Why are we stopping? We could make another half mile before noon."

"Mr. Barker said the captain has some business with a cavalry troop." She glanced around and hollered. "Hannah. Ben. Come have lunch."

While Rebecca prepared their meal, Jace watered the animals. Ben ran to the river to fetch some water for Lucy. Hannah, along with Emily, filled a basket with wildflowers growing alongside the tracks of earlier wagon trains.

At the noon break, Emily returned to her wagon and Rebecca pulled out tablets and pencils. "Come sit at the table. Time for school lessons."

Ben frowned. "Can't we wait till later?"

"No. You and Hannah get your tablets and write down the names of all the things you've seen on the trail today. See who can write the longest list." Rebecca was determined her children would know how to read and write.

Hannah said, "What if I can't spell it right?"

"Do the best you can, and we'll work on it."

When she examined their tablets, she was pleased with their work. They scribbled down everything from prairie grass, to clouds, to every kind of varmint that made the prairie their home.

CHAPTER FOUR

After lunch, Jace rode over to Bart Johnson's wagon. "Mr. Johnson, do you know what the holdup was about?"

Bart took off his hat and wiped the sweat from his brow. "Luke just told us the soldiers are searching for a gang of outlaws who may have passed this way. But he said the captain wanted to get back on the trail as soon as possible after lunch."

Jace waved a thanks. He rode back to his wagon with the picture of the scar-faced outlaw in his mind.

At the sound of the bugle, everyone stirred from their camps to travel the next seven miles. In unison, the wagons journeyed across the prairie, each family anxious to close the distance between them and their destination.

Rebecca and Jace walked alongside the oxen. She kept an eye on Ben. Hannah walked with Emily near the Webster's wagon. Rebecca untied her bandana from around her neck and wiped her forehead. From a distance away, a large cloud of dust rose into the sky from the north.

The wagon train traveled on about a quarter of a mile when Rebecca got a whiff of smoke. She whirled around when Captain Brenner yelled, "Prairie fire! Prairie fire!"

She peered to the north again. Billowing clouds of smoke filled the air. Within minutes, the red hue of the flames reflected off the sky. For an instant, the fire marching across the dry grassland like an army mesmerized her.

She hollered, "Ben. You stay right here while I get Hannah." Rebecca squinted through the smoke searching for Jace while running to get her daughter.

Not far from the wagon, Hannah ran to her with a frightened look on her face. "Mamma. Mamma."

Rebecca scooped her up and ran for their wagon. Her eyes burned and watered. She yelled for Jace. Within a few seconds, he ran toward them through the rolling fog of smoke engulfing the entire wagon train.

Through the thick haze, Luke Barker appeared beside their wagon. "Turn your team to the south. Mrs. Quaid, soak down some rags. Put them over your nose and mouth to keep from breathing so much smoke. With the wind blowing from the west, there's a good chance we're out of harm's way, but stay close to the other wagons. The direction of the wind could change any time."

While Jace pulled the lead line to the south, Rebecca and the children ran to the water barrel. She soaked several rags. "Put these on your nose and mouth and stay close to me." She ran to Jace and handed him some wet cloths. "Here, and I have some for the animals."

She spun when Carl Webster hollered from the other side of her wagon. "Mrs. Quaid, keep as close to our wagon as you can. With this smoke it's hard to keep our bearings."

"Can you tell how close the fire is to us?"

"No, ma'am."

Rebecca tried not to panic. Hank had told her stories of how grass fires could travel at a huge rate of speed and destroy everything in its path.

Rebecca closed her eyes. "Lord, don't let us perish."

Hannah cried. "Mamma, my eyes are burning. Can't you make the fire stop?"

"Grab on to my skirt and put the wet cloth back on your face. You, too, Ben. And both of you keep your feet moving."

The fire was close enough to hear the crackling of the flames. The smell of burnt grass filled Rebecca's nostrils. She squinted through the thick smoke making sure Jace was close.

Jace took the soaked rags and wiped the smoke and flying debris from the oxen's eyes and nose. Lucy, their milk cow, coughed and bellowed.

"Ben, Hannah, don't let go of my skirt and follow me." She untied the neckerchief from around her neck and ran to the water barrel. Drenching the piece of cloth, she hurried to Lucy.

Ben coughed. "Mamma, is Lucy okay?"

"Yes, she will be now."

Hannah stumbled and fell. Rebecca reached down and grabbed her hand. Rushing to Lucy, Rebecca washed the animal's face while their wagon, along with the rest of the caravan, tried to escape the hot wind and smoke of the fire.

Exhausted, with sweat streaking down Rebecca's soot-covered face, she again prayed, "Lord, by your mighty power, save us from this inferno. Save my children."

The fire raged on.

Rebecca startled at a loud crack of thunder. As it rumbled, the clouds opened and rain fell like manna on the scorched land. Wet drops extinguishing the flames roared across the plains. Over the noise of rain, she heard shouts of praise and thanksgiving, along with weeping and laughter.

God turned the tide with His mighty hand. Rebecca marveled at the great miracle she just witnessed.

She whispered, "I need one more miracle, Lord. I need Hank."

At sundown, the wagons circled the livestock. The smell of smoke lingered. The rain cleared the air somewhat, though, the wet trail would slow tomorrow's travel. And losing a day would make it much harder to reach Fort Kearney on schedule.

Rebecca tucked Ben and Hannah into bed in the wagon after supper. Their heads hardly hit their pillows before they were asleep. She dragged a bench close to the campfire and joined Jace. He sat on a stool oiling a pair of reins.

Jace rubbed the back of his neck. "Dodging that fire was exhausting. I won't have any trouble sleeping tonight." He leaned forward. "Mamma, have you ever seen anything like what happened today?"

"No, I haven't. Your pa told me about lots of prairie fires when he and his family moved to the Kansas territory."

He threw a twig into the fire. "You think Pa would've been scared?"

"Yes. He may not have shown it, but the fire was a scary thing we lived through today."

"Mamma," Jace paused, "how are we going to find Pa?"

Rebecca's first instinct was to assure him he would ride up any day now. But deep down, she feared they would never see Hank again. "I wish I knew where he was. I do know if he's out there, he's doing all he can to get back to us."

"He could be hurt," said Jace. "It could be somebody's tending to him and don't know how to find us."

"Maybe so." She rose from the bench. "We'll talk about it to-morrow. We both need some rest."

Jace got his bedroll and bedded down near the campfire.

Rebecca climbed into the wagon and tried to sleep but laid thinking about Jace. Telling him her fears about Hank would only burden him more than he already was.

Rebecca woke the next morning to crisp air and a beautiful sunrise. A flow of energy ran through the camp. Luke Barker rode up to their wagon. "Mrs. Quaid, you have everything ready to start the trail? We've got to make up some time today."

She closed the toolbox attached to the left side of the wagon near the water barrel. "Yes. Jace needs to finish greasing one more axel."

"Good, ma'am." He glanced over his shoulder. "Jace, once we get going, Captain Brenner thought you might help me ride ahead and check the trail." He turned. "That is if it's all right with you, Mrs. Quaid."

"I'm sure we'll be fine. Carl Webster has been nice enough to keep an eye on our wagon."

"Thank you, ma'am." He nodded at Jace. "As soon as I check on the herd, we'll see what's up ahead." He tipped his hat at Rebecca and rode off.

She noticed Jace didn't say anything. He didn't have to. His face glowed with excitement.

Ben ran up to Jace. "Can I go too?"

Jace shook his head. "Sorry, Ben, not this time."

"Awe, Jace. I could ride Pa's horse."

"No, Ben. You need to stay and help Mamma and Hannah. I won't be gone long." Jace saddled his horse then called out to him. "How about a game of checkers tonight after supper?"

Ben's snaggletooth smile spread across his face. "Sure, that sounds good."

Hannah jumped from the back of the wagon and laughed. "He's going to beat you again, Ben. He always does."

He waved his hand in the air. "Not this time."

Emily walked up behind Hannah and smiled at Ben. "I heard what Hannah said. Maybe we could play checkers when we stop for lunch."

Ben frowned. "No, you're a girl."

"Ben Quaid. You know better than that," scolded Rebecca, tying the sash of her bonnet.

Hannah grabbed Emily's hand. "Don't mind Ben," she said and led Emily off to a patch of purple wildflowers.

Rebecca peered down at Ben. "We've got a long way to go to-day. You can help me lead the team, okay?"

"Can I hold your staff?"

"Just be careful where you point it."

Within a few minutes, Rebecca's wagon joined the others on the trail. Jace mentioned that Captain Brenner said, with no unforeseen mishaps, they might make Fort Kearney in three days. The captain's words crept back. Her concerns for Jace if Captain Brenner chose to leave them in Fort Kearny consumed her thoughts. There was nothing left for them in Cutter Springs and certainly not in Millbury.

Rebecca's parents disowned her after marrying Hank. Now, without him, Rebecca wondered if her family was right. Not about Hank, but about her and her children's future.

Clouds intermittently hid the hot sun. Rebecca walked beside the oxen, her mind filled with questions only God could answer. *What do I do? I can't do this by myself.* Her chest tightened. Tears rose. *Lord, I'm unsure of tomorrow, and the next day, and next week. I depended on Hank for everything. I feel lost without him.*

Her thoughts were interrupted. "Mamma." Ben walked up beside her dragging the staff. Hannah and Emily trailed a few steps behind him.

"Yes, Ben?" She took her bandana and wiped her face, feeling the dampness of her tears.

"Emily said her mother wants us to come eat supper with them tonight."

"Mr. Calhoun and his wife will be there too," said Emily.

The lines on Rebecca's face relaxed. "That would be nice."

Rebecca smiled knowing supper with the Websters and the Calhouns was exactly what she needed.

The wagon train stopped at noon by a grove of mesquite trees. Rebecca was taking some pickled eggs and beef jerky from the wagon when Jace and Luke Barker rode up.

She called over her shoulder. "Are you hungry, Jace?"

Jace blurted, "Would you want to take your meal with us, Mr. Barker?"

Rebecca spun and raised an eyebrow at Jace. "He may have things he needs to take care of."

"Mamma, we have plenty." He turned to Luke. "Please stay and eat with us."

Rebecca looked at Luke. "You're welcome to stay."

"If you're sure you have enough. I'd enjoy the company." He nodded. "And Jace can tell you what the trail's like up ahead. Captain Brenner's hoping we can be in Fort Kearney soon."

"Just what's in Fort Kearney?" Rebecca asked. "And are there any families living there?"

Luke took the plate Rebecca handed him before squatting by the wagon wheel. "There're a few families who work in the mercantile and other businesses, and of course, the government troops. There's even a doctor. The cavalry took over the fort about a year ago. Before that, there wasn't much there. The Plains Indians do some trading with the post. They trade horses and food for things the people on the wagon trains bring out west. And you can post letters there too."

Hannah and Ben sat on the bench against the wagon. Ben gasped. "There're real Indians there?"

Rebecca's forehead creased. "Is it safe with Indians so close?"

"Yes, ma'am." Luke grinned. "They only want to trade for things they don't have. In most cases, they're not dangerous."

She tilted her head. "But we've heard stories about Indian raids."

He laughed. "Mostly from penny magazines written to make a good story. Not that there haven't been some situations, but they were mostly started by overzealous emigrants who took the first shot."

Ben said, "Have you ever been around the Indians?"

"Yes. The Sioux tribe has a scout who's helped several wagon trains maneuver down into Ash Hollow. Maybe you'll get to meet him. Ash Hollow's around a hundred and fifty miles on the other side of Fort Kearney."

Rebecca handed him a slice of fruit bread. "Mr. Barker, is Captain Brenner still planning on leaving us in Fort Kearney if it's just Jace to tend our wagon?"

Luke paused before answering. "Ma'am, he's the captain of this wagon train, and what he says is the law around here."

"But, Mr. Barker," said Jace, "you know I can handle anything that happens with our wagon. You've seen us stay up with the others."

He smiled and nodded. "I know. I've seen what you can do. I know the captain and he's a fair man. I'll do all I can to make sure we don't leave you behind, but his word's final." He looked at Rebecca. "Ma'am, are you a praying woman?"

"Yes, I am."

"Then you know how the Lord works. We don't know what's going to happen, but we know He does. I'll be praying your husband finds his way to the wagon train before too long. And thank you for the meal." He rose from the bench, handed her his plate, and returned to his chores.

Rebecca leaned against the wagon to catch her breath. Holding her stomach, a wave of nausea came over her. The thought of pulling her wagon from the others and watch them travel on to Oregon frightened her. She took a deep breath to clear her head.

CHAPTER FIVE

The caravan of emigrants crossing the massive plains numbered a hundred and forty men, women, and children. Families came from all walks of life leaving civilization to start up settlements in an untamed territory.

Each day on the trail became more unbearable. The wind was never-ending, along with the constant lookout for prairie rattlers. Rebecca walked beside the team and held the brim of her bonnet against the right side of her face to shield it from the blowing dirt.

"Mamma?" Hannah called down to her mother from the seat of the wagon.

Rebecca slowed her pace. "Yes, Hannah."

"Does the wind blow in Oregon?"

Rebecca chuckled. "I don't know. We can only hope for at least a calmer breeze."

"Do you think there are trees there?"

"From what I understand, there are lots of trees, and mountains, and valleys. And you can grow all kinds of things there."

"Good, because I'm getting tired of the wind blowing and no shade."

Rebecca laughed out loud thinking even a five-year-old has an opinion about most things. "I'm getting tired of it too. But in a couple of days, we'll be in Fort Kearney. Do you remember Mr. Barker telling us about Ash Hollow? Well, it's about two weeks on the other side of the fort. We'll see lots of trees there."

Rebecca's attention diverted to a number of tall clumps of prairie grass just ahead of the wagon train. However, as they got closer the clumps weren't prairie grass at all. There were hundreds of small crosses and mounds of dirt dotting the landscape not far from the trail. The numbers grew as the trail continued. Becoming queasy at the sight of so many souls left behind on the prairie, she put her hand on the yoke to steady herself. Drops of sweat accumulated on her forehead.

"Mamma, why are there so many crosses?" asked Hannah.

Before she could answer, Ben ran up alongside the wagon. "Mamma, who died?"

Rebecca took a deep breath and tried to find the words. "I don't know for sure, Ben. Things happen to people no matter where they are, but from the number of graves, there could have been some kind of illness go through the wagon train."

Ben's eyes got big. "You think Indians did this?"

"Don't go assuming something you're not sure of. Your imagination can run away with you sometimes."

"I know, Mamma, but it could have been Indians. Mr. Barker said they live all around here."

"And he said in most cases they won't bother us."

"But, Mamma—"

"What did I say?"

Jace hollered from a few feet ahead. "Ben, don't argue with Mamma."

She put her hand on Ben's shoulder. "Unless we learn how they died, we don't need to let our minds run wild. Now, go look for some firewood to fill our firebox. Watch where you step, and don't go too far from the wagon."

"Okay." He scurried off.

Holding tight to the sides of the wagon seat, Hannah bounced with every rock and hole on the trail. Rebecca noticed how quiet she and Jace had become.

She walked beside the animals trying to avert her eyes from the immense landscape of graves. Every so often she goaded the team with her staff to hurry them on. But the sight was planted in her mind. She prayed Hank wasn't buried somewhere on the prairie.

The sun blazed and dirt whipped around the wagons. Rebecca pressed her hand against her forehead to try and relieve the throbbing. Trickles of sweat ran down her back. She took her neckerchief and dipped it into the water bucket. After washing the dust from her face, she forced herself to continue. Rebecca used her staff not only to nudge the oxen but to steady herself. Every muscle in her body ached.

From the direction of Captain Brenner's supply wagon, Pete sounded the bugle for everyone to gather the livestock and make camp. She and Jace worked their wagon toward the circle. Luke Barker rode up to help get their wagon situated for the night.

"Jace," said Luke, "go on to the river and water your horses and Lucy. I'll help your mom with the wagon. As soon as I get it in line with the other wagons, you and Ben can take the team of oxen for water."

Rebecca stopped and gripped her staff with both hands. She rested her head against her hands.

Luke got off his horse and led it to where Rebecca stood. "Ma'am, are you okay?"

She raised her head. "I'm fine." Pausing, she asked, "Do you know why there were so many graves along the trail today?"

"Well, ma'am, I've been a wagon train scout for seven years. For some reason, this part of the trail is where lots of cholera cases show up. Some years are worse than others. There are a lot of reasons people die on the trail, but if an epidemic of cholera gets started, it can take out most everyone on a wagon train."

The mention of cholera gave Rebecca chills. She remembered what it did to a small community not five miles from Millbury when she was growing up.

"The captain will caution everyone to boil their water until we get to Fort Kearney."

She cooled her face with a wet neckerchief. "Do you think we'll reach the fort soon?"

"I'm sure we will if the weather doesn't slow us down."

The wagons circled the livestock. Rebecca and Jace set up their camp, along with the others, for the night. Her energy sapped after the long, hot day, she tended to her chores, finished supper, and put Ben and Hannah to bed. The campfires and familiar voices became a source of comfort to Rebecca.

She and Jace sat by their fire. "What if Pa's not back by the time we reach Fort Kearney?" said Jace.

Rebecca gazed up into the night sky and sighed. She turned her attention to Jace. "All I know to do is pray that somehow if your pa doesn't return by then, Captain Brenner will consider how you've been able to oversee our wagon up to now."

"We're only about a day and a half away." He crinkled his brow. "I know Mr. Barker trusts me to get us to Oregon."

Rebecca emptied the coffee pot over the hot ashes of the campfire and took their cups to the wooden table. "I don't know what we would do without him. Thankfully, he's made sure we were where we needed to be since we joined the wagon train." She turned to Jace. "But more importantly, he's seen how you've measured up." She peered into her son's eyes. "I'm so proud of how you've handled our situation. Your pa would be proud of you too." Rebecca paused, not wanting to voice it, but said, "I'm not sure Hank's coming back."

Jace's face turned red and he jumped up. "Don't say that. Don't ever say that." He shook. "He wouldn't leave us like this."

She grabbed his hand, but he stepped back. "Jace, sweetheart, he's been gone too long. He knows where we are. He would've gotten some kind of message to us if he was still alive." She clutched her hands together. "I don't want to give up on him either, but we can't prolong the truth." Rebecca's throat tightened.

Jace turned and ran into the darkness.

Rebecca spent a sleepless night listening for Jace's return. She was relieved to hear the bugle signal the start of a new day. To her surprise, when she stepped from the wagon into the morning sunshine, Jace was busy placing the hickory yokes on the team of oxen. She silently thanked God.

"Good morning." Rebecca walked up beside Jace. She wanted to take him in her arms.

"Morning." He gazed to the west. "Looks like we might be in for some weather today."

"Cooler weather would suit me fine." She put her hand on his arm. "Jace?"

"Mamma, we don't know for certain if Pa is dead or alive. There's no use talking about it now. I need to check the strap on the yoke."

Within minutes, the camp came alive with everyone going about their morning tasks. The smell of bacon, Johnny cakes, and coffee filled the air. Rebecca heard children laughing, babies crying, and men shouting orders working to ready their wagons.

Rebecca walked a few feet beyond the team and noticed a group of men gathered near Captain Brenner's wagon. The captain held a map while the men studied the trail.

She pulled her bonnet up over her curls and exhaled. The night's tossing and turning added to Rebecca's already fatigued body.

Ben and Hannah jumped from the wagon and ran to their mother.

"Mamma," Ben said, "did you have a bad dream last night? I could hear you crying."

She rubbed his head. "No, Ben, I was fine."

Hannah giggled. "I think you were having the bad dream, Ben."

Rebecca shooed them over to the washbasin. "Both of you need to wash up before breakfast. And Ben, you might want to get some soap and water behind your ears."

He frowned. "Oh, Mamma."

"Hurry now. We've got a lot to do before we start out today."

She and the children finished packing the wagon while Jace tended the animals. Luke Barker led his horse up beside their wagon. "Good morning." He inspected the wagon and hollered. "Jace, looks like you've got everything yoked and ready."

Jace smiled and nodded.

"Fort Kearney's about twenty-five miles down the trail," said Luke. "We should make it by noon tomorrow."

Rebecca smiled. "That's good. We're one more day closer to Oregon." She hoped he picked up on her subtle optimism of continuing with the wagon train once they reached Fort Kearney.

He tipped his hat and rode off to check the other wagons.

Rebecca called out, "Ben, help me pour this extra milk into the butter churn." They hurried to fill the churn, place the lid on top, and hang it from under the wagon. "By the time we stop for camp tonight, the wagon will have jostled enough to make fresh sweet butter for our supper."

As Rebecca and Jace lined up their team on the trail, loud sounds of whips and reins cracking filled the air. Their cargo clanged and swayed with every creak of the wagon. Ben and Hannah ran and played with the other children, the oxen snorted, and their wagon wheels turned up dust.

Rebecca grabbed her staff and slapped the oxen as she had since Hank disappeared. "Giddup!"

By noon, dark clouds hung low in the north. Streaks of lightning and the roar of thunder rolled across the prairie. The captain rode by each wagon urging the families to push their teams down the trail a little harder.

Luke," said Captain Brenner, "ride up ahead and look for a good spot to gather everyone in case the weather gets bad."

"Yes, sir."

Captain Brenner watched the clouds move closer. Years on the trail taught him how the weather could change for the worse in a matter of minutes. He took his hat off, ran his fingers through his hair, and replaced it making sure to secure it enough to withstand a strong gust of wind.

The wind picked up. Rebecca grabbed Hannah and lifted her up onto the wagon seat. "Hannah, make sure your bonnet's on tight."

To Ben, she said, "See if Lucy's rope is tied to the wagon good and tight. Looks like we may be in for some bad weather."

Ben started for Lucy, then turned and asked, "Mamma, you think Mr. Barker's close by?"

"Never mind about Mr. Barker. Just go check on Lucy."

Dirt rolled in from the storm building up just a few miles north of the wagons. Jace pulled his hat further down over his eyes. Using the yoke to steady himself, he moved closer to his mother. "You and Ben walk on the south side of the wagon. It'll keep some of the dirt from covering you up. And Hannah, crawl back into the wagon bed."

The storm hit. Rain came in sheets, racing across the prairie.

Luke appeared and hollered over the sound of the wind. "Jace, go straight for those rocks. Wedge the wagon against them as close as you can, then get everybody underneath the wagon. There's a prairie twister headed our way."

Rebecca helped Ben up into the wagon. She wiped the rain and dirt from her eyes. "Ben, you and Hannah sit tight." Grabbing the staff from the front of the wagon, she hurried to the other side of the team to help Jace while he worked the leather lead reins.

The twister roared toward them, increasing in sound and strength.

"Jace! Can you see the rocks?"

The wind pulled at her, making her staff useless. She held on to the wagon hitch to keep her balance, hollering at the oxen to move.

"The rocks are just a few yards up ahead," Jace yelled, then slapped the leather against the team again.

A bloodcurdling scream pierced the air and a frightening chill ran through Rebecca's body. Trying to see through the rain and dirt, she hollered, "Jace, somebody's hurt."

Jace yelled, "Mamma, keep pushing the team."

"But that's Sarah screaming."

More screams. Rebecca concentrated on the team, but she knew something terrible had happened.

"We're at the rocks." Jace yelled. "Turn the team to the right. We need the wagon up against rock wall."

They positioned the wagon as close to the rocks as possible. Before Rebecca could get to Ben and Hannah, the tornado reached them and thrashed against the wagon. Jace pulled her underneath the wagon by the wheel closest to the rocks. He covered her with his body. The ground shook. Rebecca put her hands over her ears thinking her eardrums would burst. All she could hear was the roar of the tornado.

Then as quickly as it came, it was gone.

Jace raised up. "Mamma, are you okay?"

"Yes, I think so. What about you?"

Before he could answer, Hannah cried out, "Mamma. Where are you?"

Rebecca scrambled from underneath the wagon and hurried to her children. Pulling herself up into the wagon bed, she found them huddled by the cedar trunk. "It's okay. The storm's over."

They bolted from behind the trunk and clung to her, rain and mud drenched dress and all.

"The loud noise hurt my ears," said Hannah.

"I know, honey, but it's gone now." Rebecca held them in her lap rocking them back and forth.

Ben popped his head up. "Where's Jace?"

"He's checking the animals." He laid his head back on her shoulder.

Rebecca wiped tears from Hannah's face and kissed them both. Reaching for a dry shawl, she said, "I need to go see about Sarah. I won't be long. Stay here with Jace. He's right outside the wagon."

She crawled from the tailgate. Putting her hand over her mouth, she gasped at the sight.

"Jace?"

He came from the front of the wagon. "I'm right here."

"Are the animals okay?"

"Yes. They're fine."

She hugged him. "I have to find Sarah. You, Ben, and Hannah stay right here until I get back."

She searched frantically for Sarah and her family. In the upheaval that surrounded her, Luke Barker rode up and startled her. "Mrs. Quaid. Are you okay? Are Jace and the children okay?"

"Yes, they're fine. We made it through the storm."

Scanning the wreckage spread across the prairie, she pulled her shawl tight around her shoulders. "I've never witnessed such devastation." She stared at the mound of mud a few feet from her, then recognized the body of Jim Bailey.

Luke frowned. "None of his family survived."

She placed her hand on his horse. "Have you seen Sarah or Carl?"

He pointed toward the west near the embankment of the ridge. "But, ma'am, I think you should know. Emily was run over sometime during the storm."

Rebecca's heart lurched. "Is she all right?"

"I'm sorry, ma'am. She died."

Rebecca's body shuddered. She turned in the direction he pointed to see Josh Webster bending over his mother.

Struggling to run through the mud and the debris, Rebecca saw Sarah holding the lifeless body of her daughter.

She bent beside her best friend. "Sarah, oh, Sarah."

"Rebecca, what am I going to do? My baby, my baby's gone." She hugged the small, still body and sobbed, along with her husband and their boys.

Rebecca wrapped her arm around Sarah's shoulders. She looked down at Emily.

Is Oregon worth this? How can any of us withstand the hardships of this trail?

CHAPTER SIX

Later, under a full moon, Rebecca made out groups of men gathering what was salvageable from the storm, along with a detail of men digging graves in the rain-soaked ground. Throughout the night she heard weeping. A heavy cloud of grief settled on her soul.

Rebecca finally got Ben and Hannah to sleep. However, each time she closed her eyes, she could see Sarah. She was so grateful her children were spared, but her soul mourned Sarah and Carl's loss. Completely exhausted, Rebecca laid gazing at Ben and Hannah too weary to sleep.

The next morning Captain Brenner climbed onto the bed of one of the damaged wagons. "Before we start for Fort Kearney, Reverend Jamison will say a few words over the souls who were lost in the storm."

The reverend stood before those forced to leave their loved ones buried along the trail. His comforting words strengthened Rebecca reminding her God has an unfailing love for the brokenhearted. She gripped Ben and Hannah's hands. Tears flowed down her face as did everyone else's.

Captain Brenner cleared his throat, placed his hat back on, and confirmed what everyone dreaded to hear. "Two families died in the storm. Jim and Clara Bailey and their two sons, Henry and Clint, and John and Evie Davis. Also, Carl and Sarah Webster's daughter, Emily, perished along with Mildred Shaw. There's damage to more than half of the wagons. We lost several head of cattle, oxen, horses, and mules."

He rubbed his forehead. "Folks, we all know how hard and relentless this land can be. We've experienced some unexpected situations that God has carried us through, this being one of them. We're still a ways from Oregon and the possibilities of more trials lay ahead of us. But with His help and a determination to finish what we started, we're going to make it to the land He's provided for us."

Rebecca and her family walked back to the wagon.

"Mamma, why did this happen? Emily was my best friend." Hannah's lower lip quivered.

"Sweetheart, let's take a walk by the river. Ben, you go with Jace for now."

The rippling water ran downstream as if the storm never happened. Rebecca stooped, and Hannah slipped into her arms. "Sweetheart, I'm so sorry about Emily. I know you loved her and are going to miss her."

Hannah put her arms around Rebecca's neck and they wept.

The wagon train inched its way toward Fort Kearney while leaving the graves of friends and family behind. Rebecca walked beside the wagon keeping Ben and Hannah close to her. She gazed at Jace working the team down the trail. The tornado took Emily from Sarah and Carl. A sob caught in her throat at the thought it could have easily been her children.

Not long on the trail, the sight of the fort appeared on the horizon. Walking near the team, Jace turned to his mother and waved his hand. "There's Fort Kearney. Do you see it? Mr. Barker described it as the closest thing to civilization since the wagon train left Missouri."

She moved out a few steps from the wagon. "Yes. It won't be long now, and we can get fresh supplies."

Hannah took her mother's hand. "Will Pa be at Fort Kearney when we get there?"

"No, honey, I don't think so." She pushed some strands of blond hair under Hannah's bonnet.

Jace patted the lead ox and walked back to Hannah. Picking her up, he carried her to the team and swung her onto the back of one of the ox. "How about riding ole' Brownie for a while." She giggled and held on to the leather strap, swaying with the gate of the team.

Ben was by his mother but ran to Jace. "I want to ride too."

Jace placed him behind Hannah. "You both hold on. I don't want to have to pick you up off the ground."

Ben turned to his mother. "I know how to ride. Don't I, Mamma?"

Jace grinned and waited while Rebecca caught up with him. Keeping pace with the wagon, he put his arm around her shoulders. "When Mr. Barker checked on us at noon, he didn't have a lot to say, did he?"

"No." She took his hand. "Once we reach Fort Kearney, I hope he'll put a good word in for you to the captain. He couldn't help but notice how you've managed things since we joined the wagon train."

Rebecca and Jace walked in silence listening to Ben and Hannah's chatter. Rebecca didn't want to face it, but she was at a fork in the road. It had been three weeks since Hank rode off to find water. Even if Captain Brenner allowed them to continue with the wagon train, the Rocky Mountains loomed before them. How was she going to get three children, livestock, and a wagon over them, even with Jace's help? And it wasn't fair to keep depending on Mr. Barker.

Rebecca let go of Jace's hand. "The sun'll be down soon. We'll be stopping to set up camp. The children need to go collect some firewood."

Jace lifted Ben and Hannah off the ox. As they ran through the scrub, Jace hollered, "Watch for prairie rattlers."

Rebecca smiled when Sarah approached their wagon and fanned herself with her apron.

"The heat is stifling today." Wiping her brow, Sarah said, "Carl thinks we should be in Fort Kearney by noon tomorrow. Did Mr.

Barker have any news for you at lunch? I noticed him and Captain Brenner talking before breakfast."

"No. He said very little, which isn't like him."

They continued together down the trail. "I know this is hard." Sarah exhaled. "But our best-made plans can sometimes go awry. I know you never dreamed you'd be entering Fort Kearney without Hank. I never thought I'd be doing the same thing without Emily."

Rebecca and Sarah looped arms and fell in step with the wagon. Rebecca squeezed Sarah's arm. "I don't believe I've ever met a woman with your strength."

Sarah rolled her eyes. "If you only knew. I'm as weak and vulnerable as they come. If I didn't know I'd see Emily again in heaven one day, I'd sit down and never get up."

"How are Carl and the boys?"

"You know men. They hold it all in, but when they look at me their eyes are full of grief. I don't know what I'd do without their strength, though." She gestured toward the Shaw wagon. "It's Grady Shaw I'm worried about. Since Mildred died in the storm, I don't think he's cried a tear trying to stay strong for his young 'uns."

"I miss her so. I'm just glad Jenny's old enough to take care of the little ones."

Sarah frowned. "That's a load of responsibility, but no more than what Jace took on. Has he faced the fact that Hank may not come back?" She gave Rebecca a side look. "And have you?"

"He won't talk about it, but Hank's been gone too long."

They walked and admired the beauty of the late afternoon sun dancing off the prairie grass. Rebecca slowed down pulling Sarah along with her and walked a ways from the wagon. She glanced over at Sarah. "Did you ever think your life could change so drastically over something you had no control over?"

Sarah laughed. "It happens all the time. I never thought I'd be walking across this dry prairie and living out of a covered wagon."

Rebecca stared ahead. "My father owns the biggest timber mill in Millbury, Massachusetts." Rebecca waved the dust from the air. "When I was growing up I had the best clothes, the best horses to ride, and the most prestigious tutors in the area. My mother worked priming me to marry a man who would be financially successful like my father."

"What happened to change your life?"

"I met Hank at a Christmas ball when I was eighteen. He was in Millbury visiting a cousin who worked in my father's mill." Rebecca's face softened. "Hank was tall with blue eyes that twinkled when he smiled. I fell in love with him the minute I saw him."

"How did your mother take it?"

"Not well. All Hank wanted was to own a ranch and raise a family. So, we married and moved to Cutter Springs. His parents died right after we married, so when his brother and his family moved to Oregon, Hank yearned to do the same."

"Do your parents know you're on this wagon train?"

"Yes. I've written them so many times, and I've never gotten a response. Not even when my babies were born." She gazed at the ground. "There's nothing I can do now but live with the decision I made to marry Hank," Rebecca turned to Sarah, "and I don't regret it. But that's not what's bothering me right now." She paused. "Have you ever pushed something down inside you so deep you could feel it festering?"

"Lots of times. But I found it never heals until you get it out in the open."

Rebecca took a deep breath, then told Sarah about the man she killed and Hank's watch.

Sarah grabbed Rebecca's arm and stopped her. "He didn't hurt you, did he?"

"No, but I could see he was going to. I'll never forget the look in his eyes and that horrible scar that ran down his face. We buried him not far from the wagon."

"Doesn't sound like you had a choice. What did Jace say about the watch when he saw it?"

"He doesn't know about it. I had to settle it in my own mind first. But before I could think, Hank's horse, Rowdy, showed up that same morning. The stranger must have ridden in on him the night before. It happened so fast we didn't pay any attention. I've tried not to give up hope that Hank's okay, but it seems there can only be one explanation." Rebecca squeezed Sarah's hand. "Except, I keep praying he's still out there somewhere trying to get back to us."

As Sarah and Rebecca resumed walking, Sarah said, "Never give up hope, honey. Stranger things have happened."

"And now I have to decide what to do next." Rebecca clasped her hands. "If Hank doesn't show up we have nothing to go back to in Cutter Springs."

"Captain Brenner said we're staying in Fort Kearney a day or two to rest up and get fresh supplies. That'll give you time to think things through, and," Sarah leaned toward Rebecca, "tell Jace about the watch."

Rebecca shook her head. "I've always been one who believed there was a purpose for every circumstance. I believe God places us exactly where He can bless us and where we can bring Him glory. But for the life of me, I have no idea where God is leading us."

The bugle sounded to circle up the wagons. Sarah sighed. "Finally. It's been a long day." She hugged Rebecca. "He'll show you the way, and I'll be praying for you."

The next morning, Fort Kearney lay only a mile down the trail. Placing her staff on the hooks fastened to the railing, Rebecca lifted Hannah up onto the slow-moving wagon, then climbed up herself to get a better look at the fort.

Holding on to Hannah with one hand, Rebecca braced herself on the seat with the other. Her palm pressed against the rough wood. Moving it, she peered down and stared at the grooves she earlier marked counting the thirty-one days before meeting the wagon train.

Hannah's eyes got big. "Mamma. Look at the trees."

Taking her eyes from the grooves, she lifted her head. "Oh my, aren't they beautiful. It looks like they've planted cottonwood trees around the fort."

Jace moved several steps to the side of the team and peered down the trail. Ben followed him and pulled on his arm. "How much longer till we get there?"

"Not long," Jace turned to his mother as he walked, "and from here, the fort looks to be good sized."

Rebecca stretched to get a better look at the fort. The morning breeze cooled her face. Maybe fresh supplies and a day's rest would overshadow her fear of being left behind.

CHAPTER SEVEN

Arriving at Fort Kearney before noon, Rebecca found it to be a collection of ramshackle wooden buildings surrounding a central parade ground having no fortified walls.

Luke Barker rode up and reined in his horse. "Mrs. Quaid, Captain Brenner and Tom Hayes, the other scout, are checking in with the fort commander. For now, the captain's ordered us to gather our wagons on the north side of the fort. He'll explain about getting supplies and trading your oxen for fresh ones when everyone gets settled."

"Thank you. I have my list of supplies we need."

A smile came across Rebecca's face then it disappeared. He may have meant the fresh supplies were for their return trip to Cutter Springs. Captain Brenner's decision was still unknown to her, but she knew it would be soon.

Rebecca helped Jace position their wagon under one of the cottonwood trees alongside Carl and Sarah's. Once in place, they hurried to the supply wagon and gathered with the others to receive instructions from Captain Brenner.

He stood at the back of the wagon. "I know everyone's tired. We all need some rest, along with our livestock. We'll be here for a couple of days so you can restock your supplies and do your needed repairs. You'll find a blacksmith, a mercantile, a gunsmith, and a place to do laundry. They even offer baths for twenty-five cents apiece."

Sam Jacob yelled, "It's about time some of you washed the prairie stench off."

Carl Webster slapped Sam on the back. "And you can be first."

Everyone laughed.

The captain continued, "You can speak to Private Quincy at the stockyard about trading your animals in for fresh ones. If you have any letters you want to post back home, the Post Office is next to the mercantile. This is Saturday, so be ready to pull out Monday morning at six o'clock."

Rebecca listened, then she and the children walked back to the wagon. Thinking about Hank, she wondered if Oregon was the right decision. And now Captain Brenner held their future in his hands. She loved Hank, but without him she found herself longing for the security of Millbury and her parents.

Ben interrupted her thoughts. "Since Pa's not here, will he know where to find us?"

"Sweetheart, your Pa will find us the best way he can." She knew she wasn't telling Ben and Hannah the truth. But for now, they would have to go on believing Hank was on his way back to them.

"Go to the stockyard, Jace, and take a look at the oxen. We have two that are limping, and Brownie's breathing too hard to get us much farther. The children and I will be at the mercantile when you're finished."

Rebecca held up her list. "Okay, let's go see what Fort Kearney's mercantile has that we might need."

Ben said, "Hurry, Mamma, before they run out of candy."

Ben and Hannah rushed into the mercantile ahead of Rebecca. "Children, stay close to me. I don't want to lose you in this crowd."

The establishment overflowed with eager shoppers checking off the items on their list. The shopkeeper and his wife scurried through the aisles gathering the supplies needed for their numerous customers.

This gave Rebecca time to examine bolts of fabric, aprons, bonnets, and lovely parasols. Standing in the center of the store, her mind flooded with memories of Millbury. Even the sound of the blacksmith two doors down pounding the hot metal brought back scenes of the town—now so far away. Taking in a deep breath, she caught the aroma of fresh coffee, spices, and tobacco. She peered at shelves stocked with every imaginable kitchen device and apparatus a homemaker would need to make the journey west. Dutch ovens and three-legged skillets lined one wall. She picked up a cone-shaped copper contraption. The storekeeper's wife came from the other side of the store. When she passed by, Rebecca inquired about it.

The pleasant woman explained. "It's a beer or ale warmer. Though you can use it for any liquid. Because of its cone-shape and handle, you can push the bottom down into hot coals and it will heat liquid much faster than with ordinary pans." She grimaced. "My husband ordered several dozen of them, but there hasn't been much interest." She smiled. "You'll have to excuse me. I'm needed at the cash register."

Rebecca replaced the apparatus on the shelf.

"Mamma," Hanna said, pointing to something on the shelf. "What's that?"

"It's an egg beater.

"Do we need one?"

"No, it would be just one more thing to keep up with."

Taking Ben and Hannah's hands, they edged their way through the throng of people until they reached the fresh produce bins.

Ben tugged at Rebecca's sleeve. "Look, Mamma." He was eye level to the jars on the counter filled with hard candy and licorice.

"Yes, I see it." She studied her list again. "If you'll be patient and let me get the supplies we need, you and Hannah can each have a piece."

After a lengthy time, Rebecca gathered every item on her list, and Ben and Hannah delighted in their sweet treats.

Rebecca and the shopkeeper were standing at the counter when Jace entered the mercantile. She waved at him and he rushed over to her.

"Mr. Horton, the shopkeeper, and I have finalized our arrangements to pick up our supplies. We'll need to hitch the team to the wagon. He said we could load them from the side door."

"This was waiting for you at the Post Office." Jace handed her an envelope. "The postmaster gave it to Captain Brenner."

She took the envelope with her name written across the front, along with Fort Kearney. Holding her breath, she leaned against the counter. Could this be news of Hank? Her hands shook and beads of sweat formed on her brow. Pushing herself from the counter, Rebecca placed the letter into her drawstring bag. She turned back to the shopkeeper. "Thank you. We'll pick up our supplies within the hour."

"Aren't you going to open it?" Jace stared at her. "The captain said the letter arrived a couple of weeks ago."

"No, not here. For now, we need to go get the wagon and load our supplies. And did you look at the oxen?"

"They look good. Mr. Barker helped me pick out the best ones. He checked their hooves to make sure they weren't cracked."

"Good. Did he say when we could make the trade?"

"This afternoon late."

"That'll be fine."

Rebecca knew Jace had an idea the letter could have something to do with Hank. But this wasn't the place. She would share it with him in her own time.

While walking back to their wagon they passed the fort's main office. A sign inviting everyone to its regular Saturday night dance hung by the door. Rebecca stopped. "Look at this. It sounds like it might be fun. I know I could sure use some."

"I heard Mr. Barker talking to Mr. Johnson and Mr. Brewer about it. He said Captain Brenner likes it when everyone attends."

"The captain must think we all need a nice diversion after the last few weeks. Meeting new people would be nice too." She gave Jace a big smile. "Let's hurry and get our supplies loaded."

The building sat near the parade ground not far from the mercantile. A large opening on one end allowed light and laughter to pour out. Dressed in his Sunday best, along with the first good bath in a while, Jace followed his mother and the children into the large, lamp-lit hall. For the next few hours, he left behind weeks of prairie dust, heat, rain-drenched wagons, and miles of walking.

Musicians gathered at the other end of the building playing fiddles, banjos, and guitars while couples twirled around the floor. Tables covered with sweet pies, freshly baked currant breads, and brown sugar cakes lined the walls.

Jace, Luke Barker, and some of the other unmarried men stood by the table near the door.

Luke elbowed Jace. "You see those girls standing by Captain Brenner? Go ask the one in the blue dress to dance."

"No. She doesn't know me."

"She's Sam Jacob's daughter. I know you've seen her since we've been on the trail."

"Sure I've seen her. But she won't dance with me. She's always with Jim Eldridge."

"How do you know she won't dance with you if you don't ask?" He gave Jace a push. "Go on over there and ask her."

Walking toward the group of girls, Jace glanced at Jim who leaned against a wall not far from where they stood. He stopped, took a breath, and continued across the floor. A few steps before he reached her, the other girls said something to her. She turned and smiled at him.

"Uh, uh, would you like to dance?" His mouth was as dry as dust.

She smiled. Her eyes twinkled. "Sure I'll dance with you. Aren't you Jace Quaid?"

The muscles in his neck relaxed. "Yes, and your Ellen Jacob. I've seen you on the trail."

She put her hand out and he took it. That was all he needed to ease him onto the dance floor.

When Rebecca saw Jace dancing, she sidled up to Sarah. "Do you mind watching Ben and Hannah for a few minutes?"

"Of course. Is everything all right?"

"Yes, I just need to take care of something. I won't be gone long."

Rebecca slipped from the crowd. At their wagon she lit the lamp hanging from the sideboard. Reaching into her drawstring bag, she pulled out the envelope and stared at her name. Hands shaking, she tore it open. Along with the letter was a small folded piece of paper that fell to the ground. Before she could pick it up, her eyes caught the words on the page.

My Dear Mrs. Quaid,

I know you must think it strange to receive this letter in the manner in which it was sent. I understand your family is traveling with the wagon train going to Oregon. If you are reading this then I know you reached Fort Kearney. I have news of your husband.

Rebecca squeezed her eyes shut. Her heart raced. She wasn't sure she wanted to continue reading. A tear dropped onto the letter. She forced herself to focus on the words written on the paper.

My husband found him just east of Creek Bend along the Missouri River. He told us three men running from the law bushwhacked him. One of them had a scar running down his face. They shot your husband, stole his horse and everything he was carrying, and then left him for dead.

For two days he was delirious with fever, but once he made sense, he talked about you and your family and your plans to get to Oregon. I am deeply sorry to tell you your husband died the 2nd of May from complications of that gunshot wound. As difficult as this news is to receive, I believe he would want you to know what happened.

Be assured, my husband and I gave him a proper burial.

Enclosed is a lock of your husband's hair. We're praying it might be a comfort to you and your children.

May God bless you and your family,
Clark and Caroline Hutchinson

Rebecca's hand fell to her side. She let go of the letter and it floated to the ground. Facing the wagon, she pounded the wood with both fists, picturing the man she killed. She struck it until her hands hurt, then grabbed the wagon wheel and fell to her knees. Struggling to breathe, she didn't want to believe what she had suspected all along. She clutched her throat. She didn't want to scream.

Not now and ruin everyone's evening. Through clenched teeth, she groaned, "That despicable man killed Hank. He killed my husband. He killed my children's father." Her body shook, then went limp. She collapsed completely and totally onto the ground where her tears pooled in the dirt. As the truth sank into her heart, she reached into her pocket and gripped Hank's watch. "Hank, I need you."

Weak from anger and sorrow, Rebecca was unsure if her legs would hold her. She sat up and leaned back against the wheel. Her eyes focused on the folded piece of paper that earlier slipped from the envelope. Picking it up, she unfolded it. A lock of Hank's auburn hair tied with brown thread fell into her lap. She jerked her hand to her mouth to cover her wrenching sobs.

Hank, how do I go on? The melody of the song she and Hank danced to at their wedding drifted from the barn. Jace, Ben, Hannah. How will I tell you your pa's dead? With a deep sigh, she pressed her hands to her face. After a minute, Rebecca pulled herself up by the wagon wheel. Retrieving the letter from the ground, she slowly walked to the back of the wagon, and tucked it, along with the lock of hair, in the cedar trunk, the one Hank made her for a wedding present.

"So now we know the truth."

Straightening her shoulders, she stepped to the water barrel and dipped her handkerchief into the cool water. She washed the tears and dirt from her face and dusted off her dress.

Rebecca exhaled. "Tomorrow will be soon enough to tell Jace and the children." For now she would allow them to enjoy the festivities.

While the dance continued into the night, Rebecca and her children returned to their wagon. Ben sat on the tailgate and pulled at his boots.

"Why does Jace get to stay and we don't?" Ben grumbled.

"Because he's older than you and Hannah." Rebecca noticed the frown on his face. "You both need more rest than he does."

After tucking them into bed, Rebecca laid down beside them.

Hannah raised up. "Mamma, will you sing to us?"

In no time, Rebecca's delicate voice lulled them to sleep.

She hoped Jace would dance until the last song. But until she heard him bed down by the campfire, she wouldn't sleep.

Now that I know the truth, what's to become of us? Her chest tightened. She sat up and held her face in her hands. We'll never see Hank again. And how's Jace going to accept the reality of Hank's death? Rebecca rubbed her temples. What will Captain Brenner do with us now?

A coyote howled in the distance. She laid down and closed her eyes. Lord, is it your plan for us to go back to Cutter Springs, or are we to continue with Hank's dream of Oregon? And how are we going to do either one without him?

The music stopped. Not long after, Jace returned to the wagon humming. When he bedded down, Rebecca whispered, "Lord, help me trust you."

CHAPTER EIGHT

To Rebecca's surprise, she woke with renewed strength. Though the letter forced her to make Captain Brenner aware of her situation, for now, she was eager to prepare a Sunday breakfast of eggs and bacon, along with skillet biscuits and redeye gravy.

Jace started the fire while she pulled down the makeshift table on the side of the wagon and loaded it with bowls and pans.

"Ben, Hannah, help Jace get some water," Rebecca said.

Her two youngest scurried from the back of the wagon and grabbed some buckets. All three headed for the river that ran not far from the fort.

Rebecca breathed in the clean, crisp air. Somewhere it had rained, and she smelled the fresh scent of wet dirt. She was grateful for the cottonwood trees which helped block the sun and ever-constant wind.

Finishing breakfast, Rebecca heard Reverend Jamison's voice ring out as he sang, *"Holy, Holy, Holy, Lord God Almighty, Early in the morning our song shall rise to thee."* The singing came from the building where the dance took place the previous evening. Men, women, and children joined in.

Hanging her apron on the back of the wagon, Rebecca called out, "Hurry children, we want to hear what Reverend Jamison has to say today."

Quickening her steps, Rebecca put her hands on Ben and Hannah's shoulders to hurry them into the building now used for a sanctuary. The same musicians from the night before played, and the congregation sang along.

Sarah waved at Rebecca from a bench midway from the front. Scooting in beside the Websters, Rebecca and her family sat just as Reverend Jamison opened his Bible.

Ellen Jacob and her family sat three benches in front of them. Rebecca noticed Jace eyeing Jim Eldridge who sat next to Ellen.

Hannah sat up on her knees and whispered in her mother's ear. "Mamma, Jace isn't listening to Reverend Jamison."

"Hannah, you pay attention to the reverend, and don't worry about Jace."

"Yes, ma'am." She sat on her bottom.

Rebecca didn't hear much Reverend Jamison said either. The burden of the letter weighed on her. She scanned the sanctuary of families who represented the wagon train. None knew her plight but sitting among them gave her some measure of peace.

Reverend Jamison concluded the service with his usual words of encouragement. Tomorrow the wagon train would soon begin a three-hundred-mile journey to Fort Laramie. He prayed they would meet the challenge with courage, and strength, and trust in the Lord to get them there safely.

After leaving the service, Rebecca was leading her children back to their wagon when she noticed Captain Brenner and several other men gathered near the blacksmith.

"Jace, take Ben and Hannah back to the wagon," she said. "I'll be there in a few minutes."

"Is there something wrong?" Jace frowned. "Does it have anything to do with that letter?"

"Just do as I say. I'll explain later."

He put his hand on the backs of his siblings. "Let's go to the wagon. We've got things to do to get ready for tomorrow."

Rebecca made her way down the wood plank walk, past the mercantile, toward the blacksmith. By this time, the men had stepped around the corner and gathered underneath one of the cottonwood trees. When she got close enough to hear them, she stopped. Her intentions were never to eavesdrop, but that's what she did.

"I know what the contract says," said Luke, "but Captain, Jace can be trusted to do what it takes to stay up with the wagon train." He knew what it would do to Jace if the captain turned them away.

Tom Hayes argued. "You know what we're facing once we leave Fort Kearney, not to mention climbing the Rockies. I know he thinks he's grown, but he's not."

Captain Brenner chewed on a piece of straw and leaned against a post. "Has Jace or Mrs. Quaid hinted that they know her husband isn't coming back?"

"No, Jace hasn't given up hope on him yet," said Luke.

Sam Jacob eyed the captain. "I know we set up rules before we left Missouri. We agreed on every one of them. But Captain, I've watched that boy since they joined us. There's something about him that tells me he'd be fine."

Luke waved his hand in the air. "He managed their wagon through that storm. And, Captain, I know this isn't our concern, but from what I get from Jace, I don't think they have any place to go back to." Luke wasn't sure if his argument was for Jace to remain with the wagon train or Rebecca.

Bart Johnson scratched his head. "What Tom said was right. You think that boy can take on what lays ahead? It's not going to be easy for any of us. From what I understand, we've got some steep hills to maneuver just getting to the Rockies."

Captain Brenner took his hat off and wiped his hat band with his neckerchief. "I know Mrs. Quaid's not sure of the whereabouts of her husband. If, by chance, he shows up between here and Fort Laramie there's not a problem." He put his hat back on. "But, I have a feeling, if he hasn't found the wagon train by now, he's not going to."

"The time's coming when Jace may have to face that possibility," Luke said. "To turn them away and leave them behind could break him."

The captain pushed off from the post. "I'll make my decision within the hour."

The next morning, Rebecca stood by their team of oxen. She put her hands over her heart which swelled with gratitude over Captain Brenner's decision to allow her family to continue on to Oregon. She was so relieved that she decided not to mention the letter for now. But if the letter caused the captain to change his mind later on the trail, she couldn't bear what it might do to Jace. She anguished between protecting Jace and being honest with Captain Brenner.

Pete sounded the signal for the wagon train to pull out from Fort Kearney and head toward Fort Laramie. Rested, Rebecca and Jace urged their team along the trail, their wagon filled to the brim with fresh supplies. The new teams of oxen seemed to plod a little faster.

Hannah ran to her mother from the back of the wagon. "Mamma, is Jace going to ride with Mr. Barker today?"

Rebecca stepped between Hannah and the plodding oxen. "Don't get too close to the team." Moving down the trail, Rebecca nudged the lead ox. "I'm not sure. I guess we'll find out when Mr. Barker gets to our wagon."

A mile down the trail, Ben raced from the Jacob's wagon to his mother. He took Rebecca's hand. "Mamma, Billy Jacob was telling me about his grandparents. They live in Oregon. Do I have grandparents?"

"Yes." She rubbed his head. "You, and Hannah, and Jace have grandparents who live in Massachusetts. That's a long way from here."

"I don't know about them. Do they know about me?"

"Yes, sweetheart. I wrote them a letter when you were born."

"When we get to Oregon can you write them, and ask them to come see us?"

"As soon as we get there and settle somewhere, I'll do just that." If God could persuade Captain Brenner to let them stay with the wagon train, He could surely work a miracle with her family in Millbury.

She could tell he was studying about something.

"Mamma, can Mr. Calhoun be my grandpa until we get to Oregon?"

"Well, I don't know. But you could ask him."

He smiled up at her, then turned to Hannah. "He can be your Grandpa too."

Rebecca listened to her children's conversation until Luke Barker caught her eye checking on the wagons. In a few minutes, he rode up and tipped his hat. "Morning. Looks like we'll have good weather today. Captain Brenner is hoping we can make a good twelve miles." Turning to Jace at the head of the team, he said, "We'll need you to take a turn herding the cattle this morning. We need to keep them behind the wagons. They stir up too much dust."

Jace hung his staff on the side of the wagon and walked to the back to get his saddle.

Speaking to Rebecca, Luke said, "If I see you need help with the team, I'll send him back, ma'am."

"Thank you." Rebecca paused then added, "And Mr. Barker, we appreciate all you did to sway Captain Brenner to let us stay on with the wagon train."

"Ma'am that was his decision. It had nothing to do with me. He and some of the other fella's noticed how Jace handles himself." He reined his horse to turn and said, "I'll check on you at noon." Before she could say anything more, he rode off.

An early morning breeze made travel pleasant, but Rebecca knew it would only last a few hours. Breathing in the sweet smell of the prairie dew, she pushed strands of hair back into her bonnet.

Rebecca smiled when Hannah and Ben ran and joined the other children. Their laughter caused her heart to yearn for Hank. Under her breath, she whispered, "Memories we'll never share." She walked beside the wagon consumed by the letter. Using the staff to steady her gate, she gazed at the flat prairie that spread for miles. They will all need to know and soon. She sighed. Along with Captain Brenner.

Rebecca peered down the row of wagons at the sudden commotion coming from Jim and Penelope Brewer's direction. Dust billowed as their wagon pulled out from the formation.

The Webster's wagon traveled beside Rebecca's. She hollered at Sarah. "Is there trouble? The Brewer's just pulled away from the other wagons."

Sarah shielded her eyes from the sun and gazed in their direction. "I see Doc Brummel's wagon headed their way." She walked over to Rebecca. "It must be time for Penelope's baby."

"Will we just keep going and leave them here?"

"Yes, for now. If it takes more than a day to deliver her baby, he and his wife will pitch a tent by their wagon. Once the baby gets here, they'll catch up with us."

Rebecca shook her head. "This being her first, I pray it goes well for her." She paused. "Making our way across this prairie is harder than I expected. I can't imagine how it's been for Penelope."

"Doc Brummel and Catherine know what they're doing. He delivered three babies before you joined up with us."

"It's a comfort knowing their traveling with us."

"From what I was told, they've only been married a few months. They're planning on starting a hospital when they get to California. He graduated from Harvard Medical School, and Catherine learned all her nursing from him."

"California?"

"Yes, when we get past Fort Hall some of the wagons are breaking off and heading for Sutter's Fort." Sarah loosened the ties on her bonnet. "Captain Brenner decided before we left Missouri that Tom Hayes would take them on to California."

"How many families are leaving us?" She tapped the ox with her staff.

"I'm not sure. I think Captain Brenner said there would be six families, plus Tom."

Before Rebecca and Sarah could finish their conversation, a troop of cavalrymen approached Captain Brenner. Sarah crossed her arms. "I wonder what they need. Aren't they the same ones who stopped us on the other side of Fort Kearney looking for a bunch of outlaws?"

Rebecca's neck stiffened. "Outlaws? I was hoping they would've caught them by now. "

"Me too. Maybe Luke Barker can tell us something when we set up camp for the night." She gave Rebecca a side glance. "Speaking of telling someone something, did you talk to Jace about the watch while we were in Fort Kearney?"

Rebecca untied her bonnet and took it off. The loose curls around her face accentuated her beauty, but the worry lines across her forehead answered Sarah's question. "No. Jace and I were waiting on Captain Brenner's decision as to what to do with us. I figured one burden at a time was all Jace needed."

Since leaving Cutter Springs in a covered wagon, Rebecca learned to appreciate the small things. Time spent visiting with Sarah seemed to help with the long hours of walking.

The cowboys continually whooped and hollered at the herd of oxen and cattle plodding behind the wagons. Men and women shouted at their teams to move a little faster while babies cried and children ran and laughed. Each wagon rang out with its endless noise of pots and pans clanging from every bump on the trail.

As most days, Rebecca and Jace walked beside the team. She gazed up into the sky. "Jace, do you ever cloud watch?"

"Only if I see a storm coming."

She walked and scanned the skies. "I have to admit, I'm captivated by them. Sometimes I pretend I have a front row seat to an array of clouds that look just like mountains. And then there are other times I think I could reach up and touch them." She smiled at Jace. "They have a way of taking my mind off the dirt and noise of the day."

He smiled back. "That's why Pa loved you. You're a dreamer."

CHAPTER NINE

The evening signal sounded. Rebecca's body ached from working to keep the team at a steady pace.

Jace inspected one of the wagon wheels while making their way into the circle. "I need to take this wheel off tonight and soak it in the river. Mr. Calhoun said he noticed the iron tire is about to come off. The wood's getting too dry."

Before Rebecca could reply, Luke Barker appeared at their wagon. "Captain Brenner said we're going to try to make up some time tomorrow. The troop of soldiers slowed us down earlier."

Jace furrowed his brow. "Are they looking for rustlers?"

"The captain said there're several outlaws in the gang. They've done more than rustle cattle. They have bounties on their heads. Three of them, the Coulter brothers, robbed and killed a scout from Fort Leavenworth, along with a shopkeeper from a settlement just north of Alcove Springs. There's no telling who else they've killed."

"And they think they've come this far west?" said Jace.

Luke took something from his shirt pocket. "They captured one of the brothers south of Fort Kearney, but the other two are still on the loose." He handed Jace some wanted pictures of the outlaws. "One of them has a scar running down his face, and one has two fingers missing from his right hand."

Jace took a look and handed the pictures to Rebecca.

"Captain Brenner told the lieutenant he'd keep an eye out for them. He's putting more night guards on patrol."

Rebecca stared at the wanted pictures.

"Don't worry, they won't be hard to recognize if they ride into camp," said Luke.

Jace handed the pictures back to Luke. After he was out of ear-shot, Jace glanced at his mother. "Did you get a good look at those men?"

"More than I wanted to see."

After supper, Rebecca put Ben and Hannah to bed and she and Jace quietly sat by the campfire listening to the livestock grazing.

Finally, Jace spoke. "Mamma, we buried the one with the scar."

"The picture wasn't that clear. We can't be sure."

He picked up a stone and threw it into the darkness. "I'll never forget the look on that man's face. It's the same man."

The time had come to tell Jace. "I have something you need to see." Rebecca made her way to the back of the wagon and retrieved the letter from the trunk. Returning to the campfire, she pulled the watch from her pocket and placed it in Jace's palm. "This fell off the man we buried."

He opened the face of the watch, and from the glow of the camp-fire saw his mother's picture. Turning it over, he read the inscription.

She handed him the letter. "This is the letter we received at Fort Kearney." As he read it, Rebecca's heart grieved.

Jace's body stiffened. He jumped up, the watch gripped in his fist and shook it in Rebecca's face, tears welling up. "Pa's not coming back." He threw the letter to the ground. "The man we prayed over killed Pa." He said through clenched teeth, "I'm glad you killed him."

"Jace, you don't mean that."

"Yes, I do. An eye for an eye, Mamma."

"No, it doesn't work that way. Your pa would tell you that."

"Well, he can't now, can he." His voice rose with every word. "He's dead." He let the watch drop to the ground then whirled and ran toward the river.

Rebecca knew nothing she could say would take away the pain. Only Jesus could soothe his soul right now. He was at a crisis in his life, and whether he knew it or not, how he reconciled himself to the reality that his pa was gone would have a bearing on the rest of his life.

She put her face in her hands. "Help him, Lord."

❧

The morning signal sounded. From inside the wagon, she heard Jace yoking the oxen to the wagon. Ben and Hannah were sleeping so soundly she hated to wake them.

Rebecca softly patted them. "Ben, Hannah, time to wake up." They both dug deeper into the feather mattress. "We're a day closer to Oregon."

Hannah's eyes opened. "Mamma, will Pa be there when we get to Oregon?"

Rebecca brushed her daughter's hair back. "No, honey, he won't."

Thankfully, Hannah drifted back to sleep. Rebecca waited another minute, and then nudged them both again. "You sleepyheads better hurry if you want breakfast. Captain Brenner wants to get started early this morning. Ben, didn't Mr. Calhoun say he had another story he wanted to tell you? You don't want to miss that, do you?"

Ben crawled out from under the covers, yawned, and rubbed his eyes. He put his shirt on and worked to button it. "Mamma, Mr. Calhoun said he killed and skinned a bobcat one time. And he's going to teach me how to whittle."

"That's good. Now, you and Hannah hurry up. You both have lots to do before we get on the trail."

He rambled on. "And someday he said we'd go rabbit hunting. Did you know he can make music with a string and a twig?"

"Ben," Rebecca scolded, "you need to quit talking and get to work."

"Yes, ma'am." He grabbed his boots, and then glanced over at his sister. "Hannah, Mr. Calhoun told me his wife is making you a surprise."

She sat up wide awake. "Did he tell you what it is?"

"No, but he said you'll like it."

They both bounced out of the wagon. Rebecca grabbed a slab of bacon, some coffee, and a jar of dried apricots then climbed down from the tailgate of the wagon.

"Ben, Hannah, grab those buckets and bring me some water."

Luke Barker rode up to their wagon. "Good morning."

"Morning." She smiled.

He waved at Jace. "Everything ready for the trail?"

Jace returned the wave. "Just need to get this wheel back on the wagon."

"Need any help?"

"No, sir. I've got it, but thanks."

Luke rode on to the next wagon. When Jace finished repairing the wheel he headed for the washbasin to clean his hands. Rebecca looked up while cutting a thick slab of bacon when he walked past her.

Rebecca wasn't sure if she should bring up the wanted pictures or not. "I'll have breakfast ready soon."

She and Jace continued their chores without speaking, the tension between them palpable. She reminded herself he was no longer a boy, but a young man.

When breakfast was ready, Ben and Hannah sat on the ground eating while Jace ate his breakfast by the toolbox. He stood with his back turned to his mother. She poured herself a cup of coffee, and slowly walked over to him. Rebecca put her hand on his shoulder. "Jace, I wish I knew the words to help you. I don't understand any of this either." A pronounced silence settled between them before she spoke again. "All I know to do is keep going. That's what your pa would want us to do."

Jace swallowed hard. He turned and faced Rebecca, then grabbed her and hugged her tight. Rebecca held him close wishing she could take on his pain. When he pulled away, she wiped away his tears.

"Mamma, I'm sorry I said what I did to you last night. I was mad at that man, but I meant no disrespect to you. I was so wrapped up in my grief I didn't think about you or what you're going through."

Rebecca noticed how tall and strong Jace stood. Looking up at him, she smiled through her tears. "Jace, sweetheart, I love you." She glanced in Ben and Hannah's direction and whispered. "And it's going to take both of us to tell Ben and Hannah about your pa, not to mention Captain Brenner."

He lowered his voice. "I know. I thought about it all night. Maybe we can talk to the captain tonight after we make camp. Tomorrow will be soon enough to tell Ben and Hannah."

Rebecca placed her hand on his cheek. "We'll just have to pray he sees fit to let us travel with the wagon train all the way to Oregon."

"Once we tell Captain Brenner about Pa, I'll talk to Mr. Barker and see if he can't persuade him. I'm pretty sure he swayed the captain's decision in Fort Kearney."

"Whatever happens, we have to believe God has His hand on us."

"Pa wanted us to go to Oregon." He stepped back. "We have to get there. This wagon train's our only hope."

"Sweetheart, our hope is in Jesus. If He wants us in Oregon there's nothing that can stop us." She hugged him again. "And He's gotten us this far, hasn't He?"

Jace straightened his shoulders. "Yes, Mamma, He has."

For a brief moment Rebecca's heart was a little lighter knowing Jace would be okay. However, her concern now was Captain Brenner. The news about the outlaw they buried was one thing. Hank was another.

Rebecca turned to finish packing the wagon. "When we get on the trail would you find Mr. Barker and ask him if he could meet us at our wagon at noon?"

"Does this have something to do with the wanted pictures?"

She put a black skillet on the table. "We're going to have to tell him and the captain which one is buried back on the trail. They'll need to get word to the cavalry."

Jace frowned. "Once the cavalry finds out what we did, what will they do?"

The noon sun beat down. Rebecca and the rest of the emigrants had traveled five long miles during the morning. Between answering Ben and Hannah's questions and keeping the team going, there was little time to ponder how she would tell Mr. Barker she killed a man or Captain Brenner about Hank. A few minutes before Pete sounded the bugle for the noon break, Jace rode up the trail to find Mr. Barker.

Rebecca started a fire, then measured out flour to make Johnny cakes. Ben and Hannah stood by the table arguing about who was going to help stir the batter. She was about to scold them but stopped when Jace and Luke rode up. Jace didn't say anything, just got off his horse.

Luke tipped his hat. "Mrs. Quaid, Jace said you have some information about the outlaws the lieutenant and his men are looking for."

She wiped the flour from her hands on her apron. "Yesterday when you showed us the wanted pictures of the three men." She paused and looked at Jace.

"Ma'am, what about them?" Luke adjusted his hat.

"Mr. Barker, Jace and I saw the man with the scar a couple of days before we joined the wagon train."

"Were his brothers with him?" He got off his horse.

"No, he was alone. He rode into our camp one night after dark."

"He was on Pa's horse," said Jace.

"Are you sure he was the same man on the wanted picture?"

"Mr. Barker," Rebecca said, "I'll never forget the man's face and the scar running down his jaw."

Jace blurted, "He's the man who shot Pa."

Rebecca stepped over by Jace. "When he realized it was just me and the children, it became clear he was dangerous. Mr. Barker, I shot and killed him. He was carrying Hank's pocket watch."

He flinched. "He didn't hurt you, did he?"

"No, but by the look on his face, there was no doubt he was about to."

"We buried him on the plains," said Jace, "south of where we met up with the wagon train."

"From what the lieutenant said, he was dangerous. I'm sorry." He reached out to touch Rebecca's arm, but drew back. "I know shooting a man is a hard thing to live with no matter the situation." Luke got back on his horse.

"Will you tell Captain Brenner so he can alert the lieutenant?" asked Rebecca.

"Yes, ma'am. We know they have one of his brother's jailed at Fort Kearney. Maybe they've caught the other one by now."

"I certainly hope so. Oh, and Mr. Barker, is there a good time for Jace and me to talk to Captain Brenner?"

He put his hand on the saddle horn. "Well, ma'am, I can't promise, but I'll see if he can make some time for you. He's waiting on Tom Hayes to ride back with information concerning the South Bend River. We'll be crossing it soon."

"Please tell him it's important. There's something we need to share with him."

"Ma'am. I'll do what I can."

Rebecca waved toward her work table. "Would you like to stay and share our meal? We've got plenty of Johnny cakes and side pork."

"Thanks, ma'am," he paused, "but with Tom gone I need to check on the herd."

"That's fine." She smiled up at him.

CHAPTER TEN

After supper, Rebecca walked the children over to the Calhoun's wagon. For the last few evenings, Zeb had been teaching Ben how to tie all sorts of knots. And of course, Ben didn't waste any time tying knots in every piece of string, cord, or rope he could get his hands on. And Clara had been reading Hannah stories from a book her mother had given her when she was a little girl.

Rebecca and Jace made their way to the captain's wagon where she reminded Jace, "Whatever happens we're going to be okay. Just remember that."

He breathed in and looked straight ahead.

When Rebecca and Jace reached the wagon, Luke, Captain Brenner, and Tom were crouched by the campfire drinking coffee. All three stood when Rebecca and Jace neared.

The captain gestured to a bench by the fire. "Mrs. Quaid, have a seat." He nodded at Tom. "Go on to the chuck wagon. Pete's got your supper ready."

Rebecca sat and folded her hands in her lap. "Thank you for seeing us. I hope we're not intruding."

"No, ma'am," said the captain.

Rebecca glanced at Jace, then back to Captain Brenner. "We've come to share with you a letter I received while we were in Fort Kearney."

The captain stared at Luke and then turned to Rebecca. "I understood this was about the outlaws we were alerted about. Luke told me what happened."

"Yes, but there's something else you need to know."

The captain nodded. "Go ahead."

Rebecca took a deep breath and exhaled. "I'm afraid I've done something that was unfair to you and this wagon train." For the next several minutes she told him about the letter informing her of Hank's death and the outlaw bearing the scar she killed. "I'm sorry I didn't tell you about this earlier. I know your decision to keep us with the wagon train hinged on my husband's return."

She pulled the letter from her pocket and handed it to the captain. His eyes scanned the page. His demeanor led her to believe he suspected as much. When he finished he handed it back.

"Ma'am, I'm sorry about your husband. But the truth is, the governing body of this wagon train has wrestled with your situation from the day you rode in. As you said, the premise that your husband would eventually return was what allowed you to join up with us in the first place."

Rebecca started to speak.

He held up his hand. "Mrs. Quaid, if we thought you or your son couldn't handle the trail, we'd have left you back in Fort Kearney." He leaned against the wagon. "Mr. Barker, Carl Webster, and several others agreed Jace was capable of keeping up with the other wagons and taking on the responsibilities that went with driving this wagon train."

Rebecca gave Jace a look and her body relaxed.

The captain pushed off from the wagon. "But I want you and Jace to understand, from here on, the trail will get much more difficult. We'll help you as much as we can, but you and your son will be facing some serious challenges."

Rebecca stood. "We understand and can't tell you what this means to us. As it turns out, we have no other direction to go but west. Whatever the trail holds for us, we'll do our best to cause no undue burden."

"Pa had a dream for our family," said Jace. "Our intentions are to make that dream come true the best we know how."

The captain nodded his head at Rebecca. "Mr. Barker and I will do all we can to help you finish what you and your husband started."

Two weeks passed since the wagon train left Fort Kearney. The realization that Hank was buried someplace near Creek Bend settled on Rebecca and her family. All of them grieved, each in their own way, but Ben and Hannah handled it much better than was expected. Of course, they cried and asked a million questions.

For Rebecca, the monotonous routine of rising before sunrise, feeding and watering animals, and walking beside the wagon ten to twelve miles a day became more grueling as time went by. She found the wind to be continuous and storms unpredictable. At times she endured sweltering heat during the day, then wished for the warmth at night.

Fortunately for all, Penelope Brewer delivered her baby during the time Ben and Hannah were dealing with their father's death. Little Mary Martha was a bright spot during a difficult time for the Quaid family. Having the Brewers and their new baby back with the wagon train reminded Rebecca life still held joy.

The Brewers was situated two wagons over from Rebecca's. From inside the wagon, Rebecca and Hannah held to the wagon rail while peering at the tiny bundle in Penelope's arms. "Oh, Mamma, look at her. She's so little."

Rebecca smiled at the sleeping baby. "She's beautiful." She looked at Penelope. "She has Jim's dark curly hair." Mary Martha opened her big blue eyes then closed them and was asleep again.

The rushing water of the South Bend River roared in the distance. "Hannah, let's go. We need to get back to our wagon. We'll come back after supper and see Mary Martha again."

Leaving the Brewer's wagon, Rebecca and Hannah walked up beside their wagon and their lumbering oxen. They caught up with Jace about the time Carl Webster hollered. "We're coming to the river crossing. Can you see a ferryboat up ahead?"

Jace climbed up on the wagon seat to get a better look. "No, sir. Do we need to turn the team to the north when we get closer to the crossing?"

"No, all you need to do is stay close to our wagon. Captain Brenner will give us the signal where to steer our wagons."

Within a few minutes, Luke Barker appeared. "Jace, Captain Brenner's decided we're going to camp on this side of the South Bend tonight. We're losing daylight and it's too dangerous to cross it after dark."

"How does the river look to you?" Rebecca asked.

"It's running pretty fast. We hit it after some big rains, and it looks like it swelled to about a half-mile wide. There aren't any ferryboats at this crossing. It'll take most of tomorrow to get all our wagons and livestock across." He turned to Jace. "Have you ever taken a wagon across a river when the water's rushing downstream?"

"No, sir, but if you'll just tell us what to do I know we can manage."

"You'll do fine, son," said Luke, then turned to Rebecca. "Ma'am, try and get a good night's sleep. Tomorrow will come early and we all need to be rested."

"Mr. Barker," said Jace, "you and the captain don't have to worry about us. We'll do fine."

"Son, we'll all worry until we get this wagon train across that river."

Rebecca hardly slept. Through the night she listened to the water rush downstream. She tried to recall every scripture passage that dealt with fear. Before daylight, she lay mulling over in her mind what the day might hold. "Lord, we need you to carry us safely to the other side of the river."

"Mamma?"

"Yes, son."

Ben crawled over and nudged up beside his mother.

"What if we get in the middle of that river and something happens? I can't swim."

"I know you can't swim, but we're going to trust the Lord to help us." She hugged him close. "And from what I understand, Mr. Barker has crossed this river as many times as you've had birthdays."

His little body relaxed against hers. She smoothed his hair from his forehead wanting to savor the moment. It seemed only yesterday Jace was Ben's age and now he's almost grown. Holding him, the memory of Hank's warm smile and reassuring embrace flashed through her mind.

Ben gave his mother a sweet smile. "I'm not scared about that river anymore. It'll be like riding on a boat in the ocean. And when we get to the other side, Mr. Calhoun is going to teach me to whistle the way he does."

She laughed and hugged him close. "Well, we better get busy before Mr. Barker rides up to check on us. Hannah, breakfast will be ready soon. You and Ben get your chores done so we can cross the river today."

They said in unison, "Yes, Mamma."

Rebecca stepped down from the wagon and noticed Jace and Carl Webster standing at the edge of the river along with several other men. Luke, Captain Brenner, and Tom studied a large map and scanned the other side of the South Bend River.

Jace smiled when he returned to the wagon for breakfast. "The bacon and hot coffee smell good, and I'm hungry." He cleaned his hands in the washbasin. "Captain Brenner said we'll cross the river at the bend just south of those rocks. We'll go across at a diagonal. Mr. Barker said it's not running as fast this morning, but there are some places that are deeper than they've seen before. He didn't think the team would have any trouble getting across, though." He dried his hands and sat on the bench by the wagon.

Rebecca handed him a cup of coffee. "Did they say how many wagons can go across at one time?"

"Mr. Hayes thinks we can all travel across together." She brought him his breakfast. "Thanks. It looks good." He took a bite of bacon. "Each wagon will follow the one in front. Captain Brenner's chuck wagon will go first to forge the way. The cattle will be the last to go across."

Hannah crawled down from the wagon seat and stood by Jace. "What about Lucy? Will she be all right?"

Jace tugged on her hair. "Don't worry about Lucy." He waved his hand toward the river. "By tonight, we'll all be standing on the other side." Finishing his breakfast, he pitched the rest of his coffee in the fire. "You and Ben hurry and help Mamma gather everything up."

Within the hour, all the wagons were lined up. Captain Brenner gave the signal and Pete, his chuck wagon boss, slapped the reins and gave a loud yelp.

Rebecca waited in line watching how each wagon eased into the river. Captain Brenner, Tom, and Luke hollered orders when each wagon rolled down the bank. Jace rode alongside their wagon making sure they stayed on course.

"Mamma," Jace hollered. "Do you see how the wagons are going in at an angle? Just stay close behind Mr. Webster's wagon, and drive the team as hard as you can. Tell Ben and Hannah to hang on tight. Three more wagons and we'll be floating across."

Rebecca slapped the lead lines and hollered at the oxen as loud as she could. Their wagon traveled between the Webster's and the Jacob's.

The sun's glare reflected off the water making it hard for Rebecca to keep her bearings. Easing into the river, she held tight to the lead lines while water sprayed onto her dress.

She yelled over the roar of the river. "Ben, Hannah, hold on tight."

As far as Rebecca could tell, everything was going well until halfway across the river a scream and a splash came from the direction of the Jacob's wagon.

Rebecca yelled, "Jace. Can you see what happened?"

Someone bobbed up from the water a few feet to the left side of their wagon and swept downstream. "

"Someone's in trouble," hollered Jace.

Sam Jacob yelled. "It's Ellen. She's fallen from the wagon." He jumped in the river.

Jace threw his hat to Rebecca and jumped from his horse into the rushing water. He swam toward Ellen. The current pulled them down stream.

Rebecca struggled to keep her eyes on them until they rounded the bend and went out of sight. She screamed for her son. Her arms ached from gripping the reins, and now her body shook with fear.

Ben and Hannah hollered, "Jace! Come back, Jace!"

Several of the wagons were already on the other side of the South Bend. The Calhouns, along with others, stood on the bank hollering and pointing Luke in Jace and Ellen's direction. Riding up from the water, he spurred his horse and raced down the river bank. Cody Jacob rode past him yelling for his sister to hang on.

Rebecca worked at getting their wagon to the other side of the river. But her mind kept replaying the sight of Jace being taken down the fast running river.

CHAPTER ELEVEN

Getting their wagon across South Bend River took every ounce of strength Rebecca could muster. Several places were so deep that water seeped up into the wagon. Lucy, along with the other animals, found herself swimming a good part of the time.

After hours of waiting for Luke and Cody to return with Jace and Ellen, Rebecca sat on the bench by their wagon rocking Hannah trying to comfort her. Holding her close, she softly patted her back and wiped the tears from her face.

"Mamma," cried Hannah, "what if Jace doesn't come back?" She wrapped her arms around Rebecca's neck and bathed her mother's shoulder in tears.

Ben put his arm on Rebecca's. His chin quivered. "Jace won't leave us like Pa did, will he?"

Rebecca drew a trembling breath. "No, Ben. Mr. Barker and Ellen's brother will find them. We have to believe that."

"But what if—"

"Sweetheart, we have to be brave." She pulled Ben close to her.

Zeb and Clara walked up where they were sitting. Just the sight of them comforted Rebecca. Clara bent close to Hannah. "Zeb and I are praying for Jace."

Hannah sat up in Rebecca's lap and wiped her face. Clara put her hand out. "Why don't we let your mother rest a bit? I've got some raisin bread I think you might like. How about you, Ben. I've got plenty. "

Rebecca smiled at Ben. "You and Zeb want to get a good look at this side of the river."

Zeb put his hand on Ben's shoulder. "Your mamma's right. There may be something on this side of the river the other side didn't have. We wouldn't want to miss it."

With the children gone, Rebecca crawled up into the wagon. Alone, she took one of Hank's shirts and wrapped it around herself.

The rest of the wagons reached the north banks by late afternoon. The river was a difficult undertaking. Rebecca, along with everyone else, was soaked and worried about Jace and Ellen. She couldn't fight off the fear that Jace might as easily be taken from her just as Hank had.

After supper, she gathered with the other families for a special time of prayer. Hannah and Ben held her hands. When she knelt, she pulled her children close to her.

Hannah put her arm around Rebecca's neck. "Will God help Mr. Barker find Jace?"

"Sure, He will," said Ben. He looked at his mother. "Won't He, Mamma?"

Rebecca smiled. "We have to trust that He will."

Her soul eased with the prayer Reverend Jamison lifted to God.

The next morning, Rebecca was relieved when Captain Brenner announced the wagon train would camp there for a day or so to rest. Crossing the South Bend pushed the livestock to their limit.

Waiting on Luke and Cody to return, Rebecca paced beside her wagon. Ben and Hannah sat quietly watching their mother. She stopped, put her hands on her hips, and looked at her children. "Ben, Hannah, my pacing isn't going to bring them back any sooner. Run fetch me some water from the river."

She reached for the washtub hanging on the side of the wagon, took it down, and started a fire. A wicker basket sat inside the wagon filled with items to be laundered. The children helped Rebecca fill the tub with water. When the water began to boil, she concentrated on her task and Ben and Hannah ran to play with the other children.

"Mrs. Quaid."

Rebecca looked over her shoulder to see Captain Brenner standing with his hat in his hand. Catching her breath, she dropped the laundry paddle. He stepped forward, picked it up, and handed it to her.

"Captain Brenner. Is everything all right?" She looked around. "I haven't seen Mr. Barker ride up yet."

He held his horse's reins while it nibbled the grass behind him. "I'm sorry. I didn't mean to upset you. I wanted you to know I sent Tom out to see if he could find them."

She leaned the paddle against the wagon. "Thank you, Captain. I have to believe Jace is okay."

"Mrs. Quaid—"

"Please, Captain, call me Rebecca."

He nodded. "I know everything that's happened since you've been on the trail has been hard. This country can be awfully unforgiving."

Rebecca remembered his compassion when he learned of Hank's death.

"Ma'am, I'm praying Jace and the others get back soon."

"Thank you." She peered up at him.

He paused. "But there's something more. You might want to sit."

She lowered herself on the bench against the wagon. "Is it Jace?"

"No. It's about the man you shot. A messenger from Fort Kearney just rode into camp and said Frank Coulter, his brother, was being held until the circuit judge could get to Fort Kearney." He stepped closer. "I'm sorry to tell you he escaped two days ago. I just want to warn you of any strangers riding up. Ma'am, he was heard to say he would find whoever killed his brother."

She glared at the captain. Her brow creased. "There's no way he could know for sure I shot his brother, is there?" She grabbed the laundry paddle and gripped the handle.

"The messenger just said Frank told his cellmate about a man he and his brothers ran up on near Creek Bend. He made mention of a picture in a pocket watch he and his brothers stole."

Her grip on the paddle tightened. "Those outlaws took it from my husband before shooting him."

"The lieutenant thinks he's meeting up with his younger brother and they're headed in our direction. Somehow they knew your husband was joining up with our wagon train." The lines on Captain Brenner's face deepened.

"Hank must have told them. Figuring Hank's horse would lead them back to our wagon, he may think Jace killed his brother." She frowned. "I don't understand. Why was it only the one with the scar who rode into our camp that night?"

Captain Brenner shifted his weight. "Earlier the Coulter brothers robbed a bank in a settlement about ten miles south of Creek Bend. From what the lieutenant said, right after meeting up with your husband, they separated and were going to join up again close to Rock Creek."

Rebecca stood and looked in the direction the river took Jace. "I know Mr. Barker will be back with Jace soon. I'll tell him about the Coulter brothers then." She straightened her shoulders. "Thank you for your concern."

The next morning after breakfast, Rebecca and Hannah sat in cane bottom chairs brought from Cutter Springs. Rebecca used her work table to finish folding their clean laundry while Hannah drew pictures on her tablet. Rebecca couldn't keep her mind on her chores thinking about Jace.

She looked up at the sound of Sarah's voice. "Rebecca? Where are you, because it's not here?"

"Rebecca rubbed her eyes. "I guess my mind drifted off. I'm trying to fill my thoughts with happy memories. I didn't hear you and Millie walk up."

Millie pulled up a bench and sat. "Sometimes it's nice to daydream about other times and places. I often think about the family we left behind in Missouri. I miss them terribly."

Sarah joined Millie on the bench and placed her sewing basket on the table. "It's never a bad thing to keep your memories close to you." She took Rebecca's hand. "I know you're worried about Jace. But I was taught all my life to never give up on God." Tears glistened her eyes. "Even when we lost Emily, Carl and I knew God was the only one who could get us through that dark time. He still carries us today." She squeezed her hand. "And I know if anybody can find Jace and Ellen, Luke Barker can."

"Ben boy." The ladies turned when Mr. Calhoun called. He approached the wagon carrying two cane fishing poles. "Ben boy, where are you?"

"Mr. Calhoun." Rebecca, Millie, and Sarah smiled at the jolly man. "Ben's gathering firewood down by the creek. He hasn't been gone long. I'm sure you can still find him there. "

"I thought he might like to do some fishing this afternoon. We'll see if we can't bring back some supper."

Rebecca grinned. "He would love that. It might take his mind off Jace."

Hannah looked up from her tablet. "Mamma, can I go too? I like to fish."

Rebecca shook her head. "Not this time. But how about us visiting Mrs. Calhoun when I get through with my mending. And you can pick some wildflowers for her while we walk."

Zeb waved. "My Clara loves wildflowers."

That brought a smile to Hannah's face.

Rebecca and the ladies finished their mending, and Millie and Penelope encouraged her not to lose hope over Jace. When they left, Rebecca's spirits lifted, she and Hannah headed for the Calhoun's wagon. Rebecca carried a pan of fruit bread while Hannah searched for flowers.

Clara waved at Hannah and Rebecca when they got closer to her wagon. She sat on the shady side of the wagon in her rocking chair crocheting.

Hannah gave her the purple larkspur and hugged her neck. "Why, Hannah, how beautiful." Rebecca handed her the fruit bread and Clara breathed in the aroma. "And this smells wonderful. My goodness, it feels like my birthday. Thank you."

She got up from the rocking chair and headed for the back of their wagon. "And I've got a surprise for you Miss Hannah." She opened a wooden trunk and brought out a bundle wrapped in red and blue muslin. "I hope you like it."

Clara handed the package to Hannah, then sat again in the rocking chair. Hannah looked at her mother. Rebecca motioned for her to unwrap the gift. When she did, Hannah squealed with delight. "Mamma, look. A doll."

The quilt doll had blue buttons for eyes and an embroidered smile across her face. Her hair was yellow yarn the color of Hannah's hair.

Hannah hugged her new doll. She stopped and edged up to Clara. "Mrs. Calhoun, did you make her just for me?"

"Yes, I did." Clara smiled. "I thought you needed a new friend. Now, what will you name her?"

Hannah scrunched up her face. "Uh, I think I'll name her...Betsy." Again she looked at her mother.

Rebecca touched the doll. "I think that's a wonderful name. She looks like a Betsy."

"You're right," Clara said. "She reminds me of a little girl I knew when I was about your age. Her name was Betsy, and she had blue eyes."

Hannah danced holding Betsy, twirling her around. Clara's face beamed at Hannah's joy.

Rebecca bent and hugged Clara. "Mrs. Calhoun, you couldn't have made Hannah any happier if you would have given her a store-bought doll. Thank you and Mr. Calhoun for being so kind to my children."

"Why, it's not hard to love Ben, and Hannah, and Jace. You know Mr. Calhoun and I could never have children. And your sweet babies give us so much joy." She looked into Rebecca's eyes. "And I know our prayers will be answered. Jace and Ellen will come home to us."

CHAPTER TWELVE

The small pond fed by the South Bend River was perfect for an afternoon of fishing. Ben stacked the firewood he had collected by a willow tree growing near the water. The tree's leaves cast a nice shade over the pond.

Ben's eyes widened when he looked out across the water. "Mr. Calhoun, have you ever seen so many fish jumping in the water?"

"Lots of times back in Tennessee."

Zeb put his pipe in his mouth, then worked a piece of bacon on his and Ben's hooks.

"You think we can catch any of them?"

"Why, sure. I know just how to trick them into nibbling on this bacon." He handed Ben his pole. "Put your hook in the water and keep it real still. When you feel a little tug on your line, jerk your pole out of the water as fast as you can. Now, you try it."

For the next hour, Ben worked at trying to snag the big catfish swimming near his pole. After a while, he sat and leaned back against the willow tree.

"Mr. Calhoun, do you have any grandchildren?"

"Well, Ben boy, my missus and I never had any children to speak of."

Ben kept his eyes on his line. "Mamma told me I have grandparents back in Massachusetts, but I don't know them."

Zeb sat, smoked his pipe, and listened to Ben.

"She said when we get to Oregon she's going to write them and have them come see us." He paused and furrowed his brow. "Mr. Calhoun, I was wondering if you might want to be my grandpa until we get to Oregon." Ben slowly looked over at Zeb.

Zeb took his pipe out of his mouth. "No one's ever asked me to be their grandpa."

Ben forgot about the fishing. "Would you think about it?"

A wide smile spread across Zeb's face. "I don't have to think about it. I'd be honored to be your grandpa for as long as you'd like."

"Well, then, Mr. Calhoun, can I call you Grandpa?"

"Sure you can. And I know my missus would take kindly to you and Hannah calling her Grandma."

"Grandpa..." Before he could say another word, Ben's pole jerked in the water.

"Ben boy, you have a bite. Pull your pole out of the water. Let's see what you caught."

Zeb couldn't bait Ben's hook fast enough. "Grandpa, this is the best spot to catch fish. Look at this one." Ben pulled another from the water.

"Your mamma's going to be pleased how you've taken to fishing." He started to bait Ben's hook again when Ben said, "Let me try. I think I can do it."

After an afternoon of fishing, they filled their basket with fish, and Ben gathered his firewood. He and Zeb started back toward the camp when Ben said, "Grandpa, do you like to play checkers?"

"Oh, that's one of my favorite things to do." He rubbed Ben's head. "Besides fishing."

"Well, maybe we could..." Ben jerked around.

Horses were coming up the river bank.

Ben realized who approached and yelled, "Jace is back. Mr. Barker found them."

He ran to meet Jace and waved his hands. "Jace! Jace!"

As soon as Luke got close enough, Jace jumped off Luke's horse.

Ben ran into his brother's arms. "Jace, where did you go? We've been waiting and waiting for you to come back."

Jace knelt beside him. "Ellen and I were carried downstream. It took us a while after we reached the second curve to swim to the north bank."

Ben hung on his neck. "Mamma and Hannah are going to be so happy to see you."

Jace looked up at Luke. "Thanks, I'll walk the rest of the way."

Zeb chuckled. "Boy, your mamma's going to be dancing with joy when she sees you. You boys better hurry to her as fast as you can. The missus and I'll bring some fish by later."

"Yes, sir." Jace picked Ben up and swung him onto his shoulders.

"See you later, Grandpa," hollered Ben.

Jace glanced up at Ben. "Grandpa?"

꘎

Rebecca and Hannah were at their wagon washing potatoes when Ben hollered, "Mamma! Hannah! Jace is back!"

Rebecca whirled. Seeing Jace, she dropped a potato she had been peeling into the water and ran to him. "Jace. Thank God you're back safely." She grabbed him. Holding him tight, she wept out loud.

Her legs buckled under her. Jace caught her before she hit the ground and gently laid her down. "Mamma? Ben, go get the doctor. And hurry. She's unconscious."

When Rebecca opened her eyes, Dr. Brummel was staring down at her. Catherine placed a cool cloth on her head. "I…where am I?" She looked around. "How did I get in our wagon?" She sat up. "Jace. Where's Jace? And the children?"

"They're right outside the wagon with the Calhouns. Now lie back," said Dr. Brummel.

"Jace and Luke Barker carried you and laid you in here," Catherine said. "You needed to be out of the sun."

"But…, what happened? Did I faint?"

"Mrs. Quaid, have you been feeling dizzy or nauseated lately?"

Rebecca hesitated a minute. "Yes, but the last six weeks have been hard. I'm overly tired."

He looked down at Rebecca. "Mrs. Quaid, when was the last time—"

She gasped. "Dr. Brummel. Are you saying—"

"Mrs. Quaid, from your symptoms, I believe you're with child."

She grabbed his arm. Squeezing her eyes shut, Rebecca sobbed. "No, Doctor. This can't be. Not without Hank."

Dr. Brummel took her hand. "You cry as much as you need."

"Rebecca," said Catherine, "I know it doesn't seem like it right now but believe me everything is going to be all right. You're still young and healthy."

Rebecca caught her breath. "Doctor, are you sure?"

Dr. Brummel looked at Catherine. He softly put his hand on Rebecca's shoulder. "Catherine and I estimate you're several weeks along." He closed his medical bag. "You need some time to process this. I know you'll want to talk this over with Jace. But for now, please try to rest."

Dr. Brummel and Catherine climbed from the wagon. He turned back to Rebecca. "I'll be by in the morning to check on you. Again, please rest."

Jace stood by the tailgate of the wagon when Dr. Brummel and Catherine stepped down. The doctor looked at Rebecca then at Jace. "Your mother's going to be fine. She just needs some time to get used to the idea of having another child." He put his hand on Jace's shoulder. "If you need anything, you let me know."

"Thank you, doctor." Jace shook his head. "I really don't know what we need right now."

He tilted his head and nodded. "Take my word for it. Everything's going to be fine."

When the doctor left, Rebecca sat up and reached for Jace's arm. "We were so worried about you and Ellen. I'm forever grateful to Mr. Barker."

"Really, Mamma, we're okay. What about you? Are you feeling better?"

She smiled. "I just fainted, that's all. But I'm afraid I've added another burden on you."

"Don't worry." Jace took Rebecca's hand. "We'll manage."

Rebecca looked past Jace when Clara walked up behind him. "Clara, thank you for taking care of the children."

"Jace," she smiled, "why don't you go over to our wagon? Zeb's cleaning fish for supper. You and the children eat with us tonight."

Jace left, and Clara said, "May I talk to you for a minute? I know you're tired, but I won't take long." She paused. "I'm afraid Zeb and I were close enough to hear what the doctor was saying. We didn't mean to eavesdrop, so please, forgive us." She took Rebecca's hand in hers. "The truth is, you've been given a gift from God."

Rebecca laid back, covering her face with her hands.

"Dear, I know this was the last thing you wanted, but try and see it through God's eyes. The truth is, He never makes mistakes. And as much as your heart aches for your husband, this baby is a part of him. It's God's way of keeping Hank close to you."

She uncovered her face. "But Mrs. Calhoun, I can't do this without him."

"I've watched you. Your faith is strong. Don't let the devil plant doubt in your heart. And remember, there's not a soul on this wagon train that won't do what they can to help you and your children, especially Sarah and Millie. Why, honey, we're your family now. Zeb and I love you and the children as if you were ours."

Rebecca wiped her face with her apron and exhaled. "Mrs. Calhoun—"

"Now, child, call us Zeb and Clara."

Rebecca grabbed Clara's hand. "You and your husband are so important to us."

Clara put her hand on Rebecca's cheek. "No more than you are to us. Now, don't you worry. Jace and the children are taken care of." She laughed. "We're having the fish Ben caught this afternoon." She squeezed Rebecca's hand. "You just try to get some rest. I'll be back in a little while and check on you."

After supper, the Calhouns, Luke, Cody, Jace, Ellen and several others gathered at the Webster's wagon. Jace sat by Ellen near their campfire.

"I've never been so scared in all my life," said Ellen. "The river was washing over me faster than I could get my breath." She could still picture Jace working to rescue her.

"There were a couple of times I lost sight of her," said Jace, "but then she would bob up from the water. At one point, I got close enough to yell for her to work her way to a clump of rocks just beyond the bend in the river." He took her hand.

Her heart fluttered and she smiled. "If he hadn't been there, I'm sure I would have drowned. He kept yelling for me to swim to the rocks."

"How'd you get from the rocks to the river bank?" Zeb asked.

Jace gestured to his left. "Mr. Barker and Cody. We were both hanging on to the sides of the rocks when I saw them ride up. We weren't that far from the bank, but the water was rushing too fast."

"I didn't notice them," Ellen said, squeezing his hand, "until Jace waved to get their attention. The sun was about down. The darker it got, the louder Cody kept yelling for us to hang on."

"The only way to get them out of the river," said Luke, "was to rope them and pull them through the river current."

Cody laughed. "I've never thrown a rope as many times as I did that night. I threw until my arm ached, but I was determined to get them out of the water."

"Thank goodness." Ellen grinned at her brother remembering how many times he had made her mad. "I never thought I would say this, but I was so glad you were there."

"Well," said Zeb, "evidently you were able to rope them in because here they are."

Luke smiled. "We weren't about to come back without them."

Ellen glanced at Jace, still smiling.

Rebecca got very little sleep but was glad to hear the bugle sound the next morning. Now that Jace and Ellen were with the wagon train again she faced the never-ending routine of breakfast, greasing wagon wheels, milking cows, and loading up campsites to start the day's long journey.

Placing the can on the bench, Rebecca emptied the remaining milk from the pail. She turned. "Ben, take this pail to the river and rinse it out."

He jumped from the wagon seat about the time Sarah and Millie walked up with curious looks on their faces.

She nudged Ben on the shoulder. "Hurry. And rinse it clean."

Sarah looked at Millie then back at Rebecca. "I can see you're feeling better this morning. We were worried to death about you."

Millie gave her a sly smile. "At first, we thought you were just excited to see Jace. But later on we heard there was more to it."

Rebecca tilted her head and crossed her arms. "And just how did you know what caused me to faint?"

Millie chuckled. "Ben and Hannah overheard Dr. Brummel when he was tending to you. Your news was more than they could keep to themselves."

"Well, I'm thankful the children are pleased. I wish I could feel as happy."

Sarah put her arm around Rebecca's shoulders. "I can imagine your dismay at hearing you're going to have another baby knowing Hank will never know the child."

"It may take a while for you to get used to the idea," said Millie. "But with Ben, and Hannah, and Jace, you'll soon feel better about the whole thing. And there's nothing more precious than a new baby."

Rebecca let that sink in for a moment. Without Hank, she didn't think she could face raising another child. But when she remembered holding each of her newborn babies, she straightened her shoulders. "You're right. I might as well be joyful since this must be God's plan for me. I don't understand, but I guess I have to accept that He does."

Millie smiled, her eyes twinkling. "Just think, your baby will be born in Oregon. Hank would be pleased about that."

The idea resonated in Rebecca. She smiled. "He would be pleased."

The signal sounded to get the wagons on the trail. Sarah pulled her bonnet up. "Got to go. Carl will be wondering where I am."

"Rebecca, let us know if we can help you," Millie said. "Remember, it's still a ways to Oregon."

Rebecca embraced her two best friends. "What would I do without you both?"

"You don't have to worry about that," said Sarah.

Then each headed for their wagons.

Hannah ran from the other side of the wagon where Ben hung the clean milk pail. Holding Betsy, Hannah said, "Mamma. Ben said Jace told him he could ride alongside him on Pa's horse today. I want to ride too, but Ben said no. Can he do that?"

Rebecca bent to tie the ribbons on Hannah's bonnet. "I think the boys need some time together. So, why don't you and Betsy walk with me today, and we'll plan a surprise for Jace's birthday."

Hannah clapped her hands while Betsy's arms and legs flopped from one side to the other.

CHAPTER THIRTEEN

That evening Rebecca stood by the chuck wagon with the rest of the emigrants. Captain Brenner cautioned about what lay ahead on the trail.

"From now until we get to the Oregon territory," he said, "the trail will be nothing like the flat pastures we've become accustomed to. Fort Laramie is our next supply post. Between here and the fort is the North Platte Valley and Ash Hollow. But to get to the valley, the trail will slant sharply uphill several miles. When we reach the top of the plateau on the east crest, it's a twenty-two-mile trek across a high, waterless tableland and a thirty-degree grade drop into the valley."

"When we reach the top of the plateau are we talking water rations again?" said Carl Webster.

"Yes. We leave the river until we get to Ash Hollow. Fill every container you have and don't waste a drop. And remember, our animals need water as much or more than we do."

"How about grass?" Hugh Unger asked. "If there's no water is there enough extra grain to get our teams across?"

The captain nodded. "We knew we'd be facing this. One of our supply wagons is carrying enough, along with what each of you stocked up on in Fort Kearney. We'll have to be careful, but we should make it."

The wagon train started on the trail the next morning soon after the sun peeked over the horizon. Captain Brenner hadn't exaggerated the change in terrane. By mid-morning Rebecca struggled with the constant uphill journey. Ben and Hannah complained about the climb as well.

Earlier Jace and Luke headed up the side of the incline to get a feel of the stress it posed on the animals. Rebecca was glad to see them ride back around noon.

Luke reined up at Rebecca's wagon with Jace right behind. He took a long drink from his water canteen and wiped his mouth on his sleeve. "Captain Brenner said there's no stopping for lunch until we reach the crest of the hill. When on top, the animals need feed and water first. Do the best you can to keep your team moving." Leaving Jace to take care of their wagon, he rode to check on the others.

Jace got off his horse. "Ben, you get on my horse. I'm going to saddle Rowdy. We'll hitch our horses to the yoke to help the team climb the hill. When I get everything ready, you ride as hard as you can. We don't have far to go, so don't let up until we reach the top."

Ben climbed on Jace's horse. "We'll get them to the top, Jace. Just watch and see."

Rebecca smiled knowing Ben would do all he could to show Jace he was capable as any to do the job.

As treacherous as crossing the South Bend River was, climbing to the top of the plateau proved to be as difficult and exhausting. The animals snorted and huffed while being pulled, pushed, and prodded up the sharp incline.

One of the McCain's oxen dropped dead on the trail.

Along the trail were remnants of family heirlooms, trunks, and other possessions thrown from wagons to lighten the load.

Rebecca couldn't remember a harder day.

After supper, Jace walked over to the Jacob's wagon to visit Ellen. Rebecca sat in the cane bottom chair near the wooden table and closed her eyes. Ben and Hannah played checkers by the campfire. She dozed off, but was startled when Luke Barker softly call out, "Mrs. Quaid?"

She opened her eyes. "Oh my, I'm afraid I drifted off to sleep." She stood but found herself a little lightheaded.

He reached out and took her arm to keep her from falling. "You might want to sit back down."

Embarrassed, she allowed him to help her settle back in the chair. "I'm fine. The day was hard and I'm just tired." She motioned to the bench on the other side of the table. "Please, sit down. Would you like some coffee? It's still hot from supper."

"Thank you, ma'am, I could use some."

Ben and Hannah looked up from their checker game.

"Ben," said Luke, "you did a good job today. The captain noticed how you worked to get your team and wagon up the hill."

"Thank you." He beamed.

"Tomorrow will be an easier day," said Luke. "Our only concern for the next few days is water. So, Ben, Hannah, we need to conserve all the water we can until we get across this plain."

Ben asked Rebecca, "Where's Jace?"

She grinned. "Where do you think he is?"

"Ellen Jacob again?" He frowned. "Why would he want to talk to her?"

"Never mind about Jace. You and Hannah need to get ready for bed andyou're your prayers."

"But Mamma—"

"Now, Ben." She pointed to the back of the wagon. "You, too, Hannah."

Luke finished his coffee. "Tell Jace we'll need him to take his turn herding cattle tomorrow. I'll keep an eye on your wagon."

She looked up into the star-filled sky and sighed. "Have you ever been so covered in burdens you didn't think God could see you?" She blushed. "I'm sorry. I don't know why I shared that."

He leaned forward and rested his arms on his knees. "Don't apologize. And yes, but you have to remember feelings can take you down the wrong trail."

A light breeze blew across the campsite. She brushed her hair from her face. "The last two months have tested my faith. I'm not sure about anything, except going to Oregon." She laughed. "And then I'm not certain what we'll do when we get there. We have family in Willamette Valley, but I found things can fall apart without any warning."

He smiled. "The Lord only gives us one day at a time. And He's faithful to prepare us for what the day brings. Crossing the country with bare necessities and the hardships it presents can wear on anybody." He stood and adjusted his hat.

Her legs stronger, she stood to see him off. "There's no way to express how much we appreciate you and Captain Brenner. And, if you would, please call me Rebecca."

"Yes, ma'am, if you'll call me Luke."

She glanced up at a falling star streaking across the night sky. "Did you see it?"

He looked up and grinned. "I know God has you in His sights, especially now."

With little grass on the dry plateau, the constant plodding of the livestock caused dust to boil up with no wind to blow it down the road. It made breathing hard. Rebecca found herself wishing for the prairie winds.

Hannah pulled at her skirt. "Mamma, Betsy's thirsty."

"I know, honey. It's not long until noon. We can get a sip of water when we stop. I know the animals are thirsty too."

"How long is it before we get to water?"

"Mr. Barker seems to think we'll be across this plateau by tomorrow evening. That means we'll be getting close to Ash Hollow. He said there are lots of trees and cold, spring filled ponds."

"By that time will it be Jace's birthday?"

"Well, it'll be close. It's only a week away. We'll surprise him with a birthday cake."

Hannah's eyes got big. "A real birthday cake with icing?"

"Well, we'll see. But you know how he loves brown sugar cakes."

"Umm." She rubbed her tummy. "So do I."

Hannah and Rebecca whiled away the morning talking about Jace's birthday, how wonderful living in Oregon will be, and the stories Grandma Clara shared with Hannah. For that brief time, the conversation took their minds off the dust, the heat, and the fact that Betsy was thirsty.

When the bugle sounded to stop for lunch, Rebecca tightened her grip on the lead lines. She slowed the team and hollered over her shoulder. "Ben, when we get stopped, grab the bucket hanging on the other side of the wagon. I'll pour some water in it and you can give Lucy a drink. Try not to spill any, okay."

"Okay, Mamma," he said.

Jace filled some pails to water the oxen. As he carried them, he said to Rebecca, "I'll check the wagon wheels to make sure the wood isn't getting too dry."

After lunch, Ben and Hannah ran to visit with the Calhouns for a little while before starting out again. Rebecca sat in a chair sewing a button on one of Ben's shirts while Jace sat on a bench and leaned against the wagon. She could tell by the look on his face he had something on his mind.

"You worried about something?"

"No, but if it's all right with you, there's a group of us who are going to gather at the Brown's wagon after supper tonight. I asked Ellen if she would go with me. We won't be late."

"That's fine." She looked away then back at Jace. "Ellen seems like a very nice girl."

His face turned red. "She's just someone to spend time with."

Rebecca smiled and nodded.

He changed the subject. "Mr. Barker said he would check on you, and Ben, and Hannah after supper tonight."

"That's nice of him, but there's really no need. We'll be fine."

"I know. I told him, but he insisted. Said it wasn't any trouble at all."

She put her hand over her heart. "I don't know where we would be right now except for him."

He laughed. "I know. Back in Fort Kearney. I wish Pa were here."

For the first time, he mentioned his pa since Rebecca had shown him the pocket watch. She hesitated before asking, "Do you think about Hank much?"

He lowered his head. "Every day." Then looked up. "There'll never be a day I won't miss him. But I have to believe he'd be proud that we didn't give up on settling in Oregon."

Before Rebecca could say anything, the signal to get back on the trail sounded. A few minutes after Ben and Hannah returned to their wagon and pulled out on the trail, someone screamed out in pain.

Jace whirled around. "I think it came from that clump of sage. It looks like someone's down." He ran toward the sage. He hollered back. "It's Jamie Gaines!"

By the time Jace reached him, Carl Webster and Bert Ingles were crouched down beside Jamie. Hal Gaines aimed his gun at the ground and shot. He yelled. "Get the doc! My boy's been snake bit!"

The prairie rattler lay dead only a few feet away.

Jamie screamed and thrashed on the ground.

Hal said, "Jamie, stay still if you can. Where did it bite you?"

"My…leg, just above my ankle."

Jace jerked his bandana off and wrapped it tightly around Jamie's calf.

Jamie did his best not to move, but Jace could imagine his pain.

Dr. Brummel ran up with his medical bag and ripped Jamie's left pant leg up the side. He gave Jamie some kind of concoction to drink. The doc cut an x across the wound and tried to squeeze as much of the poison out as he could. "Can you boys get him to my wagon?"

Jace and Carl carried Jamie to the doc's wagon. Hal and his wife, Lorna, followed with her asking between sobs, "Is Jamie going to be okay?"

Jace and Carl laid Jamie on the back of Dr. Brummel's wagon. Catherine gave him some laudanum and he was soon out. She wiped the wound. "How bad is it?"

Jace overheard the doctor. "I don't want to give them false hope. If Jamie lives, he'll probably lose his foot. Though from my experience with snake bites, his chances are slim."

Captain Brenner rode up to survey the situation. "Doc, can he make the trail this afternoon or should he be jostled around that much?"

"Go ahead and take the wagons down the trail. Tell Hal and Lorna that Catherine and I will keep him as comfortable as we can. Lorna can ride in the back of our wagon with Jamie. We'll try and keep up with you."

Jace and Carl walked back to their wagons.

"What do you think his odds are?" said Jace.

Carl shook his head.

Six miles down the trail, and not long after sunset, Jamie died.

Carl Webster and Jim Brewer dug the grave by moonlight. Everyone gathered around the small mound of dirt. Reverend Jamison spoke words of comfort to a family too broken to hear them. Hours after the service, Lorna kneeled by the gravesite and refused to leave. She never moved but wept throughout the night. Every so often Hal would go to her and plead for her to come back to the wagon and rest.

The next morning Hal knelt by Lorna at their son's gravesite. "Lorna, honey, we've got to leave. Captain Brenner is ready to pull out."

"No. No. I can't leave Jamie here in this desolate place."

Hal swallowed back his tears. "I know it's hard, but we have no choice. Please, come with me. Sally and I need you." He prayed God would move her to return to their wagon.

She pushed him away. "Hal, I can't. Not now." She glared at him with bloodshot eyes.

Hal noticed Sarah standing not far from them. After a bit, she approached and knelt. "Lorna, dear, I understand how painful this is. I've been right where you are. And though it seems you're leaving Jamie behind, you're not. He's with Emily and Scripture tells us we'll see them again." Sarah took her hand. "Please, Lorna, we have to leave now."

"Lorna," Hal begged, "please, sweetheart, we can't stay here any longer."

After a few minutes, Sarah and Hal gently pulled Lorna to her feet and walked her toward the wagon. Lorna sobbed uncontrollably.

CHAPTER FOURTEEN

After traveling two more days over the plateau, the wagon train stood not far from the edge of a cliff. The steep slope dropped three hundred feet into the North Platte Valley where Ash Hollow laid.

Jace saddled his horse. "I'll ride up and see what the captain has to say. You all stay here and rest until I get back."

He approached the captain standing alongside Carl Webster, Jim Brewer, Luke, and some others peering off the side of the cliff. When he got a look at the steep incline he understood the men's concern.

"It'll be a miracle if we get all these wagons down that slope without a calamity," said Carl.

Jim gazed down the sharp incline. "How are we going to manage such an undertaking?"

A few more men gathered around the group. Captain Brenner put his hand up. "Folks, don't let this discourage you. Luke and I've maneuvered quite a few wagons down this drop. But for now, we'll make camp about a hundred yards to the south. By this time tomorrow, we'll have most of the wagons down in that valley."

"What about the women and children?" Jim asked.

"For now, get your wagons settled. We'll gather after supper, and I'll tell you how we're going to get these wagons, the livestock, and everyone's family down the hill."

Luke walked over to Jace. "Tell your mother to tie down everything that's loaded in your wagon. I'll be by in the morning after we meet with the captain to check everything."

Jace looked down at Luke from his horse. "The cliff looks too steep for the animals."

"Don't worry." He took his hat off and slapped it against his leg. Dust boiled into the air. "The animals will make it down the hill easier than the wagons. Right now everybody needs to set up camp and get a good night's rest." He grinned. "But you've got night patrol until midnight. I guess that means you and Ellen won't get to spend much time together after supper."

"Why do I have to keep reminding you that she's just a friend?"-Jace flushed. "There's nothing wrong with that, is there?"

"Nope, not at all." Luke raised an eyebrow. "I just noticed she's not spending time with Jim Eldridge anymore." He laughed and swatted the back of Jace's horse with his hat.

After supper, while the men talked with Captain Brenner, Rebecca, Sarah, Millie, and Penelope gathered at the Webster's wagon. Their children played while the women talked.

"Are you all right, Sarah?" Rebecca could sense Sarah's uneasiness. "You look worried."

"It's Lorna. She's not good." Sarah frowned. "I've tried to talk to her, but I can't seem to get through. I can hear her weeping at night from across the campsite. I know everyone's heard her scream out at times."

Penelope held her baby close to her. "I don't know what I would do if I lost Mary Martha." She gasped and glanced at Sarah. "I'm sorry. I didn't mean to—"

"It's okay." Sarah reached out and patted her hand. "I miss Emily every day, but I have no choice but to go on. I wouldn't wish it on my worst enemy. And I worry as much for Hal and Sally as I do Lorna."

"Lorna looks like she's sleepwalking most of the time," said Millie. "I'm frightened for her."

The men gathered at the supply wagon. Captain Brenner stood with Luke and Tom to explain the procedure on how to safely maneuver the wagons down into the North Platte Valley and Ash Hollow.

The captain approached one of the wagons. "Each of you will need to lock the front wheels. To do that," he held up some chains, "you'll wrap these around the tongue of your wagon then to your wagon box. We'll tie ropes together and attach them to the sides of the wagon. The ropes will be long enough to reach the bottom of the hill. Then we'll slowly skid it down the side."

Captain Brenner took his hat off and rubbed his forehead. "The thing we have to worry about is making sure the ropes don't pull apart. If they do, the wagon will tumble down the hill."

"Will livestock need to go down before the wagons do?" asked Carl.

"Yes," said the captain. "That's usually the best way, so we can get them settled before the wagons start down. The animals will be able to make it to the bottom on their own. We just have to make sure they don't get too scattered." He paused. "It'll take every man we've got and most of the day to get down in that valley. To stay on schedule and have some time to rest in Ash Hollow, I'm praying we can ease each wagon down with no mishaps."

"What's the best way for our families to get down to the valley?" Jim removed his hat and wiped the sweat with his sleeve.

Luke waved his hand toward a large cluster of brush. "There's a trail cut over on the other side of that sagebrush. It's not an easy path, but it's the safest way for the women and children to make the slope."

Zeb Calhoun shook his head "As far I'm concerned, if we ever needed the hand of God, it's tomorrow getting these wagons into that valley."

Rebecca opened her eyes after a restless night. The sun wasn't up, but she heard activity going on in the camp. She knew Pete would be sounding the bugle soon.

"Mamma?" Hannah reached over and put her hand on Rebecca's face.

"Yes, honey."

"If we have to leave our wagons and go down another trail, where are we going to sleep tonight?"

"Don't worry." Rebecca smiled. "By the time we get to the valley, our wagons may be waiting for us."

Ben sat up in bed and giggled. "I wish I could ride our wagon down the mountain. That sounds fun."

Jace stuck his head into the back of the wagon. "Hey, what are you all waiting on? The sun'll be up soon, and Captain Brenner wants everyone ready to go by six." Then he disappeared.

Rebecca and the children stretched and crawled from the wagon. She hurried breakfast while Ben and Hannah did their chores.

Jace walked his horse beside the wagon where his mother fried bacon. He tightened the cinch on his saddle. "I'm going to ride to the captain's wagon in case there's anything else I need to know. I'll be back by the time breakfast is ready."

He hopped on his horse and rode off. Rebecca gazed at him. She smiled. He is everything his pa would have wanted of a son.

Sarah walked up while Rebecca filled Ben and Hannah's plates with scrambled eggs and bacon. She took in a deep breath. "The coffee smells wonderful."

Rebecca grabbed the coffee pot. "Here, let me get you a cup." She poured and handed it to Sarah. "Are Carl and Josh at the captain's wagon?"

Sarah sat on the bench. "Yes, they hurried through breakfast, then headed that way. Carl didn't sleep last night worrying about getting all these wagons down that hill."

Rebecca poured herself a cup of coffee and joined Sarah on the bench by the table.

"Did you ever think it would be this hard to get to a place we've never seen?" said Rebecca. "I know we've heard wonderful things about Oregon, but sometimes I wonder if it's worth it."

Sarah took a sip. "This was Carl and the boy's dream. I could have lived out my life right where we were. But after Emily died, I made up my mind I could be happy anywhere Carl, Josh, and Toby wanted to live. Oregon seems to be where they chose."

"Jace has his heart set on Oregon" She stared at her coffee. "He and Hank spent hours talking about what they heard and read from people who had been there. And now Jace is convinced getting to Oregon would honor Hank's memory."

Before Rebecca and Sarah finished their second cup of coffee, Jace and Luke rode up. Luke tipped his hat. "Morning ladies. The captain's ready to get started. After you finish getting everything secured in your wagons, Captain Brenner will tell you what you need to do to get down into that valley."

Sarah put down her coffee cup and left the wagon calling over her shoulder. "Finally, we can get this journey going so Carl can get a good night's sleep tonight."

Captain Brenner pointed to the south ridge of the cliff. "Tom, you and the boys take the cattle down the trail where it slopes closer to the North Platte River. Try and keep them together but let them go at their own pace. They'll be able to make their way down."

Tom Hayes slapped his coiled rope against his leg and yelled. "Giddup, there!"

The cattle turned and headed toward the crest of the hill. A hundred and twenty-five oxen, thirty milk cows, and forty-two head of cattle snorted and bawled when they stepped onto the thirty-degree slope.

The captain rode about two hundred yards north of the cattle herd. He pulled his horse up near the first wagon in line to drop off the cliff and met with Reverend Jamison. Dismounting, Captain Brenner used his hat to point to a flag flapping in the wind. "Do you see the flag Luke planted beside that clump of sagebrush? He staked a rope on it to help get down that trail. Tie the other end of that rope around your waist and ease yourself down the trail."

"Will there be enough rope to get me to the bottom?"

"There'll be plenty. Once the line's taut, signal the ladies to hold on to the rope to guide them down. While you and Jim lead the women and children, we'll begin lowering the wagons."

From the northeast, a small band of Indians rode up to the group of men. Carl grabbed his rifle, but Luke stopped him. Hal, Hugh, and the others stood near the first wagon.

Captain Brenner made a sign. "Wiconi. Welcome."

The Indian raised his hand. "Captain. Brought help to lower wagons."

Captain Brenner turned to the group of men standing ready to hoist the first wagon down. "These are nomadic Sioux scouts from a tribe that lives in and around the valley. For years Wiconi has helped us get the wagons down this bluff into the valley." He nodded toward the Sioux scout. "As soon as Wiconi and his men check the chains and are satisfied, we'll push the first wagon over the crest of the hill. Let it slide down slow and easy. Use the ropes to guide it."

Captain Brenner called to the men positioned at the bottom of the cliff he had sent down earlier. "We're sending the first wagon down. When you have the ropes untethered from the wagon, wave your hats and we'll pull them back up."

After Wiconi and his tribesmen examined the chains, the men holding the ropes at the edge of the cliff eased the nose of the wagon dipping it forward. From that point on, the men worked at making sure the wagon didn't turn sideways and tumble down the hill.

When the first wagon got halfway down the cliff, Captain Brenner yelled, "Slack up on the right side a bit."

While the men worked at lowering the wagons, Rebecca and her children stood in line behind Millie ready to make the trip down the cliff. Rebecca held to the rope used to guide them. The air was thick with dust from all the activity.

Rebecca stepped to the edge of the bluff. "Hannah, Ben, hold on to the rope. And stay right behind me."

Rebecca followed Millie down the narrow, steep path. Clumps of sagebrush and bramble made it hard to maneuver without fear of falling. Only a few feet on the trail, Hannah lost her grip on the rope, tripped, and rolled several yards. Rebecca gasped. "Hannah. Hannah."

"Mamma."

A clump of sagebrush stopped her before she rolled further down the trail. Rebecca half-ran, half-slid toward her. "Hannah, are you okay?"

"I dropped Betsy! She cried. "She's back there somewhere."

Rebecca looked over her shoulder. "Ben."

"I'm right here." He called from a few feet up. "And I found Betsy."

Holding on to the rope with one hand and Betsy with the other, Ben hurried down to his mother and sister.

Rebecca untied her neckerchief and dabbed at the skinned places on Hannah's elbows and arms.

"Ouch." Hannah squirmed. "That hurts."

"We'll clean these up better when we get to the bottom." Rebecca brushed the dirt from Hannah's dress. "Now, you and Ben hold on to the rope and watch your step."

When Rebecca reached the bottom, she was relieved to see several wagons sitting unscathed a few yards from the landing. The livestock grazed on lush, green grass.

After washing Hannah's scrapes, Rebecca joined Millie, Penelope, Sarah, and Clara underneath a grove of trees by the pond. She marveled at the sight of the meadow. "Have you ever seen such beauty?" She slipped her bonnet from her head and took Hannah's hand. "Oh, honey, look at the yellow blossoms on the bushes." She took in a deep breath. "The cool breeze reminds me of springtime back east."

Several different varieties of roses, along with jasmine, filled Ash Hollow. Rebecca and the ladies examined the grapevines and currant bushes growing wild throughout the valley. And the cool shade helped them forget the hot days on the prairie.

"We better enjoy it," said Sarah. "Captain Brenner told Carl once we leave Ash Hollow, Fort Laramie is our next stop. After that, we start up the cold Rocky Mountains."

❧

By late afternoon, only half of the twenty-nine wagons had reached the valley. The sweat-bathed men on the top of the ridge continued to struggle lowering the remaining.

The captain motioned for the next wagon to pull up to the edge. With ropes attached, the men rolled it forward. But a rope severed. Carl hollered. "The wagon's slipping!"

Hugh Unger yelled when the loose rope he was holding jerked his arm. His elbow popped. "My arm." The bone just above his right elbow punctured through the skin. He fell to the ground moaning. "It's broken."

The wagon turned on its side then plunged down the steep slope. Its contents flew in every direction. Dishes shattered. Pots and pans clanged and rolled down the hill. With each bounce, the wooden bed splintered into pieces. The axle broke and threw the front two wheels ten feet into the air. When it settled into the valley below, the canvas cover lay in shreds.

Dr. Brummel hurried to Hugh. "Get me something to wrap Hugh's arm with and quick."

Captain Brenner knelt beside Hugh. "The doc will get you fixed up. Just don't move for now."

The captain rose and walked over to the rope laying on the ground. Examining the frayed end, he turned to Luke. "We'll have to fix this before we can go any further." He blew out a deep breath. "Let's hold off until the morning. We'll all be fresh and maybe we can finish without another mishap."

Clyde Russell walked up and Captain Brenner put his hand on the man's shoulder. "You and Harriet can use our extra supply wagon. What we can't salvage from the wreck, we'll all pitch in and help with your necessities. Let's try to rest up tonight." The captain turned to Luke. "When Doc Brummel gets Hugh where he's able to be moved, you and Carl take him down the same trail the women used. I'll send ten men down to guard those in the valley. The rest of us will stay here tonight."

CHAPTER FIFTEEN

Rebecca and the other travelers found dropping into the fragrant meadow of Ash Hollow well worth the backbreaking toil it took to get the wagons down the steep hill. Even the burden of Rebecca's daily chores lightened with the scent of wild roses and flowering shrubs. The valley offered the first shade Rebecca had seen in weeks. She savored the cold, clear water that fed into the pond near the meadow.

Standing over the campfire the first morning in the valley, Rebecca stirred a boiling pot of lavender scented lye soap.

Hannah ran around from the other side of the wagon. "Mamma, I picked you some flowers."

"Oh, how beautiful. Thank you." She pointed to the wagon. "Mamma's got to keep stirring the soap. Can you help me by getting a jar for the flowers?"

After a few more stirs, Rebecca doused the fire under the pot of soap. "We'll put the flowers on the table tonight when we gather with everyone for supper. Remember, we're celebrating Jace's birthday." She put her fingers to her lips. "Can you keep the secret?"

Hannah giggled. "I haven't forgotten. I have a surprise for him too." Before placing the flowers in the jar, she pulled something from her pocket. "I found a stone near the pond that's perfectly round and flat." She showed it to her mother. "I shined it and it looks like a jewel." She returned the stone to her pocket. "Don't tell him. I want it to be a surprise."

Rebecca put the flowers in the jar and filled it with water. "I know he'll love it. What about Ben? He's been awfully secretive lately. Has he been working on a present for Jace?"

"Yes." Hannah ducked her head. "But he made me promise not to tell."

"Then keep your promise because I want to be surprised too."

Hannah put her hand over her mouth.

Rebecca placed the soap molds on her work table. "Go find Ben. I think he and Grandpa are at the pond."

Working to fill the soap molds with the hot liquid, Rebecca found herself humming.

"You sound happy."

She turned at the sound of Luke's voice.

Luke grinned and took off his hat.

"I guess I am." She poured the soap into the last mold.

"Ben told me it's Jace's birthday." He shuffled his feet. "Sixteen is an important milestone."

"I suppose so. I just know I can't treat him like a little boy anymore." She wiped her hands on her apron. "Would you like some coffee?"

"Coffee sounds good."

She grabbed two cups from the table. "Pull up the bench and have a seat."

When he didn't say anything, she asked, "Are you looking for Jace? He's watering the team right now."

He looked down then back up at Rebecca. "Uh, no. I'm not here about Jace."

"Is there something else?"

He put his cup down. "Rebecca." He rubbed his forehead. "Tonight after supper there's going to be some fiddle playing and dancing." He looked off then back to Rebecca. "I don't know if it's proper in your condition, but would there be a chance you'd dance with me?"

Her eyes widened. "I...uh, I suppose it would be all right."

He let out a breath and smiled. "I'll see you then? I'll walk you over if that's okay."

"No, that's fine. The children and I will meet you there."

"I'll look forward to it."

After he left, she stood staring after him then folded her hands over her stomach. "What have I done?"

The crowd gathered near the meadow. Rebecca and Hannah joined them with arms filled with Jace's favorites. Ben left them for the Calhouns to work on his gift for Jace. Under the shade tree, cloth-covered tables were set up near the pond. Each one of them with delicious smelling meat pies, buffalo steaks, potato cakes, currant breads, and dried fruit pies. Nearby, several lanterns hung from stakes to designate the dance floor. And on the bench near the chuck wagon lay Bart's guitar and Jim's fiddle.

Sarah hurried over to Rebecca. "And where is the birthday boy?"

Rebecca gestured toward the Jacob's wagon. "He went to get Ellen."

Sarah stared up into the sky. "Isn't it a beautiful evening?" She pressed her hand over her heart. "It's been a while since Carl and I have felt this lighthearted. Being around friends and family has a way of easing life's troubles."

"As hard as this trail's been, I would have hated not knowing you, and Carl, the boys…and Emily." Rebecca hugged Sarah. "You've been so kind and helpful to us."

"When you travel in these conditions, everyone has to look out for each other."

"Well, that certainly held true for Clyde and Harriet." Rebecca's eyebrows raised. "I can't imagine losing nearly everything you own in one quick swoop down the side of a cliff."

Sarah put her palms together. "And enough was gathered to supply their wagon until we get to Fort Laramie. That's what makes us family."

From the center of the dance floor, Clyde Russell shouted, "What are we waiting for? Reverend Jamison, if you'll bless this feast, we can all dig in."

Sarah squeezed Rebecca's arm and left to stand by Carl.

Hannah tugged at Rebecca's skirt. "Mamma, when are we going to give Jace his gifts?"

"In a little while, sweetheart. But for now, let's enjoy this wonderful meal." She glanced over and noticed Ben and Zeb sitting on the Calhoun's tailgate working on something.

After the meal and before the music got started, Rebecca and some of the ladies sat on benches near a hedge of lilac bushes. Rebecca glimpsed Jace and Ellen talking by the pond.

Becky Franks leaned over to Rebecca. "I know exactly what you're thinking." She nodded in the direction of Jace and Ellen. "I can see it in your eyes. Children grow up much too fast."

"Don't they though." Rebecca sighed. "It seems only a few months ago he was trailing behind Hank, and now look at him."

"Yes, look at him. He's turning into a fine young man. You and your husband did a good job raising him. From what I've seen, he's handled your family's situation as well as any grown man. You should be proud of him."

"Thank you. I am, and I know Hank would be too."

Bart strummed his guitar.

"Sounds like Jim and Bart are ready to get everyone dancing." Becky stood.

Rebecca's pulse raced. She inhaled then under her breath scolded herself. "Luke hasn't asked me to dance yet, for heaven's sake. Why am I so nervous?"

Becky's eyebrows lifted. "He hasn't what?"

She blushed. "I'm sorry, it's nothing. I was just thinking out loud."

"Oh, excuse me, Rebecca," Becky waved, "it looks like Alvin's wanting to make a few rounds on the dance floor—if you can call this a dance floor." Rushing off, she called over her shoulder. "I think the man could dance all night."

Rebecca sat enjoying the night air and the music. Jace whirled Ellen around the dance floor keeping time to the waltz. She could hardly believe how Jace resembled Hank.

"Rebecca?" Luke walked up beside her. He removed his hat. "Would you like to dance?"

She glanced at the dancers then back at Luke. "I...I suppose so."

He put his hat back on and took her hand. Reaching the dance floor, he wrapped his arm around her waist as she placed her hand in his. For the next few minutes, Rebecca left her worries behind. She let Luke lead her around the dance floor and got lost in the music.

"It's been so long since I've danced. I was afraid I might have forgotten how."

He smiled. "You haven't forgotten."

Hannah stood by Grandma Clara and waved to them.

"I think Ben and Hannah are more excited about Jace's birthday than he is," said Luke. "Ben's got some big secret he's holding on to."

"Hannah too. She has a gift for Jace and she can hardly hold her excitement."

The waltz stopped, but Luke continued to hold her. Standing in the middle of the dance floor, Rebecca blushed. "I believe the music's over."

He smiled. "How about another dance?"

The music resumed, and Rebecca's feet barely touched the ground. Luke twirled her around and around.

When the last note played, Captain Brenner made his way to the center of the dance floor. "I think it's time to announce what we're celebrating tonight. Jace, come on over here."

Rebecca winced at his embarrassment.

Jace walked over to the captain.

Captain Brenner shook his hand. "Jace, this is an important milestone for you. It's not every day a boy turns sixteen." Jace removed his hat. "Several of the women baked their favorite cakes for this occasion."

Jim and Bart struck their instruments, and everyone sang happy birthday.

Jace's face reddened. He shifted his weight from one foot to the other. "I won't forget this day or the road we've traveled together for the last couple of months." He looked down then back at the crowd. "My pa would have been pleased to know all of you."

Before he could say anything else, Hannah ran up to him. "I have a surprise for you."

Ben was right behind her.

Jace knelt on one knee.

Hannah beamed when she handed Jace her prize rock.

"Did you find this just for me?"

"Yes, I found it near the pond. It's shiny and you can carry it in your pocket."

He hugged her. "Every time I look at it, I'll think of you."

Ben fidgeted. "Jace," He whirled his gift from behind his back. "I made this for you. It's a whistle. I whittled it out of a piece of wood."

"You made this yourself?"

"Well, Grandpa helped me a little. But it really whistles. Just try it."

Jace blew into the wood piece and, sure enough, it made a whistling sound. He ruffled Ben's hair. "I've never owned a whistle before. Thank you."

Jace stood and Captain Brenner put his hand on his shoulder. "Congratulations. I'm happy we were all here to celebrate with you." Then he slapped Jace on the back. "You better grab Ellen before someone else does."

After the excitement of Jace's birthday, Ben and Hannah slept soundly while Rebecca sat in a chair by their wagon listening to the night sounds. She closed her eyes, humming the melody that flowed through her mind.

Jace walked up humming the same tune. "Mamma, why are you still up?"

"Waiting on you." She motioned to the bench next to her chair. "Come sit with me for a while. Did you enjoy tonight? Ellen looked so pretty."

"She's a nice girl." He pulled a medal from his pocket. "She gave me this to remember her by. She won it when she came in first place at her school's spelling bee."

"How nice." Rebecca reached behind her and took a pouch from the work table. "I wanted to wait until after the excitement of the party to give you this." She placed the gift in his palm.

He opened the pouch and his forehead wrinkled. "Mamma, I can't take Pa's watch. It's the only thing you have of his."

Rebecca covered his hand with hers. "Sweetheart, I want you to have it. He would want you to have it." She squeezed his hand. "And I have you, and Ben, and Hannah, and a new baby."

He stood. "But, Mamma—"

"Never forget how much your pa loved you." She stood and put her arms around him. "And I love you so."

His voice broke. "Thank you, Mamma. I love you too."

CHAPTER SIXTEEN

The signal sounded to begin their journey down the sandy banks of the North Platte River. Fort Laramie lay a hundred and fifty miles down the trail.

Jace put the bit in Rowdy's mouth then threw the saddle on his back. "Mr. Barker sent Nate with a message saying he needed to talk to me this morning before we get on the trail." He finished cinching the saddle and mounted his horse. "I shouldn't be too long."

"We'll have everything packed and ready by the time the wagons move out," said Rebecca.

Hannah jumped from the wagon seat. "Why do we have to leave Ash Hollow? I like it here."

Ben raised his head from the washbasin and scoffed. "That's silly. Why would you want to stay in Ash Hollow? Pa wanted us to go on to Oregon." He twisted his head toward Rebecca. "Right, Mamma?"

"Yes, Ben."

Rebecca stooped and gave Hannah a smile. "Ash Hollow was the perfect place to celebrate Jace's birthday." She adjusted Hannah's bonnet and tied a bow under her chin. "We won't ever forget it, will we?"

Hannah made a face at Ben. "No, we won't." Then turned and put her hands on her mother's face. "You're so pretty, Mamma."

"Thank you, sweetheart. So are you." She hugged Hannah and stood. Rebecca tied her bonnet on securely and grabbed her staff. Ben ran to the Calhoun's wagon while Hannah pretended Betsy was her little girl.

By noon, the sun's reflection glared against the rushing water of the North Platte River. Though the grade was only slightly uphill, it caused the oxen, along with the group of travelers, to breathe a little harder. With each step Rebecca took, the sand found its way into every fold of her clothing.

She removed her bandana and wiped the sweat from her forehead and neck. Drops of moisture trickled down her back. Though she had only been on the trail a few hours, Rebecca was anxious for the noon break.

Finally, the bugle sounded. "Ben, you need to water Lucy," said Rebecca. "Jace will help you. And Hannah, help me with the biscuits. I'll start a fire in the pit and get the coffee going."

The boys grabbed four buckets and headed for the river. Three trips gave ample supply of water for Lucy, the team, and the water barrel.

"Jace, what did Mr. Barker need with you this morning?"

He took a sip of coffee. "As soon as I eat my lunch, he needs me to check on the other wagons for any problems."

She furrowed her brow. "Is he okay?"

"He told me the council's holding a meeting to settle a dispute about a stranger who rode into camp late last night and was caught taking a couple of Bert Ingles' horses."

Rebecca swung a glance at Jace. "He's not one of the outlaws they've been looking for, is he?"

"No, I don't think so. But we're still a ways from Fort Laramie, and the council needs to decide what to do with him. They don't know if he acted on his own or he's a part of a gang."

The scar-faced Coulter brother flashed in Rebecca's mind.

"Captain Brenner is going to double up on the night guards." He put his coffee cup down and assured Rebecca. "Don't worry. I know what you're thinking, but the Captain and Mr. Barker will keep an eye on us all."

She clutched her throat. "I know." Then gave a stern look and pointed her finger at him. "Jace, you stay away from that stranger."

"I will. Captain Brenner's keeping him away from everyone." He finished his coffee and grabbed his hat. "Mr. Barker said he would check on you when we get back on the trail." Jace made sure his cinch was tight, then climbed on and headed up the trail.

Remembering Ash Hollow, Rebecca's heart stirred at the mention of Luke's name. She peered down at her wedding ring and her fingers pressed against it. *I don't understand, Lord, I'm lonely and I need my husband.* She pressed the palms of her hands over her eyes. Lowering her hands, she raised her chin and took a deep breath. *I'm carrying Hank's child. I can't have these feelings for Luke and I won't.*

Sarah came around the back of the wagon with an arm full of quilts. "You okay? You look flushed."

"I'm fine. Jace was just telling me about the stranger and Mr. Ingle's horses." She put her hand on her belly.

Sarah laid the quilts on the back of the wagon. "Are you sure you're all right? Is it the baby?"

"No." Rebecca rolled her eyes. "Well, yes, in a way."

"Do I need to get Dr. Brummel?"

"No, it's not really the baby. I'm just struggling about Hank." She exhaled. Her shoulders sagged. "Why is this happening? Hank should be here with us. We need him."

"I know, honey." Sarah's brow crinkled. "You never imagined you would be in this situation. But God has the strangest ways of blessing us."

Rebecca shook her head. "You're right. He knows what's best for us."

"And what you need right now is to rest before we get back on the trail." She ran her hand over the top quilt. "These are for you and your family. The closer we get to the Rocky Mountains, the colder the weather will be at night."

"Are you sure you have enough to share?"

"My, yes. I couldn't bear to leave all these beautiful quilts back in Missouri, so I brought them all. Believe me, we have more than we need."

Rebecca clutched Sarah's arm. "What would I do without you?"

Sarah hugged her then stepped back and pointed her finger in the air. "Oh, and something else. Speaking of that stranger, Carl said for you to keep your revolver loaded. Tell Jace to do the same with the rifle. Carl doesn't expect any trouble, but you never know."

"We'll make sure they're loaded. And thanks for the quilts."

When Sarah left, Rebecca sat on the bench by the wagon wheel. Closing her eyes, she remembered Hank when they first married. She missed his playful smile and strong arms. She folded her hands and pressed them against her brow when she recalled him riding off never to return again.

"Rebecca?"

She opened her eyes, reluctant to leave her memories of Hank. Shielding them from the sun, she glanced up to see Luke standing in front of her.

"Rebecca, we're about to move out. Can I help with anything?"

Irritated at how his voice caused her heart to flutter, she snapped. "No, Mr. Barker. The children and I can manage."

He frowned and pulled his chin in. "Are we back to Mr. Barker? I thought after Ash Hollow we were closer friends than that."

"I'm sorry, Luke. But my condition makes things different now."

She saw the confusion in his eyes. She knew he didn't understand how her heart still ached for Hank. And now with her pregnancy, Rebecca was even more uncertain. But there was something about Luke that drew her to him. Until she could reason out in her mind how she would deal with it all, she couldn't let herself fall in love with Luke.

"Why would that make any difference?" He gripped his reins. "I didn't know Hank, but I do know he would want me to look after you and your family until we get to Oregon, especially now." He swung up into the saddle and over his shoulder said, "You know where I am if you need anything."

Three days after leaving Ash Hollow, the wagons slowly moved in a caravan style rather than side-by-side up the river toward Fort Laramie. Jace bounced from taking care of the constant repairs to their wagon, to his turn at night guard, to herding cattle. He also rode with Luke to scout out the trail when he could.

Ben, on the other hand, possessed the knack of asking more questions than Rebecca could answer. Though, having Zeb and Clara helped fill the gap.

By mid-morning, Rebecca's team of oxen slowed their pace making it hard to keep up with the other wagons. She nudged the oxen with her staff. "Giddup."

"Is Jace herding the cattle?" asked Hannah.

"He and Mr. Barker are helping Hugh Unger fix his wagon wheel. It came off the tire iron earlier this morning."

"Is Mr. Unger's arm still hurt?"

"Yes, and he needs everyone's help until it heals." Rebecca pulled Hannah closer while they walked beside the oxen. "It's a blessing when we get to help each other."

The Calhoun's traveled a couple of wagons ahead of theirs and Rebecca caught sight of Ben and Zeb. Ben motioned with his arms and Zeb let out a big belly laugh.

Hannah tilted her head to see. "What's Grandpa laughing at?"

"I don't know, but I'm sure it's something Ben said."

Hannah giggled and wrinkled her nose.

Rebecca took her eyes off the trail and studied the sky overhead. "Hannah, look at those clouds. The long fluffy ones remind me of the white seagulls along the beach back in Millbury."

Hannah squinted. "I've never seen a seagull. Is that what they look like?"

"Well not exactly. You have to use your imagination."

"What's that?"

"It's something you do with your mind."

Hannah pointed up the trail. "No, Mamma, what's that tall thing over there?"

Rebecca focused down the trail. "My, I have no idea."

"Grandpa," Ben threw his hands up, "do you see it? What is it?"

In the distance, appeared a tall formation of earth and rock. Ben gazed at the strange object. "Have you ever seen anything that tall, Grandpa?"

"No, boy, I haven't."

By late afternoon, the wagon train was close enough to make out the formation.

Ben ran ahead of Zeb a few steps then ran back. "Look Grandpa. Wonder what it is."

Zeb took a puff from his pipe. "You know, son, I remember reading about it in a magazine article written by a fur trapper who traveled this trail back in 1843. He said someone dubbed it the Court House. From the details he gave, that's got to be it. The trapper said he tried climbing the thing. He was only halfway up when he nearly fell. He estimated it to be around four hundred feet high."

"Wow, what's it made of?"

"The article said clay and volcanic ash."

Ben swung his head around, eyes widened. "There's volcano's around here?" He turned a circle looking around. "Mamma taught us about volcanos."

"But there's more to the story. The old trapper wrote that he carved his name on the side of the rock while he dangled from the side. I'll bet it's still there if we had a mind to climb up that thing. In fact, it wouldn't surprise me if that rock bears the names of thousands of emigrants who've traveled this trail."

Ben's eyes danced. "Grandpa, when we get closer, do you think we could carve our names on the side of it too? We wouldn't have to climb it."

"I don't know why not. Then when those who come after us get a close look at that rock, they'll see we've been here."

The ground rumbled and Ben grabbed onto Zeb. "Grandpa." A cloud of dirt rose from the north. "Is it another storm?"

"No, boy. Can you see them? It's the biggest herd of buffalo we've seen so far. Looks like hundreds of them headed northwest." He emptied the tobacco out of his pipe and put it in his pocket. "That's the first big herd we've seen yet." He placed his thumbs around his suspenders. "Back east, I read a news article where buffalo herds on the plains are disappearing. Ben boy, you need to remember what we saw today. By the time you get my age, there may not be a single buffalo roaming these parts. I'll be surprised if we see another herd that big again."

Sitting by the campfire after supper, Rebecca, Jace, and Hannah listened while Ben told them about the fur trapper. He reared up on his knees. "Grandpa said we're going to carve our names on the rock when we get closer."

Hannah burst. "Me too?"

"That's a good idea," said Rebecca, smiling. "And I have another good idea. Why don't you and Hannah get your school tablets and draw a picture of the tall rock. That way you'll have a reminder of it when we get to Oregon."

Racing to the back of the wagon, Ben said, "I'd a lot rather draw a picture on my tablet than do my arithmetic."

"I heard that, Ben Quaid." Rebecca glanced over at Jace. "You'd think learning to read, write, and do their numbers was from the devil himself."

Jace laughed. "I remember thinking the same thing." He drank the last bit of coffee and grabbed his hat. "I told Ellen I'd be by after supper for a walk by the river. You don't have to wait up. I won't be late."

"It's a beautiful night." She gazed up at the sky. "Just look at all the stars." She tossed him his jacket. "You may need this. It's getting cooler each evening when the sun goes down."

CHAPTER SEVENTEEN

A day's ride from the Court House, the caravan came upon another and more dramatic stone shaft that reached into the sky even farther.

Not long before noon, Ben skipped alongside the Calhoun's wagon, then stopped. He scratched his head and peered down the trail. "Grandpa, there's another one." Ben pointed to the formation. "Look how tall and skinny it is."

"It looks like a church steeple," said Zeb.

"How did those big rocks get there?"

"Well, son, God made them. But I imagine years of wind and rain have changed them from their original formations."

"But why would God put them out here all by themselves?"

Zeb pulled on his beard. "I figure He knew we would come along someday and enjoy seeing them. He does things like that. It gives God great pleasure to surprise us with all sorts of things."

"Will we get to see it up close like we did the Court House?"

"I'm sure we will. We may carve our names on that one too."

Ben grinned, his eyes lifted up at Zeb. "Everybody's going to know we've been here, right Grandpa?"

"That's right. In the summer of 1857. And years from now when people begin to populate this area, they'll see Ben and Hannah Quaid etched on the sides of these rocks and wonder to themselves who you were and what you did with your lives."

Most of the morning, Captain Brenner kept his eye on the dust stirred by a group of riders not too far northeast of the wagon train. He stepped from his horse when Luke rode up beside him.

Luke nodded toward the smoke. "What do you make of that?"

"I saw the smoke of their campfire at sunrise this morning." The captain took his gloves off and beat the dust out of them on his leg. "So far, they've kept a steady distance from us. But tell some of the hands to stay alert."

"It's nearly noon. You want me and Tom to ride that way and see what we can find? By the dust, it looks like it could be five or six of them."

"No. Stay close in case something happens. I think we just need to keep watch on them for now. And don't let on to any of the families. We don't need to scare them unnecessarily."

The captain got back in the saddle and rode up beside the chuck wagon. Pete sat on the wagon seat hollering at the team of mules to move a little faster. Captain Brenner waved to get his attention.

"Pete," he pointed to the supply wagon that Nate, his right-hand man, had converted into a makeshift jail. "I'm going to tell Nate to pull that wagon just far enough in front of the wagons so we can watch the prisoner while keeping him separated from the others. He and a couple of the cowhands can take turns driving that wagon till we get to Fort Laramie."

Pete hollered over the noise of the creaking wagon. "Captain. Our prisoner had lots to say this morning when I took him his breakfast."

"Anything about the men trailing us?"

"As a matter fact, yes he did. Said for me not to worry about breakfast tomorrow morning. He seems to think those fellas are going to make sure he rides out sometime during the night."

"I'll have two of the cowhands guard the prisoner tonight."

"Oh, and Captain," he spit some tobacco out the side of his mouth, "he mentioned some brothers by the name of Coulter. Said they're looking to make good on a promise to avenge their brother's death. Seems to think his killer's on this wagon train. I don't have a good feeling about this."

Without saying a word, Captain Brenner whirled his horse around and rode back toward the cattle herd.

Throughout the day, the dust from the riders continued to follow the wagon train. Rebecca noticed it, along with what seemed to be more activity than usual by Captain Brenner, Luke, and the trail hands.

After she fed Hannah and Jace at noon, she handed Hannah a jar of sweet relish. "While we're stopped for lunch, will you take this to Clara for me? And see if they would like to have supper with us tonight. While you do that, Jace and I are going to run over to the Webster's wagon."

Hannah jumped from the tailgate. "Since Ben's been with Grandpa all morning, can I tell him it's his turn to look for firewood this afternoon?"

"Yes, but you two don't argue in front of Zeb and Clara."

Rebecca and Jace headed for Carl and Sarah's wagon. "Carl, do you and Sarah know what's going on? Luke's been acting strange today."

Carl untied his bandana and wiped the sweat from his face. "Nobody's said anything, but it's not hard to see riders are keeping up with the wagon train." He waved his hand at the cloud of dust. "You and the children stay close to your wagon in case whoever they are decide to show themselves. And, Jace, you be careful."

Returning to their wagon, Rebecca glanced in the direction of the riders then turned to Jace. She gripped his arm. "You don't think that prisoner's gang knows I killed one of the Coulter brothers?"

"How could they know?" He straightened his shoulders. "But I'll check the rifle in case we need it."

Rebecca walked to the front of the wagon worried others might be in danger because of her. She climbed up on the seat and reached for the loaded pistol. Holding it in her hand, she remembered how it jerked the last time she fired it.

During the night, Rebecca kept waking up thinking she heard strange noises. When she stepped from the wagon the next morning, Jace had the coffee going.

"You're up early," said Rebecca. "Did you hear noises last night?" She got a cup from the chuck box and poured herself some coffee.

Jace pulled his gloves on. "No, but Mr. Barker rode by earlier and said the captain pulled the prison wagon farther from the wagon train. Until we get to Fort Laramie, he's putting another night guard on him."

She pulled some strands of hair behind her ear. "He say anything else?"

"No. Just said the captain would feel better if that outlaw was in a cell at Fort Laramie where he belongs."

Rebecca started breakfast, but her mind wasn't on it. As confused as her emotions were over Luke, she wished he would ride up. His presence brought her more peace than she realized.

Ben bounced out of the wagon.

"Get the pail and milk Lucy. And tell Hannah to help you."

He rubbed the sleep from his eyes. "Yes, Mamma."

Jace was checking the tongue of the wagon when Luke rode up. "Jace, the captain has orders for you to stay close to your wagon today. And don't let Ben or Hannah stray away from the wagon either."

"Has it got something to do with that prisoner?"

"Until we get closer to Fort Laramie, just keep your rifle close to you."

Rebecca stepped up beside the team. "Do you have any idea how long it will be before we get to Fort Laramie?"

"Ten days or more."

Sensing Luke's frosty demeanor, Rebecca kept further comments to herself.

Three more days on the trail and they could still see the outlaws following them. From the makeshift jail, the prisoner shouted threats. Some of them indistinguishable, some clear and frightening.

Rebecca walked alongside the team but turned her head toward the prison wagon when the outlaw's voice rang out. "Frank and the others are gonna bust me out of this place. And he's gonna take care of whoever killed his brother."

Jace came from the other side of the wagon and caught up with his mother. "Don't listen, Mamma. He doesn't know what he's talking about. There's no way any of them know who killed his partner's brother. Anyway, when we get to Fort Laramie, the troops will take care of the whole sorry lot."

"It can't be soon enough for me. I feel like we've put everyone on this wagon train in jeopardy."

"Captain Brenner and Mr. Barker will make sure those outlaws don't get near the wagon train."

She wiped her brow with her bandana. "I'm sure you're right."

"Don't worry." Jace put his arm around her. "Mr. Barker will keep his eye on us. I noticed he was camped not far from our wagon last night."

Rebecca jerked her head around. "Are you sure?"

"Yes, ma'am. He waits till everyone's down for the night. He was up and gone this morning before anyone else stirred. I wouldn't have known it, but I heard something last night. When I went to look around I saw him."

"Jace," she grabbed his arm, "don't you be wandering off in the night. You know what the captain said."

"I know, but my rifle was loaded." He gave her a smile. "Nothing's going to happen to me."

She straightened and pulled her shoulders back. "As much as I want to believe that, I'm not so sure. Those men following us are no better than the man we buried." She shook her staff. "They're dangerous cold-blooded killers. And have one thing on their minds. To kill their brother's murderer."

As cool as the nights were, it didn't take long after the sun rose for the heat to wear everyone down.

Rebecca peered down the trail and longed to see Fort Laramie. She quickened her pace and caught up with Jace. "Did Mr. Barker say how much farther it is to Fort Laramie when you talked this morning?"

"It depends on which trail we take at Scotts Bluff. If we go around the bluff, it could add a couple of more days."

"So by early next week we should be close, if not there." She stared in the direction of the gang of men trailing them. "It's hard enough to get through a normal day on the trail, but that awful prisoner and his gang are making it worse."

Pete sounded the bugle for the midday break.

"Thank heavens," said Rebecca.

She turned to Ben and Hannah riding on the wagon seat. "Get the buckets and water Lucy."

"I'll take care of the team," said Jace.

A few minutes after the wagons stopped, Rebecca caught sight of Sarah slump and crumple to the ground.

"Sarah!" Rebecca threw her staff to the ground. Slapping her bonnet from her head, she held her skirt up and ran toward her. Rebecca knelt over her. "Sarah." She called to Hannah. "Run for the doctor."

Rebecca rushed to their water barrel and drenched a cloth for Sarah's forehead. She ran and knelt pressing the cool cloth against her face. "Sarah? Sarah, can you hear me?"

Carl ran from the other side of the wagon. He fell on his knees beside them. "Sarah, honey." He took her hand. "It's Carl. I'm here."

Rebecca felt her face when she didn't move. "She's burning up with fever."

Hannah and Dr. Brummel appeared from the front of the wagon, along with several others.

"Doc," said Carl, "there's something wrong with my Sarah. She's burning up."

The crowd stepped back while Dr. Brummel examined Sarah. "Carl, we need to get her out of the sun. Let's get her in your wagon?" Carl scooped her into his arms, and Dr. Brummel helped lift her into the back of their wagon.

Penelope and Millie ran and huddled with Rebecca waiting for news from the doctor.

"When Carl carried her to the wagon," said Rebecca, "she never made a sound."

Penelope wrung her hands. "This morning when I brought her those quilt pieces she said she'd had a sore throat for several days. I should have made her go see the doctor right then."

"Now, don't take on any guilt." Rebecca gripped her arm. "If she thought she was that sick, she would've gone herself. I'm sure Dr. Brummel can give her something. She's probably just exhausted from the trail."

The doctor stepped from the wagon. Rebecca could read his face. Something was seriously wrong with Sarah.

He grimaced. "I've told Carl and the children Sarah has contracted an infection. I'm not sure how contagious at this point. However, it'll be necessary to quarantine the whole family until we see how she gets along. I'll tell Captain Brenner."

Rebecca stepped toward the doctor and placed a hand on his arm. "Is she going to be okay?"

Penelope and Millie leaned in toward Rebecca and the doctor. He shook his head. "I'm not sure just now. We need to give her body time to fight this off. But until then, no one should come near their wagon." He paused. "I suggest you pray."

Rebecca's breath caught. She gripped his arm tighter. "Dr. Brummel."

He put his hand over hers. "I wish I could be more encouraging, but it'll be a few days before we know how serious this is."

Millie, Penelope, and Rebecca stood dazed while Carl pulled his wagon from the trail. Rebecca wrapped her arms around her waist. "Sarah has to get better. We all need her."

Penelope lowered her head. "She's who I go to when I'm not sure about things."

"Well," said Millie, her eyes filled with tears, "Sarah needs our prayers along with Carl and the boys." She laced her fingers and gripped her hands. "We have to believe she'll be well soon."

CHAPTER EIGHTEEN

Late evening the following day, Rebecca walked near the team and glanced toward the Webster's wagon to make sure it wasn't lagging too far behind. Two of Captain Brenner's cowhands rode not far from it as protection from possible danger.

Turning her attention to the team, Rebecca called to Jace when she noticed a cloud of dust coming toward the caravan. She strode up beside him then stopped. "It's not the outlaws, is it? Surely they wouldn't be so bold as to ride up in broad daylight."

She took a step forward to get a better look. "It's soldiers." She turned to Jace. "Thank the Lord." Rebecca studied them. "Do you think they're from Fort Laramie?"

"Could be," said Jace. "We're too far from Fort Kearney."

Rebecca stood on her tiptoes and put her hand up to guard her eyes from the sun. "Captain Brenner's riding out to meet them." She gazed at the Webster's wagon. "What about Sarah and Carl?"

"Mr. Barker said the two cowhands guarding their wagon are watching for anything unusual. He knows not being in the circle makes them an easy target."

The signal to halt the wagon train sounded. Within a few minutes, Luke rode up. "Captain Brenner's talking to the lieutenant and said to go ahead and water your oxen. We're making camp for the night."

"What brought the soldiers here?" said Jace.

"A scouting troop from Fort Laramie was ordered to search for a gang of outlaws who held up a government dispatcher delivering their payroll. The captain told the lieutenant about our prisoner and the riders following us."

Rebecca twisted the ribbon on her bonnet. "Please say the lieutenant will take charge of the prisoner."

"He ordered three men to take him back to Fort Laramie and the rest will continue tracking the other outlaws." Luke pushed his hat back. "They're all wanted for theft and murder."

Rebecca let go of the ribbon. "Will the troops be able to round them up before we get to Fort Laramie?"

"We're getting close to Scott's Bluff. Fort Laramie is about five days from there." Luke smiled at Rebecca. "Wouldn't surprise me if the troops have them behind bars before we get there."

She sighed. "That would certainly be answered prayer." Before Luke could turn to leave, she asked, "Does Captain Brenner know anything more about Sarah?"

He shook his head. "She's still in a bad way. The fever hasn't broken yet. The captain's just thankful Carl and the boys haven't come down with it." He took his hat off and wiped the sweat from his brow. "I've seen this kind of thing on nearly every wagon train I've been on. We just have to pray she's strong enough to fight it off."

"If it's one thing Sarah is, it's strong." Rebecca's eyes watered. "I just pray the infection doesn't last much longer."

"Keep praying." Luke smiled down at Rebecca. "That's the best medicine she could have."

She hesitated then raised her eyes to him. "Would you like to take supper with us tonight? It's been a while since the children have heard your stories about Indians and scouting for the wagon train." If she were honest with herself, it was Rebecca who missed Luke's company.

"Thank you, but Captain Brenner wants to map out the trail through Scott's Bluff. Maybe some other time."

By noon the next day, Rebecca, along with others, stared at the unnatural twists and bends of rock walls, towers, and gulches known as Scotts Bluff. The late afternoon sun glared behind the wide, steep ledge of sand and clay dividing the trail.

Rebecca and the children stood by Clara and Zeb looking up at the tallest natural wonder she had ever seen. "Zeb, how long do you think the bluff is?"

He rubbed his whiskered chin. "I don't know, but it could well be a half-mile long."

She gazed at the bluff. "There's a fork in the trail at the base of the bluff. It looks like one goes off around the southern end while the other passed directly over the peak."

"The one going over the peak looks awfully steep," said Zeb.

Rebecca shaded her eyes. "Luke and Jace are riding this way." Her heart fluttered at the sight of Luke, though she tried to dismiss it.

Reining their horses up by the Calhoun's wagon, Luke said, "The south route around the bluff will get us within four days of Fort Laramie."

Rebecca asked, "There's no way to go over it?"

Luke stroked his horse's neck. "Going over the bluff is too dangerous. Some wagon trains have done it but at the price of damaged wagons and dead animals. Captain Brenner decided it's not worth the risk."

Rebecca peered at the bluff. "It looks like the trail leaves the river. Did the captain say anything about another water supply up ahead?"

"There's a spring about two days ride from here. We'll meet up with the Platte River when we reach the other side of the bluffs. Until we make it to the springs, we'll have to ration water again," said Luke. "Traveling over this part of the trail is hard and slow. It's covered in ravines and dried up gulches."

Rebecca laughed. "From the time we set foot on this trail, nothing's been easy."

"You're right," said Luke. "Some parts are harder than others and this is one of them." He swung his horse around. "Have a good evening."

"I wish Pa could see this bluff," said Jace.

Ben said, "You think he can see it from heaven?"

Hannah chuckled. "Sure he can."

Rebecca pressed her hand on her stomach when she felt a stir of movement within her.

ঔ

Late that afternoon, Luke rode back to the wagon train after scouting the trail. He had spent most of the morning looking for a possible water supply knowing the spring was a good two days ride, but with no success.

When he neared one of the supply wagons, he caught a fight erupting. Jim Eldridge reared back and knocked Jace to the ground. Luke spurred his horse.

Jace jumped up and rammed Jim's body against the wagon wheel. Jim got Jace around the neck and pulled him to the ground.

Luke jumped from his horse, reached down, and grabbed both of them by the collars.

"Whoa, break it up." Luke jerked them off the ground.

The boys scrambled to get free from his grip. Jim took another swing.

"Boys, I said break it up. What's going on?"

Jim wiped blood from his lip and glared at Jace. "He started it."

Luke stared at Jace. "Is that right? Did you start it?"

Jace slipped out of Luke's grasp and stared at Jim.

"Answer me." Luke glowered at Jace. "Did you start it?"

"No, sir."

Jim scowled. "He took the first swing."

Luke picked up Jace's hat and handed it to him. "Is that right, Jace?"

"I might have taken the first swing, but I didn't start it." He rubbed his knuckles.

Luke glared at one boy and then the other. "You both need to cool off. Whatever's going on, you better work it out before it gets out of hand." He grabbed Jace's shoulder. "But for now, you come with me."

Jace scowled at Jim.

Luke nudged Jace. "Leave it alone for now. I need to talk to you." Luke took the reins of his horse and he and Jace headed toward the chuck wagon.

When out of earshot from anyone, Luke gave Jace some time, then asked, "Are you going to tell me what that was all about?"

"It's nothing."

"Yeah, I could tell by the way you were swinging it was nothing. You want to tell me the truth?"

"Jim was right. I did throw the first punch."

"Jace." Luke cocked his head. "I know you. There must have been a good reason why you and Jim were fighting."

Jace stopped short and faced Luke. "He said something about Ellen. I'm not going to tell you what he said, but he won't say it again if I have anything to do with it."

Luke held back a smile and raised a hand. "I understand defending a lady's honor, but you need to remember we have a long way to travel before we get to Oregon. Somehow you and Jim have to work this out."

Reaching the chuck wagon. Luke grinned and leaned against it. "But from what I saw, you may have fixed the problem."

"It's fixed all right as long as he doesn't shoot his mouth off again."

Luke stooped and plucked a blade of grass. "I figure he knows now to keep his comments to himself." He chewed on the grass while Jace cooled down.

Jace dusted the dirt off himself. "I need to get back to my wagon. Mamma'll have lunch ready and she doesn't need anything else to worry about, especially my getting into a fight with Jim."

"She'll understand."

"I hope so." He headed toward their wagon.

Pete walked from around the chuck wagon with a pot of coffee.

"I could use some of that," said Luke.

Pete poured him a cup and chewed on a mouth full of tobacco.

"I had to break up a fight between Jace and Jim Eldridge." He waved his cup toward Jace. "It's hard growing up without a pa. He's at the age he needs him."

Pete spit and said, "Jace is a good kid. But what about Jim? Is he okay?"

"Jim's fine. The only thing hurt was his pride."

The added miles around Scott's Bluff proved to be more difficult than Rebecca expected. Men shouted and animals strained to maneuver the deep, V-shaped ravines and gulches now dried up from fast running streams. Rebecca and Jace worked their wagon over the rough terrain watching for detours around the wide gaps in the ground. Rebecca shook her head at the never-ending challenges the trail held.

Just before noon, Captain Brenner rode near Rebecca's wagon. "Turn the wagons to the south. The ravines are not cut so deep further down that way."

She glanced over and saw Jessie McCain's wagon tip sideways crossing a deep gulch.

The captain hollered. "Tom, you and Nate help Jessie before he spills everything from his wagon. He needs to slow his animals down and ease his way over that gulch."

When he rode off, Rebecca said, "Ben, you and Hannah don't get too close to the wagons. And watch where you step. The prairie grass makes it hard to see the ravines. You don't want to step crooked and hurt yourself."

A few minutes later and not far from where Rebecca worked the oxen, Ben jumped and darted toward the wagon. He scurried up the side and grabbed the loaded Colt revolver laying under the seat. Jumping from the wagon, he hollered, "It's a rattler," but his foot caught and he plunged to the ground. He landed on the gun. A shot went off.

"Ben!" When Rebecca got to him, he was lying face down beside the wagon. She fell to the ground and turned him over. The Colt was smoking. The scent of gunpowder filled her nostrils.

"Somebody get Dr. Brummel! Hurry!"

Ben lay unconscious while Rebecca searched for any sign of a bullet wound. She leaned over his motionless body and lifted his shirt, but there was no blood. "Ben. Ben, it's Mamma. Open your eyes."

Jace, Luke, and Grady Shaw ran to where Rebecca knelt over Ben. She whirled around when a gunshot went off. Bert Ingles dangled the snake from the end of his gun. Rebecca gasped and turned back to Ben.

Jace crouched beside his little brother. "Can you hear me, Ben?"

Dr. Brummel rode up and jumped from his horse.

Ben opened his eyes and moaned.

Rebecca looked to the heavens. "Thank you, Lord." She caressed Ben's face. "Are you okay?"

"Where's my gun? I've got to kill a snake." He mumbled.

Rebecca was relieved one minute and furious the next. "Young man, you may get a seat warming like you've never experienced before. You know you're not supposed to touch that gun."

"But Mamma—"

"Ben," scowled Rebecca.

Dr. Brummel examined him. "He has a bump on his forehead, but he'll be fine."

Ben slowly got up while Jace picked up the gun and headed for the wagon. He peeked back over his shoulder at Ben and his mother. "I've never seen Mamma so mad. If you know what's good for you, you'll tread lightly around her for the next few days."

Rebecca laid her hand on Ben's shoulder. "You better listen to your big brother. And you don't leave my side for the rest of the afternoon. Furthermore, you have extra chores for the next week."

CHAPTER NINETEEN

At the end of the first day circling Scott's Bluff, Captain Brenner, Luke, and Tom sat by the campfire near the supply wagon. From the light of the fire, they studied a map. A pot of coffee simmered on the fire.

"We should reach Fort Laramie in two to three days," said Tom, "if the weather holds out."

Luke pointed to the west. "The springs are about five miles up the trail. We've got to get the livestock to fresh water. The heat and the mosquitoes are making the trail intolerable."

Captain Brenner motioned down the trail. "There's an Indian trading post close to the springs. My horse threw a shoe, and there's a makeshift blacksmith at the post. We'll need to have some of the other horses shod while we're there. It'll be a good place to rest. A good drink of water will help. We've been pushing everyone hard."

Luke slapped his hat across his chest. "I think some tempers are beginning to flare. The heat and these infernal gnats and mosquitoes are driving us all crazy."

"After we get to the Rockies, it won't be a problem," said the captain, grimacing. "But what's in some of these wagons might be. When we leave Fort Laramie and head for the mountains, we'll need to conserve all the energy these animals can muster, and that means lightening the load of these wagons."

"Well, that may be easier said than done." Luke grinned. "Some of those fancy carved bureaus hold more sentimental value than they're worth. If those ladies have to leave them on the side of the trail, we'll probably see lots of tears."

"When we're in Fort Laramie, I'd like to persuade them to sell some of their goods. It would make things a lot easier on them and the wagon train."

Tom lifted the coffee pot. "Want any more coffee?"

"I'll take some." Luke tossed him his empty cup. "I've got the first shift of night patrol."

Tom poured him a cup and handed it to him.

Luke took a sip and said, "We should reach the springs by late tomorrow. That'll put us in Fort Laramie by Sunday or Monday maybe."

"Tom," said the captain, "make another round of the wagons before you bed down. And this is the last night you'll need to check on Carl's wagon. He and the boys never caught what made Sarah so sick so I'm bringing them back into the caravan tomorrow. Even with extra guards, five days is too long and too dangerous for them to be separated from the rest of us."

After Tom left, Luke leaned back on his elbow. "Captain, how many more times are you going to make this trip? Have you ever thought of settling somewhere?"

"A thousand times. I just haven't found the right spot yet, or the right person to settle down with. I guess when I find them, I'll give this up and never look back." Captain Brenner smiled. "I always say after making that cold, hard hundred miles from Fort Laramie to South Pass it's my last." He glanced at Luke. "What about you?"

"The thought has run through my mind. I've made this trip more times than I want to count. We'll see how things look in a few months."

The captain emptied his coffee cup. "We have to get over the Rocky Mountains first." He stood. "I wouldn't want this known, but there are some on this trip I'm not sure are going to make it."

The wagon train reached the springs late the next afternoon. Rebecca, along with the other ladies, took advantage of the clean, clear water to do laundry.

Bent over the wash bucket, Rebecca stood when Jace and Ben walked up beside the wagon. "Ben, you go with Jace and take the horses to the blacksmith."

"Mr. Barker," said Jace to Ben, "is waiting for us, so we need to hurry."

"I want to go," said Hannah.

"No, you need to stay here and help me. You need to wash Betsy's dress."

When the boys left, the noise of an approaching wagon caused Rebecca to turn. Hannah hollered. "Mamma, they're back."

Carl and Sarah waved from the wagon seat.

Rebecca's back ached and the frigid water from the springs caused her hands to chafe, but she forgot her discomfort when she saw Sarah. Rebecca had missed her terribly.

"Hannah, when the Websters get settled we'll take them the fresh berry cakes we baked earlier."

Hannah slapped at the swarm of mosquitoes hovering around her.

"But before we do that let's go to the wagon and get some lard ointment. That'll keep the mosquitoes off you for a while."

Hannah whined. "No, Mamma, that stuff stinks."

"But it'll keep the gnats and mosquitoes from tormenting you."

"It's greasy." Hannah moaned. "It makes the dirt and sand stick to me."

Rebecca didn't blame them. "I know, honey. It's greasy because it's made from hog lard and tallow which doesn't smell very good. But it's better than scratching the whelps they leave." She took the jar of ointment. "Now, let's put this on you and then go see Sarah."

Carl maneuvered their wagon back into position. Rebecca could hardly wait to see Sarah. Carrying the cake, Rebecca and Hannah hurried to their wagon.

When Sarah stepped down from the wagon seat, Rebecca stopped and pressed her hand to her chest.

"Rebecca, Hannah." Sarah hugged them both. "I'm so glad to see you."

Rebecca was shocked at how the illness took such a toll on her body. Sarah's once rosy cheeks were gray and sunk in. The dress she wore hung from her shoulders.

"I know." Sarah grabbed Rebecca's hands. "I don't look like I did before I got sick. Dr. Brummel said it would take some time to get my appetite back."

Rebecca put her arm around Sarah and could feel her shoulder blades protruding through the cotton dress she wore. "Sarah, I've missed you. I prayed every day for you."

"Thank you." Sarah's eyes watered. "I missed you and the children." They both sat on the bench by the wagon. "Dr. Brummel warned me not to expect too much."

"You don't worry about anything. We'll all make sure you have what you need. All we want is for you to take care of yourself and get completely well." She hugged her again. "I've missed your sweet laughter."

❦

That evening, Jace and Ellen stole a few minutes to walk down by the springs. Ellen gave him a side glance. "What about you and Jim? Are you both over the fight?"

"No. He stays away from me, and I do the same with him." Jace stooped by the springs.

"I don't know what happened, but it's not good to be at odds with each other." She sat down beside him. "As a favor to me, would you think about mending your friendship?"

"I'll think about it."

"We still have a long way to travel." She leaned toward him. "It'll make it better for you and for Jim."

He picked up a pebble and threw it into the water. "Mr. Barker has us herding cattle together for the next few weeks. I know he's doing it on purpose."

"Well, when you're working together don't you have to talk to each other?"

"Not that much. But let's not spend time talking about Jim. It's my turn to take the first shift of guarding the cattle tonight, so I'm going to have to get you back to your wagon soon." Jace stood, grabbed Ellen's hand, and pulled her up.

"Would you like to have supper with us tomorrow night?" She squeezed his hand. "Pa said it would be okay. Mamma said she'd open a jar of peach preserves she brought from Missouri. She's been saving them for something special."

"Sure, if Mr. Barker or Mamma don't have plans for me."

Before he left, Ellen smiled up at him. "Just think about what I said about Jim."

Rebecca sat straight up in bed. She was jarred from a sound sleep by someone calling out not far from her wagon.

Ben moaned. "I heard something. What is it, Mamma?"

"Shh, go back to sleep. I'll check to see what's going on. You and Hannah stay right here."

Rebecca jumped from the wagon and woke Jace. "Jace, something's wrong."

He sat up and rubbed his eyes. "Is it time to get up?"

"No." Rebecca grabbed a couple of lanterns and lit them. "Come with me. It sounds like Hal Gaines." She peered into the night. "I see Zeb and Carl coming this way."

A lone lantern shone in the distance traversing the prairie. Carl and Zeb caught up with Rebecca and Jace. Zeb said, "It's Hal. He's calling for Lorna."

"How long has he been out there?" asked Carl.

"I'm not sure." Rebecca held up the lantern.

The captain and Luke walked into the light of the lamp.

Zeb waved his hand. "When I walked past Hal and Lorna's wagon coming this way, Sally said her dad woke up and her mother was gone. He didn't know how long though."

Rebecca gasped. "What about the outlaws? They could be out there. They may even have her."

"Sally said her pa wasn't concerned about the outlaws," said Zeb. "He's just got to find Lorna."

"Let me go talk to Hal," said Captain Brenner. "Luke, you gather up some more lanterns."

Sarah, Millie, and some others gathered with Rebecca and waited for the captain to talk to Hal. When he returned Rebecca saw the deep lines on his face. "Hal's afraid Lorna's gone," said the captain. "He's searched everywhere. She's not at the springs, unless—"

Rebecca caught her breath.

"We need to spread out and search in every direction. Carl, you and Zeb take some men out on the west side of the wagons. Luke and Jace can take some toward the north. I'll help Hal, and Pete, and Nate can search the south side. If anyone finds her, fire one shot. And Rebecca, you and some of the women might want to stay with Sally till we find her mother."

By early morning, every man had scoured the ravines and gulches for Lorna. Rebecca and the ladies pooled their resources and set up a central campfire near Pete's chuck wagon. Hot coffee simmered on the fire, along with bacon and eggs to fortify the search party.

Some of the women gathered by the wagon while others sat on benches near the fire. Rebecca scooted over by Millie keeping an eye on the coffee. She said in a low voice, "Millie, if Lorna was alive, she would have shown up by now. And some of these ravines are so deep, if she fell into one she may never be found."

Millie exhaled. "She hasn't been herself since Jamie died." She lowered her head. "From the first day we set out for Oregon, there hasn't been anything easy about this. But losing a child is just more than some can take."

"I know Sarah still grieves Emily," said Rebecca, "but there's something different about her. I've never known anyone as strong as Sarah. Her faith gives her an inner peace that helps to sustain me when I'm discouraged. I don't know what I would do without her." She laid her hand on Millie's arm. "Or you."

A cloud of dust rose not far from the chuck wagon. Rebecca shielded her eyes and squinted. "It's Luke and Jace."

Luke hollered. "We found her! She's alive!"

Rebecca clasped her hands. "Thank you, dear God." Then hugged Millie.

Millie ran, hollering over her shoulder. "Sally's with Sarah. I'll go tell her Lorna's alive."

Jace got off his horse. "Mamma, Mrs. Gaines is alive, but she didn't recognize her husband. Her mind's not there." He tied his reins on the wagon wheel. "We found her in a deep ravine sitting on her knees singing to herself."

Rebecca covered her mouth with her hand. She shut her eyes, clinching them tight. She couldn't hold back the mournful sob rising in her throat. Burying her head in Jace's shoulder, she wept over another horror of the trail.

Jace held his mother in his arms. "Mr. Gaines is bringing her back to camp. Sally's going to need you and the other ladies."

Rebecca pressed her fist against her mouth. She stepped back and turned toward the Gaines' wagon. "What's to become of Lorna?"

CHAPTER TWENTY

Rebecca climbed from the wagon the next morning to find a cool breeze. Wrapping her shawl around her shoulders, she gazed at the dry trail and let the fresh air wash over her face. The wagon train lost a half-a-day of travel but finding Lorna was more important than their schedule.

She walked over to Jace. "You made coffee. It smells good."

"Did you get much sleep last night?" He poured a cup and handed it to her.

"I keep thinking about Hal and Sally…and Lorna." She took a sip and scanned the area. "Hannah's in the wagon, but where's Ben?"

"I tied Lucy up on the other side of the wagon. He's milking her."

"Good. He's still in trouble about the gun. He can wash the milk pail when he's finished. And after breakfast, I want a double load of firewood from him today."

Hannah climbed from the wagon. "Betsy and I are ready for breakfast."

"I need some milk to make the shortcakes. Let me go check on Ben."

She walked to the other side of the wagon. When she turned the corner Ben was holding the milk pail and smoothing dirt with the edge of his boot.

"What are you doing?"

He stopped and looked up at her. "Nothing."

"Well, let me have the milk. Hannah's ready for a cup."

Ben followed his mother around the corner of the wagon with his hands in his pockets.

Rebecca dipped some milk from the pail. "Here, Hannah." She took a better look at the pail of milk. "The pail is only half-full this morning. Lucy usually gives us more milk than this." She stared down at Ben. "What happened?"

"Uh…Lucy shoved me right as I was turning to bring you the milk."

"Are you sure?" She gave him a quizzical look. "I've never known Lucy to do that before."

"Well, hmmm…maybe I tripped." He scrunched his shoulders. "I can't remember."

Rebecca set the pail down and put her hands on her hips. "Well, if you can't remember, while Hannah, Jace, and I eat our breakfast, you can sit on the toolbox and think about it. I'm sure Lucy doesn't want to be blamed for something she didn't do."

Ben's eyes widened. "But, Mamma, I'll starve if I don't eat breakfast. And you're making shortcakes."

"Yes, but until you can tell me the truth, your shortcakes are going into the pie box. You can have them for breakfast tomorrow morning."

He shuffled his feet and lowered his head.

Rebecca stood over Ben. "Are you sure you don't want to tell me how you spilled that milk?"

He pulled his hands from his pockets. "Ah, I guess it wasn't Lucy's fault."

Rebecca's eyebrows lifted. "You guess?"

"No. I left the bucket full of milk and chased a rabbit into that bramble bush. When I got back a lizard had crawled into the bucket. I splashed most of the milk on the ground trying to get him out."

"Ooh, "grimaced Hannah, "I drank that milk."

Ben frowned at her. "Oh, it won't hurt you."

Holding back her laughter, Rebecca said, "Ben, don't ever keep something like that from me again. I know you told me the truth, but your shortcakes are still going in the pie box. You can have them at lunch."

"But why, Mamma? All Hannah did was drink a little milk a lizard swam in."

"Young man, don't argue with me. Now you finish up your chores so we can be ready to go when the bugle sounds."

"I don't know what's so bad about a lizard in the milk." He shrugged and turned to Hannah. "Girls are such sissies."

Rebecca shook her finger at him. "I don't know what's gotten into you lately."

She stood glaring at him when Jace walked over and put his hand on the center of Ben's back. He led him to the team of oxen.

The South Platte River stood between the wagon train and the eastern Wyoming Territory. Crossing this river, however, proved less difficult than the previous North Platte.

By noon, Rebecca caught a glimpse of Fort Laramie. "Jace, Hannah, Ben. There it is. We're not far now."

She and Hannah walked near the wagon. Ben picked up firewood a few yards from the wagon still making up for the lizard incident. Rebecca stretched her neck to get a better look at the fort. She put her hand over her brow. "From a distance, Fort Laramie appears much bigger than Fort Kearney." The river ran not far from the fort.

Rebecca spirits lifted at the sight of the fort. "Mr. Barker called Fort Laramie the gateway to the Rocky Mountains." She smiled. "We're getting closer to Oregon."

Jace glanced back at Rebecca. "Wish Pa could see this."

"Me too. Wouldn't he have loved seeing the Wyoming grassland?"

Jace gazed out across the plains. "Looks to me like this land could feed a lot of cattle. It runs clear to the base of those mountains."

Luke rode up. "Morning. We should reach Fort Laramie by afternoon." He reined his horse. "And don't be alarmed about the number of Indians camped about."

"Indians?" said Rebecca. "They are all friendly, aren't they?"

"Well, most of them. Because of the number of people who've settled this country, a few incidents have happened, but Fort Laramie keeps this portion of the wilderness fairly secure."

"Oh my." Rebecca shook her head. "Ben will be excited. I'll have to watch him, though, or he'll be right in the middle of them."

Luke and Jace laughed before Jace said, "If any of them speak English at all, it won't take him long to wear them down with questions."

Luke smiled at Rebecca. "When we get near the fort, I'll let you know where we're going to circle up. And don't push your team too hard. The last few weeks have just about done them in. I'm surprised we haven't lost any more than we have."

"From Ash Hollow," said Jace, "through Scotts Bluff was some of the roughest territory we've traveled."

"Fort Laramie didn't come any too soon." Rebecca rubbed the back of her neck. "I've never been so dirt-covered or bone-tired. And my patience is running low." She glanced across the way at Ben.

"And we've only traveled 640 miles," said Luke. "We're a third of the way to Oregon."

Rebecca exhaled knowing the Rocky Mountains stood between them and Willamette Valley. Thinking about Lorna, she just prayed they would all make it.

The military post Rebecca longed for lay only two miles down the trail. Fort Laramie represented the first semblance of civilization since Rebecca and the emigrants left Fort Kearney.

When the wagon train got close to the fort, Ben waved his arms. "Grandpa, look at all the tepees."

"Yeah, boy," Zeb said. "The captain told me the tepees you see are homes of the Lakota Sioux and a few Cheyenne tribes who live near the fort during the summer hunting season. They travel close to the Laramie River."

Ben's eyes got big. "Is that their trading post."

"It sure is." Zeb puffed on his pipe.

"Look." Ben pulled on Zeb's arm. "There's some more buffalo."

Zeb hung his thumbs in his suspenders. "The Indians depend on them for food, clothing, and lots of other things."

Ben crinkled his nose. "Wow, Grandpa, I like this place."

"I like this place too. It seems like it took a world of days to get here, though. I'm out of coffee and good pipe tobacco. And I'm thinking you and me and everybody else could use a bath."

Ben frowned. "Don't mention that to Mamma. If you do, she'll have me in a tub of water scrubbing my skin off."

After arriving at Fort Laramie late in the afternoon, Jace made his way to the stockade, located across the parade grounds from where the wagons sat. He walked in and introduced himself.

The man behind the desk looked up from his paperwork. "I'm Corporal McCrae. What can I do for you?"

Jace removed his hat. "A little over a week ago your troops picked up a prisoner at Scott's Bluff. Is he still here?

"Is Charles Brenner your wagon train's captain?"

"Yes, sir."

"Does he know you're here?"

"No."

He removed his spectacles. "Son, I'm not authorized to give information about the business of this fort to just anyone. Is there a personal interest in this man?"

"A member of his gang shot and killed my pa."

"I'm sorry." The corporal stood and stepped from behind his desk. "If you and Captain Brenner would like to come by later, I might have some information."

"Thank you." Jace turned and left.

He walked to the chuck wagon looking for the captain and saw Nate hammering a loose board on the toolbox. Nate stopped his hammering and said the captain was at the stockyard looking for a couple of fresh mules to pull the chuck wagon.

Jace headed across the parade ground and around to the back of the blacksmith where the stockyard stood. Standing by the fence, Captain Brenner rested his arms on the top railing and studied the animals. Luke leaned against the fence beside him.

"Captain."

He turned. "Jace." He gazed back at the stock. "You ready to look at fresh oxen?"

"Yes, sir." He paused. "But I was wondering about the prisoner at the stockade. Corporal McCrae said he would need to talk to you before he could give me any information."

"Son, why waste your time?"

"Because he may have said something about the Coulter brothers."

The captain stepped back from the fence. "Okay, let's go see if we can't ease your mind. You and Luke can come back in the morning and pick out a new team for your wagon."

After breakfast, with a list of needed supplies in hand, Rebecca, Hannah, Ben, and Sarah walked into the crowded mercantile. The packed shelves held much more than Fort Kearney's mercantile. Squeezing between the shoppers, Rebecca surveyed her list then stared at the prices marked on the items.

She frowned and elbowed Sarah. "Look at what they want for a pound of salt. And the price for two cups of sugar is a dollar. That's disgraceful."

Sarah pointed at a hundredweight of flour. "We paid five dollars for that in Fort Kearney. This bag is fifteen dollars."

Rebecca crossed her arms. "I'm glad to be in Fort Laramie, but I'm beginning to think this mercantile has gouged up the prices knowing we need these supplies to get to Fort Hall." She picked up a tin of maple syrup. "This is ridiculous. I'm not going to be able to get nearly what I need."

Holding the maple syrup, she glanced up to see Jace through the windows standing on the front walk of the mercantile. "Hannah, you and Ben stay with Sarah and I'll be right back."

Walking through the swarm of people, she stepped from the store and approached Jace.

He stood with his hands on his hips. "Mr. Barker and I took the oxen over to trade for fresh ones. But—"

She frowned. "Is there a problem?"

"We traded for two oxen in Fort Kearney for what one costs here. Can we afford that?"

"How can this be? They know we need fresh animals." Rebecca wanted to stomp her foot over the inflated prices, but instead, took a deep breath and collected herself.

Jace lifted a brow. "It's obvious we're being taken advantage of."

"Well, we have to have the animals. You and Mr. Barker do the best you can. We'll load what I can afford here when you finish."

"Oh," said Jace, "and Captain Brenner told Mr. Barker there would be a dance at the far end of the parade ground tonight."

She laughed. "Surely no one would charge us to dance." She wrinkled her brow. "Or would they?"

CHAPTER TWENTY-ONE

After the first bath in four weeks, Rebecca put her best dress on for the dance. She opened the trunk that held Hank's letter and pulled out a bright pink ribbon.

Sitting on the edge of the tailgate, she called Hannah. "Come here, sweetheart, and let me tie this in your hair. We want you to look pretty tonight."

Ben scowled. "Why did I have to take a bath?"

"Because we all needed one." His mother smiled. "I can see your handsome face now that last month's dirt is gone."

He scoffed. "Jace didn't have to take a bath."

"Yes he did, and I didn't have to threaten his life like I did you."

Ben scratched his neck. "That soap smelled funny. It's making me itchy."

"You're just not used to being this clean."

Rebecca stood and pressed her hands across the folds of her dress. "Okay, are we ready?"

"You look ready to me." Luke strolled up. "Do you mind if I walk you to the dance?"

"Why, of course not." She grinned. "Did the captain give you the night off?"

Heading for the dance, Luke said, "Yes, he thinks it might put me in a better frame of mind when we get back on the trail." The children walked ahead of Luke and Rebecca.

"What do you think?" Rebecca gave him a side glance.

"It can't hurt. We all need time to think of things other than the trail." He looked around. "I guess Jace is with Ellen tonight?"

"Yes." She slowed her pace a bit to allow Ben and Hannah to walk out of earshot. "Jace told me about him and the captain meeting with Corporal McCrae. He said the prisoner's scheduled to hang next week."

"Well, horse thieves don't live long in this part of the country."

Hannah turned and ran back to her mother and Luke. "Mr. Barker, do you like Mamma?"

"Hannah." Rebecca's face turned crimson.

Luke stooped and picked Hannah up in his arms. "Yes, I like your mother, and you, and Ben, and Jace. And I'm glad we're going dancing tonight. Would you like to have the first dance with me?"

Hannah eyed her mother. "Is it okay?"

"Yes, sweetheart. We're all going to have a good time tonight and not think about tomorrow, or the next day, or the next week." She tweaked Hannah's nose then Rebecca's ears perked. "I think I hear Mr. Johnson and Mr. Brewer warming up their instruments."

Rebecca linked an arm in Luke's and walked toward the party. As they passed the stockade, she stopped. Five wanted posters were nailed beside the front door. Two of the Coulter brothers stared back at her.

Savoring the following Sunday afternoon of rest, Rebecca, Sarah, Penelope, and Millie sat on the shady side of Sarah's wagon sewing quilt pieces.

Penelope, who held Mary Martha in her lap, asked Sarah, "What's the name of the pattern you're quilting? I don't recognize it."

"There's really not a name for it. My grandmother came up with the pattern after visiting her cousin in Charleston. She said it reminded her of the sunsets by the ocean."

"It's beautiful," said Rebecca noticing how Sarah's hands trembled.

Millie threaded a needle. "Did any of you hear there are some families who have decided to turn back? Bart said Captain Brenner met with them early this morning."

"Did he say which families?" Rebecca asked.

"He didn't, but it wouldn't surprise me if Janie and Bert Adams pull out and go back to Missouri. Janie's just not cut out for this kind of journey."

Rebecca laughed. "Who is?"

The rest of the women agreed.

"I don't mind confessing, traveling on a wagon train across some of the country we've dealt with, not to mention the weather, water rations, sickness, and every kind of insect or varmint we've come in contact with, was not what I expected. And we still have a long way to go."

"As much as I love Jim," said Penelope, "when he told me we were going to Oregon, he painted a much better picture. Of course, I knew it wouldn't be easy."

Sarah rubbed her shoulders. "Captain Brenner warned us that until we get over the Rockies it won't get any better."

"Sarah, are you getting tired?" Rebecca remembered how energetic Sarah was when they first met.

"Maybe a little, but I'm enjoying the afternoon with you all."

"I posted a letter to our families back home," said Penelope. "I told them all about Mary Martha. I sometimes wonder if she'll ever get to see her grandparents."

A series of explosions went off. The ladies jumped and Mary Martha let out a scream.

"Is it gunfire?" yelled Millie.

Rebecca rushed to the other side of the wagon. Ned Morris, Jimmy Ingles, and Ben stood watching a string of firecrackers explode.

She hollered. "Ben!" She stood with her hands on her hips. "Get over here!"

He made his way to his mother.

"What in the world are you boys doing? You scared us to death. And where did you get those firecrackers?"

"Mr. Brown at the mercantile found them in his storage room. He said he'd had them a long time and didn't know if they were any good."

"Oh, so Mr. Brown gave you firecrackers he wasn't sure were good. You might have blown a finger off."

"But he gave them to us for free."

Rebecca glance up to see a group of men standing in front of the mercantile grinning. Luke, Jace, and Tom were among them.

Ben scratched his head. "Mamma, can I go and play now?"

"Yes, but you need to tell Penelope you're sorry you scared Mary Martha."

"Yes, ma'am." He headed for the group of women dragging his feet.

Captain Brenner called a meeting at the chuck wagon late that afternoon. He stepped up on the seat of the wagon, his hat in hand. "Tomorrow we resume our journey to Oregon. Sweetwater is about fifty miles west of here. It'll take us four or five days to get there if nothing goes wrong."

He paused and explained that four families were pulling out of the wagon train. Two were going back to Missouri and two decided to make their stake in a town north of the trail outside of Fort Kearney.

Rebecca and her family stood near Bert and Janie Adams. Rebecca wrapped her arms around Janie. "We're all going to miss you, Bert, and the children. But I certainly don't blame you for wanting to put down roots before we cross to the other side of the Rockies. If it were up to me and Hannah, we'd go with you, but Jace and Ben still have their hearts set on Oregon."

Janie dabbed at her eyes. "Rebecca, Bert and I'll be praying for you and your family. I hope you find what you're looking for in Oregon."

After bidding the families their farewells, Rebecca, Jace, and the children walked back to their wagon. Rebecca took Jace's arm. "It's times like these I miss your pa. I don't like saying goodbye knowing we'll probably never see any of them again."

"Did you mean what you said about wanting to leave the trail?" Jace stared straight ahead. "Have you forgotten about Pa's dream?"

Rebecca pulled Jace to a stop and turned him toward her. "No, honey, I haven't forgotten. It's just that I miss your pa so. And there are times I wonder if all this is worth it."

Without a word, Jace turned and walked on to the wagon.

At five o'clock sharp the next morning, Pete sounded the bugle. Rebecca jostled Ben and Hannah. "Breakfast will be ready soon, and Lucy needs milking." Ben moaned and buried his head in his pillow. "Ben. You and Hannah, up. Now. You don't want us to leave without you, do you?"

Zeb's spurs jingled as Rebecca stepped from the wagon. "Morning, Zeb."

"Morning, Rebecca. Where's Ben and Hannah?"

She waved her thumb toward the wagon.

Zeb spoke loud enough for them to hear. "You can tell them I have something they might want to see."

Hannah popped her head out of the back of the wagon. Ben jumped to the ground while still buttoning his shirt. "Grandpa. We're up."

He handed them his surprise. Ben's eyes got big. "It has sparkles. What is it?"

"It's what you call fool's gold. It's pyrite. I found it lying beside my wagon wheel. You and Hannah can put it in your treasure boxes."

"Thanks, Grandpa. I've never seen a rock with sparkles." He furrowed his brow. "Do we have a treasure box, Mamma?"

Zeb laughed. "If you don't, we'll find something to put it in when we stop for lunch. Now, you better get busy milking Lucy."

"Yes, sir." Ben ran for the bucket, whirled around, and hollered. "Hannah! Hurry up and help Mamma with breakfast."

Rebecca laughed. "It's amazing the effect you have on that boy."

"He's a tonic to me. Don't know what I'd do without him. Is he much like his pa?"

"Not like Jace, but I see Hank in his smile and the way his mouth turns up when he's not sure about something."

Zeb paused before he spoke. "I asked the captain if Clara and I could pull our wagon closer to yours. We'd like to be able to keep a watch on you and your children. I hope you don't think we're hovering over you too close."

Rebecca put her arms around Zeb's neck and hugged him. "I need you and Clara as much as the children do. My only regret is Hank never got a chance to meet you."

A smile showed through his gray beard. "I'll go tell Clara." He walked back to his wagon, and his familiar whistle trailed after him.

After being gone all day tracking the swift flowing creeks between Fort Laramie and Sweetwater, Tom and Luke rode into camp the first night after leaving the fort. They gave Captain Brenner a report of their findings.

Sitting around the campfire near the chuck wagon, Pete handed them their supper. The captain studied Luke's markings on the map and asked, "Are these the deepest points of the creeks?"

"Yes, these two are where the water is knee deep. The rest are just small tributaries."

Tom said, "The trail's incline is enough to cause the livestock problems though."

Captain Brenner raised his brows. "You boys remind everybody not to drink any of the creek water."

Pete laughed. "It won't take but one sip to know to spit it out. But I know some will have to learn the hard way. One swallow of alkali water will turn their gizzards upside down."

"Captain," said Tom, "how far are we going before we need to lighten the loads on their wagons?"

He rubbed his forehead. "I'd hoped they would get rid of some of their things at Fort Laramie, but no one listened. Every day we get closer to the Continental Divide the harder it is on the animals." He studied the map again. "By day after tomorrow, some things will need to be unloaded."

That next morning, the wagon train trudged up the trail toward Sweetwater River. As pretty as the white blooms were along the trail, the thick shrubs of greasewood, along with the sagebrush, made walking slow and hard. The oxen struggled to stay in the tracks of the previous wagon trains.

Rebecca stumbled and caught herself. "These wretched weeds."

Sarah called out. "Don't fall."

"I won't, but it's hard to keep your footing with all these clumps of growth. I can't see what keeps them alive. It's awfully dry here."

This part of the trail proved to be the roughest the wagon train had encountered. Not a person rode in the wagons. Rebecca used the staff to keep her balance.

"Not only is the trail filled with overgrown shrubs," said Rebecca, "but look at all the bureaus, bedsteads, and chests of drawers strewn in every direction. Some look like they were bought from nice furniture stores back east."

"Have you ever seen anything like this?" Sarah shook her head. "There's everything from churns to clothes to fine china."

"Our oxen are breathing hard. We may have to do the same thing before long." Rebecca wiped her brow with her sleeve. "I can feel the uphill slope getting steeper every day."

Sarah grimaced. "We'll find out soon enough. But what a shame to see all these lovely things discarded like rubbish."

Rebecca moved over by Jace to walk by him for a while. "It breaks my heart to see family heirlooms tossed about and left to ruin. Every item represented a part of someone's life."

"I'd rather see stuff scattered everywhere," said Jace, "than all these dead carcasses. I've never seen so many rotten oxen, mule, or cattle."

Rebecca tried to avert her eyes and concentrate on keeping pace with Jace.

That evening after supper, Captain Brenner called a meeting to discuss what he knew was on everyone's mind. He had heard their comments and seen their faces when they passed all the discarded items along the trail. Everyone gathered at his wagon.

He scanned across the crowd. "We've had two days of hard travel. This part of the trail, as we get closer to the Rockies, will present us with a new obstacle." He pointed in the direction of the Rocky Mountains. "Until we get to the Continental Divide, the trail will be a constant ascent. And we have several swift flowing creeks to cross. Your animals can only pull so much weight."

Daisy Jenkins raised her hand. "What if we need everything we've brought?"

He glanced at Luke then back at Daisy. "You need to think about what you can unload from your wagons that would spare your oxen the strain of pulling it up that mountain." He let that soak in for a minute. "Pete will sound the bugle at the same time in the morning, but we'll leave an hour later than usual. This will give you time to discard any items you can live without. Remember, if you lose an animal for the sake of a family heirloom, that piece of furniture won't get you over those mountains."

"How far are we from decent water?" asked Hugh Unger.

"Only three days," said the captain. "And, by the way folks, Sweetwater River got its name honestly. There's no alkali in it."

Hannah pulled on her mother's skirt. "Mamma, I don't have to throw Betsy off our wagon, do I?"

"No, honey, Betsy's safe."

Rebecca knew if Hannah was forced to leave Betsy on the trail, they would be in big trouble.

CHAPTER TWENTY-TWO

Perched in their wagon after supper, Rebecca said to Jace, "Okay, you and I can go through our things and get rid of anything we don't need. And I'd rather do it tonight." She waved her hand. "Ben, Hannah, you need to jump out of the wagon so Jace and I can work. Hannah, see if you can beat Ben at checkers."

Jace dug through their wagon for a few minutes. "We brought a bunch of stuff we really didn't need, didn't we?"

"Yeah, and those are the easy things to get rid of." She opened the cedar trunk to unpack it.

Sitting on the other side of the trunk, Jace frowned. "What are you doing? You can't throw this trunk out." He closed the lid. "Pa made this for you. It's a part of him we still have."

She ran her hand over the smooth wood. "Jace, sweetheart, you know how I love this trunk, but even without it we still have Hank with us. Every time you hold his watch in your hand you're holding memories of him. I can see his face right now, and you and I both know he'd be the first to say this trunk has to go."

Jace's shoulders slumped. "I guess, but it seems a shame."

She stretched her arms across the trunk. "One thing I've learned walking across this country is you have to put everything in perspective. The people we've gotten to know and you and the children are more important to me than any piece of furniture or family treasure." She squeezed his arm. "We forget that worldly possessions are just that. God provides us with what we need." She paused. "I'd give every material possession I own to have your pa back again."

Rebecca and Jace stopped and stared at each other when Daisy Jenkins, two wagons away, wailed. "No! No! That was my mother's bureau. It came from Europe. You can't throw it out."

In a minute another loud wail rang out. "Joseph, no. That's my grandmother's hand-rubbed mahogany table."

Rebecca raised an eyebrow. "I'm afraid we may hear a lot of crying for the next few days."

Two days of dodging prairie bramble, crossing chalky-watered creeks, and tears shed from leaving heirlooms abandoned by the side of the trail, caused tempers to flare. The constant uphill slope drained Rebecca's energy, along with the team of oxen.

The cursing and loud sounds of whips popping during the afternoon soon became too abrasive for the women. Rebecca and her children, along with Millie, Molly, Sarah, and Penelope walked a good piece to the north of the wagon train to save their ears from being scorched.

Molly laughed. "I'm not a swearing woman, but if I thought it would have gotten us to Oregon faster, I would've let the words fly the minute we left Independence, Missouri." She slid her bonnet to the back of her neck. "I've watched those poor animals all day long, and not one curse word has hurried their gait any faster."

Penelope walked around a large clump of sagebrush. "Do you reckon the oxen know what those words mean because I sure don't recognize some of them?"

Mary Martha was wrapped in a small blanket bound with leather straps around Penelope's shoulders. The baby's sweet-natured babble soothed Rebecca's ears. Such a welcomed relieve to hear the cooing of Mary Martha after all the wailing and crying over leaving their possessions on the trail, plus the men's course language.

"We've all been stretched to the limit," said Rebecca. "We're anxious about Lorna. Her mind's still confused. We're running out of fresh water. The nights are getting colder while the sun beats down on us during the day. And with every mile, the trail gets harder."

Rebecca noticed Sarah gazing at the mountains in front of them.

"Ladies," said Sarah, "have any of you thought about how far we've come and realized what we've accomplished?" She used a piece of a broken hoe handle for a cane to steady herself. "I never thought I would be able to keep a family fed in the conditions we've endured. We've lived through frightening weather, swarms of insects, river crossings, and drought. And I sure never imagined going weeks at a time without a bath. But look at us now. If you ponder on it very long, you have to believe this is where God planted us for a season."

Rebecca smiled at Sarah then a roar of hooves and a cloud of dust overtook them. Several cowhands galloped by headed toward the herd of animals at the back of the trail.

Millie coughed and waved her hand in the air. "My goodness, didn't those cowboys see us walking out here? You'd think they would've been taught some measure of manners." The women dusted themselves off.

"I don't think manners," said Rebecca, "were what Captain Brenner was looking for when he hired them."

Mary Martha let out a cry. Penelope hurried her steps. "I think somebody's hungry. We ought to be hearing the bugle any minute." She pulled her shawl tighter around her baby. "It's beginning to get cool."

Pete sounded the signal to stop for the night.

Rebecca said, "I never knew a sound could be so glorious. It's come to mean rest, food, and fellowship for those of us who have an ounce of energy left."

"Carl thinks we'll get to the Sweetwater River tomorrow," said Sarah.

"Well, it won't be too soon for me," said Penelope. "I would trade my mother's fifteen-piece silver tea set for a fresh drink of cold water." Then she laughed. "Oh yeah, I forgot. It's laying on the trail two days ride behind us."

Rebecca laughed, along with the other women, at Penelope's comment. "If there was any trading to be done, we'd all be in trouble. We're down to the bare necessities as it is," said Rebecca.

Carl was right. The wagon train reached Sweetwater River late the next day. The river flowed through a lush, green valley alongside a huge rock formation called Independence Rock.

She waited for Jace to lead their team back to the wagons from the river after their animals drank until their bellies hung low. Sweetwater River was exactly that…sweet.

After supper, Rebecca and Jace sat around the campfire while Ben and Hannah played checkers by lamplight at the table.

Rebecca gazed at the valley. "This area is a lot like Ash Hollow." She took in a deep breath and exhaled. "Have you ever smelled anything more glorious? And just look at that huge rock formation." She pulled her shawl tighter. "After so many days of bramble bush and dirt, this is heaven."

Jace sat on the ground and leaned back on one elbow. "This valley has everything a person would need to make a home. Water, grass, and plenty of timber."

"Are you saying you'd like to settle here?"

"No. Pa always said Oregon has this and more."

Luke's horse whinnied when he rode up. "Evening. Hope I'm not intruding too late."

Rebecca sat up straight. Her heart seemed to flutter more each time Luke came near her. "Not at all. We were just admiring the valley."

"Captain Brenner wanted everyone to know we're having a Fourth of July celebration tomorrow night. He's having some of the hands butcher a steer for the meal."

Jace gave a quizzical look. "July fourth has passed."

"I know, but sometime in July is usually when most wagon trains reach this valley. That's where Independence Rock got its name. It's another landmark on the Oregon trail."

"How long do you think we'll be here?" Rebecca asked.

"We'll pull out day after tomorrow. The nights are getting colder so we may be racing against time to beat the winter weather. Even though it's July, our nights are beginning to feel more like October."

Luke reined his horse around. Before he left, Rebecca stood and walked over to him. She placed her hand on the stirrup leather. "Have you or Captain Brenner seen any sign of those outlaws who were following us earlier?"

"No. And I don't want to frighten you, but until they're apprehended, we can't let down our guard." He leaned forward and put his hand on hers. "Just be careful of incoming riders."

The next evening, Rebecca and the children gathered with the crowd near Independence Rock and celebrated. Beef roasting over a pit whet her appetite. She placed a pan of cornbread and three jars of sweet pickles on the table beside the savory sage hen and rabbit pies swimming in rich gravy. There were current breads, dried apple pies, and pound cakes to feast on.

Soon after everyone ate and right before sunset, Rebecca strolled over to Independence Rock to read the names etched all along the edge. "Ben, Hannah. Come look at this. It reads Jeremiah Lincoln 1841."

Zeb walked up beside her. "This is a monument to those who came before us. It's a historical account that will be here forever."

"And we get to be a part of that history," said Rebecca.

Before he could respond, Jim and Bart played an introduction and their music floated across the valley. Zeb smiled. "Time to grab my Clara and take her for a whirl."

Rebecca joined the ladies who were sitting close enough to watch the couples dance the grass down to the dirt. She sat patting a foot to the rhythm when Luke approached her.

"Would you like to dance?"

She smiled up at him and stood. "I would love to." Taking his hand, Rebecca followed him to the patch of beaten down grass. He held her in his arms and pulled her close.

"Captain Brenner thinks we'll be over the Continental Divide and at South Pass in about two weeks."

Rebecca sighed. "I wish we could just settle by this river. There's timber and grass for cattle, and we could lay down some roots. I long for a home again."

He gazed into her eyes. "You'll have a home as soon as we reach Willamette Valley. Jace told me all about his plans to make a homestead just like his pa described to him. He paused. "Rebecca, there's something I…"

A shout rang out. "Emigrants. Will you allow this mountain man to come into your camp?"

From across the way, a man rode toward their camp. Captain Brenner, Luke, and Pete walked out to meet him before he could get too close to their group. "Who are you and where do you come from?" inquired the captain.

"I'm called Trapper Dan. I live along the Missouri River."

Captain Brenner waved him in. Between his fur-covered head and his gray-speckled beard, peered steel gray eyes and a half-hidden smile. He carried a load of pelts, a few beavers, but mostly wolf and badger tied on the back of his horse. He smelled of bear grease and pine needles.

"I was under the notion that beaver trapping was pretty well wiped out a few years ago on the mountain," said Pete.

"You're right, mister. There's still a few, but not many. Now I get what I can, and I lead expeditions through the mountains."

"Where you headed with these pelts?" said the captain.

He lumbered off his horse. "I'm planning to take the shortcut through Sublette's Cutoff to Soda Springs, then on to Fort Hall."

The captain gestured toward the campfire. "Come sit, and Pete will get you some supper."

"Thank you, pilgrim. I could use a good meal about now."

The crowd gathered around the stranger.

"How long you been trapping?" asked Captain Brenner

"Most of my life. I have a cabin about three weeks ride up in the northern Rockies."

"So you're taking the shortcut rather than going down through Fort Bridger?"

"Yeah, going through Sublette's Cutoff shortens the trail by about eighty-five miles."

"But the trail's not that clear, and the water is all alkali. Since I've been leading wagon trains this way, we've always gone down to Fort Bridger."

"Young man, I've been making that trail for thirty years. I know every inch of it."

The captain leaned toward Trapper Dan. "We'd be obliged if you'd ride along with our wagon train to Fort Hall. We could use your knowledge going through Sublette's Cutoff."

He grinned through his wild whiskers. "Well, I'd be pleased to enjoy your company."

Rebecca turned from the group when Hannah ran to her crying. "Betsy's gone. I can't find her."

"Sweetheart, she's around here somewhere. We just need to look." She turned to Trapper Dan. "I'm sorry. I need to help Hannah."

He laughed. "You go right ahead, young lady. You need to help the little missy find her friend, Betsy."

Luke caught Rebecca before she left. "Can I come by your wagon later?"

She smiled. "I'll have some coffee for you." Then turned and took Hannah's hand. "Now where did you see Betsy last?"

Thirty minutes later, Rebecca found Betsy near Independence Rock where the children had been playing. She took Ben and Hannah back to their wagon where they each crawled into bed without any arguments. Starting a fire, Rebecca made some coffee.

Jace walked from the back of the wagon with Rowdy. "I've got night guard for the next three hours."

Rebecca smiled at Jace. "Did you have a good time with Ellen?"

"Yes." He grinned at his mother.

She hugged him. "Please be careful."

"Don't worry. I always am. You'll be asleep by the time I get in. I'll see you in the morning."

He rode off and Rebecca sat in a chair by the wagon. She removed her hair combs and let her hair cascade down her back. She pulled her shawl tighter around her shoulders. Leaning her head back, Rebecca closed her eyes and breathed in the night air. The sound of the Sweetwater River lolled her to sleep.

"Rebecca?"

Startled, she opened her eyes and straightened her shoulders.

"Luke, I didn't hear you ride up." She gestured toward the bench near the fire. "Sit down and I'll get you some coffee."

She poured them both a cup. He pulled a chair for her to sit near the fire and he sat on the bench. Luke took a sip before he said, "I don't know if everyone realizes what a gift we received. If Trapper Dan can lead us through the cutoff, it'll shorten the trail by seven days."

"So, the captain thinks that's the best route?"

"Yes. The weather's going to be a huge concern when we get closer to the Rockies, so gaining a week of travel can help." He put his hands near the fire and warmed them. "The sooner we get over the Continental Divide, the closer we are to Oregon."

She raised an eyebrow and sighed. "Oregon seems so far away. It's all been much more difficult than I thought it would be."

"When we get over the divide and a few miles on the other side of South Pass we'll be close to the Oregon Territory."

She gazed at the star-filled sky. "Just think, in a month or so we'll have walked across a big portion of this continent." Rebecca turned to Luke. "I would never want Jace to hear me say this, but sometimes I wish Hank had never heard of Oregon."

"Once we get to Oregon, you'll feel different." He moved closer to her. "Rebecca, it takes a strong-willed person to endure this trail." He paused. "I'm glad your husband wanted to settle in Oregon. If not, I wouldn't have ever known you."

Rebecca's heart trembled. Her cheeks warmed.

Luke placed his hand under her chin and raised it. He caressed her lush, brown hair then took her hand. "I know you haven't known me long, and your life took a strange turn when your husband died. But, Rebecca, I've never known anyone like you. I…"

She pulled her hands from his. "Don't, Luke." She stood and stepped away. "I'm confused. I'm not sure how to deal with any of this." Rebecca pressed a hand to her stomach. "I have another child to think about now."

Luke stood and moved closer. "I'm not here to make things worse for you. I want to help you, and Jace, and the children any way I can. Please don't push me away."

She shifted her weight and turned her back to him afraid of what she might say.

Luke put his hands on her shoulders. He turned her around and peered into her eyes. "You're tired and this trail's been a long, hard journey. But trust me, everything's going to work out all right." He pulled her close and gently held her.

Rebecca leaned into his strong arms. When she looked up at him, he pulled her to his lips this time. She clung to him accepting his warm embrace.

CHAPTER TWENTY-THREE

After the camp settled in for the night, Captain Brenner and Trapper Dan sat on benches and talked over coffee at the chuck wagon. Pete readied the wagon for the next day's travel.

The captain called out. "Pete, got any of that coffee left?"

"There's plenty." Pete poured them both a cup.

Captain Brenner took a sip and asked Trapper Dan, "Have the snows started up in the higher levels yet?"

The mountain man placed his leg across his knee. "My prediction is we're in for a hard winter. The peaks are covered with new snow already." He eyed the captain. "You might know this but coming down into the meadow before I met up with your wagon train, I noticed a gang of men tracking you from a distance. From my vantage point, I spotted you several days ago, along with them."

"Captain," Pete said, "you don't think it's that no-good gang of horse thieves, do you?"

"We haven't been able to see their dust with the wooded terrain." The captain's expression darkened. "Pete, tell Nate to keep his rifle handy, and you do the same."

After Trapper Dan bedded down, Pete asked the captain. "You think we can trust him? He could be a part of that gang. The route through Sublette's Cutoff could be a way for them to bushwhack us."

A crease formed on Captain Brenner's brow. "I'll double up on night guard again and tell Tom and the hands to keep a sharp eye out for anything unusual."

Another week on the trail and Rebecca sensed how the weather played an integral part of their journey. The deeper the Sweetwater River led the wagon train into the mountains, the more spectacular the scenery. But the wind grew colder and the nights became frigid.

After supper, Rebecca, Jace, and the children sat by the campfire. She pulled her jacket collar up and walked to the wagon. Reaching in, she said, "Jace, here's your Pa's wool coat." She threw it to him. "You're going to need it for night watch." Rebecca shivered. "I can tell we're getting closer to the Continental Divide."

"This altitude makes it harder for me to breathe," said Jace. "And the oxen can only pull our wagon about ten miles a day at best."

Jace put on the coat and swung onto Rowdy. "Keep the pistol close, Mamma." Then he headed toward the herd.

As Jace rode off, Millie rushed to Rebecca's wagon out of breath. Her face was pale. Reaching her, she asked, "Have you talked to Carl today?"

"I just waved to him early this morning when we pulled out on the trail. Why?"

"Penelope and I both noticed how frail Sarah's become lately. This cold weather isn't doing her any good. We think there's something wrong."

"Well, it's been so cold at night and then hot during the day it has us all on the verge of sickness."

Millie motioned toward the Webster's wagon. "Did you see Sarah walking beside their wagon today?"

"No." Rebecca's eyebrows furrowed. "I noticed she rode in the wagon."

"I don't want Carl to think we're busybodies," Millie frowned, "but I'm worried about Sarah."

Rebecca grabbed Millie by the arm and pulled her across the way. Carl and the boys were eating their supper beside their wagon when the women approached.

Carl appeared startled. "Rebecca, Millie, is everything okay? You look worried."

"We are worried," said Millie.

Rebecca frowned. "We're concerned about Sarah. We noticed she didn't leave the wagon today. Is she all right?"

He glanced at his boys then at Rebecca. "Dr. Brummel was here before daylight. She has the same symptoms she had earlier. He knows she's not contagious, but he said to keep her as warm and quiet as possible."

"Does he know what caused Sarah to become ill again?" said Millie.

"No, but he's hoping she'll get better if she rests."

"Can we see her?" Rebecca stepped closer to the campfire.

Carl led them to the rear of the wagon and pulled the canvas back. "Sarah, honey, Rebecca and Millie are here to see you. Are you feeling well enough?"

"Yes, their visit is just what I need." Her voice sounded weak.

Rebecca grabbed Millie's arm when she saw Sarah.

Leaning inside the wagon, Rebecca put her hand on Sarah's forehead. "You feel hot and there's no color in your face. We're worried about you."

Sarah said in a stern voice, "Now, both of you get those anxious looks off your faces. Dr. Brummel just wants me to rest. He gave me some kind of concoction he swears will cure what ails me. I'm fine, really. I'll be all right after a night's rest."

Rebecca took her hand. "I'm going to hold you to that."

"Please let us know if we can do anything for you," said Millie.

"I will. By tomorrow I'll be much better." She teased. "In no time we'll be telling stories and laughing."

Millie caught Rebecca's arm when they left the Webster's wagon. "She's not well. She doesn't even look like the Sarah I met a few months ago."

"I know. This weather isn't doing her any good either."

Rebecca shook her head. "Carl and the boys have been through so much. Seeing Sarah, I can only imagine what's going through their minds."

Three days from Independence Rock, Rebecca and Jace worked their wagon across Sweetwater River for the fourth time. The river meandered in a zigzag formation all along the trail.

Bringing the wagon up out of the water on dry ground, Rebecca laughed. "Every time I do this I get a little better at it."

Lucy snorted when she followed the wagon to the river bank.

"Pa would be proud of you," said Jace.

When the wagon reached dry ground, Rebecca halted the team. Jace took Rowdy and tied him to the wagon while Rebecca climbed down from the seat and took her staff in hand.

She caught sight of Sarah not far ahead of their wagon and waved. "You look better this afternoon."

Sarah waved. "I'm losing count on how many times we've crossed this river." She smiled back at Rebecca. "I'm feeling much better."

From the Calhoun's wagon, Ben and Hannah ran to Rebecca holding pieces of ice.

She questioned. "Where did you get that?"

"Grandpa and I found it. It's just up the trail," said Ben.

Hannah grabbed for the ice. "I found it too."

"How about giving me a piece," said Jace.

Luke rode up. "Did Ben and Hannah show you what they found?"

"Yes," said Rebecca. "Where did the ice come from in the middle of the summer?"

"A place called Ice Slough. You can find ice forming about a foot underneath the top of the soil."

"But wouldn't it melt during the heat of the day?"

"We've reached the Continental Divide. The altitude is so high it can't melt." Luke pointed west. "South Pass is about three days up the trail. Then four more miles is Pacific Springs. It won't be too many days until we'll ride into what's considered the Oregon Territory."

Rebecca caught her breath. "You mean we're that close?"

"We're still a good ways from Willamette Valley, but Fort Hall will put us at the eastern border of the Oregon territory."

Rebecca smiled. "Ben, take that bucket and gather some of the ice. I'll wash it and put it in our water barrel."

She smiled down at Hannah. "Isn't it amazing how God sprinkles surprises all along the trail? From gigantic mounds of rock and ash to beautiful green meadows, and now ice to cool our throats."

Hannah giggled. "Like finding a buried treasure."

Rebecca sighed. "So is getting to Oregon. Your pa's dream is becoming a reality."

Rebecca continued to keep track of the number of days she and her family had lived in a covered wagon. Though it seemed a lifetime, the journey from Cutter Springs, over the Continental Divide, and then to South Pass added up to three months and twenty days. Their next stop was Pacific Springs where Sublette's Cutoff laid.

Reaching the cutoff, Rebecca dreaded having to ration water again because of the alkali in the streams.

Well before sunrise, Jace had the wagon ready. He walked over to his mother. "I've filled every container we have with fresh water. We'll need to remind Ben and Hannah not to waste any."

Rebecca narrowed her eyes. "Is Captain Brenner sure we should take Sublette's Cutoff? Sarah said Carl seems to think it would be worth traveling 130 miles by way of Fort Bridger to get to Fort Hall."

Jace gripped the side railing of the wagon. "I trust Mr. Barker and the captain. Trapper Dan said he knows the trail. He said it's fifty miles of dry, grassless prairie, but we have just enough water and grain for the animals if we're careful. And it can save us a good week's travel. He assured the captain that Green River is at the far west side and has good water."

She exhaled. "All right then. We'll have to trust Captain Brenner and Luke…and Trapper Dan."

The signal sounded. The wagon train pulled out on the trail toward Sublette's Cutoff. Clouds covered the sky most of the morning which delayed the sun from taking the chill out of the air.

Ben and Hannah walked beside Rebecca while Jace worked the team. "The dust is bad today." She reached into her pocket and grabbed two bandanas. "Let me tie these on your faces to keep the cold air and dust from getting in your lungs.

Rebecca turned from Hannah and saw Ben pull his down. "Ben. Get the bandana over your face and now."

"Oh, Mamma."

Before Rebecca could scold him, Clara rushed toward them waving her arms as though something was wrong. Out of breath, she told Rebecca that Sarah was calling for her.

Rebecca turned to the children. "You both stay with Jace. I'll be right back."

She and Clara hurried to the Webster's wagon. Carl had pulled their wagon to the side of the trail. He and his boys stood at the back of the wagon.

Rebecca rushed to them. "Clara said Sarah is ill again."

Carl's eyes narrowed and his brow lowered. "Doc Brummel is tending to her. She collapsed a few minutes ago. But she insists on seeing you."

"Carl, how serious is she?"

Before he could answer, the doctor stepped from the wagon. "Rebecca, she's asking for you. Try not to tire her out. She needs to rest."

"I'll only stay a minute."

She climbed into the wagon past Toby and Josh and took Sarah's hand. "Sarah, I'm here."

Sarah opened her eyes and pulled Rebecca closer. She whispered. "Rebecca, pray for Carl and the boys."

Rebecca swallowed hard. "Don't talk like that."

Sarah stared at Rebecca. "I can't do this anymore."

"You just need some rest, that's all." Rebecca pressed a hand on Sarah's face. "You'll be fine in no time." Her hand trembled. Sarah's breathing was shallow and rapid. "Do you hear me?"

Sarah lifted a hand, but it fell to her side. "I hear you, but you don't understand. Dr. Brummel doesn't give me any hope."

A sob caught in Rebecca's throat. She leaned down. "No, Sarah, please don't."

"Listen to me, Rebecca. My body's wasting away, but my spirit's strong. You can't see it, but on the inside, I'm ready to enter the gates of heaven."

Rebecca's chest tightened. She squeezed Sarah's hand.

Sarah's brow furrowed. "Don't cry for me, cry for Carl and the boys."

"And me. Sarah, you're my strength."

"No, honey, Jesus is your strength. He's walked every mile of this journey with you. He promised us in His Word He would never leave us."

Rebecca's body rocked with grief.

Sarah's voice weakened. "Are Carl and the boys here?"

Carl took her hand. "Yes, sweetheart, we're right here." Josh and Toby gathered in close and put a hand on their mother.

"Carl, Josh, Toby, I love you." Sarah gazed past them. "Emily's waiting for me."

Carl's voice broke. "Sarah, honey, no."

CHAPTER TWENTY-FOUR

Sarah's funeral service was a blur. Rebecca lay awake through the night thinking about her. How she had welcomed Rebecca and her family the first day on the trail. She knew her soul was in heaven but leaving Sarah behind broke her heart.

Captain Brenner ordered the wagons to move out the next morning for Sublette's Cutoff. After getting on the trail, Rebecca walked beside the team with Jace next to her.

He put his arm around his mother. "I'm sorry. I know how you loved Mrs. Webster."

Ben and Hannah held her hands. Hannah said, "Is Emily's mamma with her now?"

"Yes, she is."

Hannah sighed. "I still miss Emily. She was my best friend." She looked up at Rebecca. "I guess Mrs. Webster was your best friend, right Mamma?"

Rebecca peered down at Hannah and nodded. "But they're both in a place they can rest now. There's no dirt, or heat, or sickness where they are."

Rebecca, Jace, Ben, and Hannah walked the next mile in silence.

To add to Rebecca's despair, Trapper Dan was right about Sublette's Cutoff. Though it shortened the journey, a desolate tableland stretched as far as the eye could see and bleached bones and bloated carcasses of abandoned oxen, mule, and cattle littered the trail.

Rebecca trudged beside the wagon. Ben and Hannah kept close to their mother. Jace worked the wagon over the dry ravines and gulches.

Two days on the cutoff, Luke rode up midway through the morning. "How much water do you have?"

She pulled her bonnet down to block the sun. "Not much. Maybe a day's worth."

"Green River is about three miles on west. We'll reach it before sundown."

Luke spurred his horse and rode up beside Jace. "When we get to Green River move your wagon alongside Carl's and unyoke your team. Let them run free to drink all they can."

He doubled back to Rebecca. "We'll have fresh water soon."

"How long will we stay at Green River? Our supplies are near to nothing?"

"The captain said we'll camp there tonight and pull out again in the morning. We can rest and fill our barrels and our animals with water. We need to make Fort Hall as soon as we can. Everybody's tired and still grieving Sarah's death. Tempers and emotions are raw right now." Luke rubbed his face. "I haven't noticed a cloud of dust following us the last few days. But Trapper Dan says those outlaws are still out there. You and Jace keep your guns loaded."

Rebecca was relieved Trapper Dan knew the trail through Sublette's Cutoff and was accurate about Green River. Melted snow running from the high peaks of the Rocky Mountains supplied the river.

Except for the scattered carcasses, Green River was tranquil after a long, scorching day. A gentle breeze drifted down from the mountains and the sound of the flowing river soothed Rebecca's mind.

She stood over the campfire that evening stirring a simmering kettle of savory rabbit stew while Ben and Hannah played marbles by the wagon.

Jace came from the river with two jugs of cold water just before Luke rode up.

Rebecca turned to Luke and smiled. "I hope you're hungry."

He got off his horse and tied the reins to the wagon. "Smells great. I've never turned down a good meal."

Hannah jumped up and ran to Luke. She took his hand. "You can sit on the bench here by me."

He took his hat off. "I'd be proud to."

Ben scooted on the other side of Luke and stuck his tongue out at Hannah.

"Don't be acting that way toward your sister," scolded Rebecca.

Jace pulled a chair up to the table by Ben. He nudged his little brother with his elbow. "I think it's your turn to bless the meal tonight."

Ben frowned and bowed his head. "Dear Lord, thank you for letting me find the bullfrog at the river today. I'm sorry I stepped on him and killed him. I didn't mean to. I'm just hoping he's in heaven with you. Amen."

Rebecca chided. "What about our meal?"

He bowed his head again. "And thank you for the rabbit Jace killed so we could have supper. Amen."

Rebecca shook her head.

As they ate, the subject turned to the families leaving the wagon train for California. Rafter River was their jump off and it lay a few days or so on the trail after leaving Fort Hall.

Jace stirred his plate of stew to cool it. "Is the trail any better going to California?"

"No, not really," said Luke. "Their biggest obstacle is getting through to the Sierra Nevada and across the mountains before the winter snowfalls."

Rebecca ate a spoonful of stew. "And what about our trail from Fort Hall to Fort Boise?"

"It's about two hundred and thirty miles. But there isn't much there now. Floods destroyed Fort Boise a couple of years ago. We still use it for a campsite, though."

Rebecca's brow crinkled. "What about supplies?"

"We'll have to double up on supplies at Fort Hall. There's not anything between there and the town of Dalles except for a few Shoshone trading posts who like to trade fresh fish from the Snake River for trinkets."

"Mamma," Jace said, "don't worry. We'll be all right."

"We still have thirty or so head of cattle. If we can keep them from wandering off or being killed by wolves we'll be fine."

Rebecca frowned. "There are more wolves around here than any place we've been before. I hear them at night howling. They sound so close."

"Wolves usually keep their distance unless the area's low on varmints. That's when our stock is vulnerable."

Jace finished his supper. Rebecca noticed him fidget. She grinned at him. "Ellen's probably waiting on you. You better hurry on. And don't forget your coat."

He jumped up. "I won't be gone long."

Hannah and Ben pulled out the checkerboard while Rebecca and Luke enjoyed coffee around the campfire.

She blew on the hot coffee. Taking a sip, she said. "If I understand, we'll go through Soda Springs before we reach Fort Hall."

"Yeah, it's about seventy miles from where Sublette's Cutoff merges onto the trail again. We'll be traveling alongside the river once more. We should reach it in a few days or so." He rubbed his knees. "Captain Brenner wants to stay ahead of any early snows. Willamette Valley is at least another hundred days on the trail."

Rebecca stared at her cup. "A hundred days. That seems a lifetime."

Rebecca woke to a dreary, rained-soaked trail. She buttoned her jacket and wrapped a scarf around her neck. "Ben, Hannah, you stay in the wagon so you won't get soaked." She climbed from the tailgate.

Though the rain continued to fall, the wagon train started the slow move westward while their wheels bogged in the mud. Jace held to the side of the wagon to keep from sliding under the wheels. With his other hand, he slapped the staff across the back of the oxen and yelled, "Giddup, there!"

The morning sun continued to hide behind thick, white clouds. Rebecca walked up behind Jace and touched his shoulder. "The only thing that makes the rain and mud-soaked trail tolerable is the gentle descent since we crossed the Continental Divide."

He pulled his hat lower and hollered over his shoulder. "Not far ahead is another mountain."

"Has Captain Brenner said how many more mountains we have to cross?"

"No, but I'm hoping not many more. We're going to need a new team of oxen when we get to Fort Hall."

Rebecca slipped then caught herself and mumbled. "Please, Lord, let there be a green valley on the other side of one of these mountains, and make it soon." Her thoughts diverted to the noise of several men loudly cursing their teams to plod a little faster.

Jace peered over his shoulder at his mother and grinned. "Don't worry, Mamma. I'll pick kinder words to talk to our team."

Because of the rain, what should have taken four days to reach Soda Springs took six. Captain Brenner and several of the cowhands struggled to pull wagons and teams out of the thick mud.

Arriving at Soda Springs, Captain Brenner noticed a company of horseman off in the distance. He and Tom rode out from the caravan in their direction. Upon meeting up, the lead horseman introduced himself as Corporal Baines. "We're from Fort Hall. We're tracking a band of rogue Sioux Indians who've been raiding settlements in this area."

Captain Brenner said. "A mountain trapper joined our wagon train on the other side of Sublette's Cutoff and said he'd noticed a gang trailing us. He didn't say anything about them being Sioux. But we haven't seen anything of them in the last week or so."

"We've got another company of men about thirty miles up on that north ridge," said Corporal Baines. "But for now, you might want to keep an eye out."

Captain Brenner nodded. "Thanks. We're on our way to Fort Hall. Good luck on your search."

Riding back to the wagons, the captain ordered Tom to make sure the cowhands were aware of what was going on.

Luke rode out and met the captain and Tom. "Doc Brummel said we've got two cases of measles, Phoebe and Mary, Bob Allen's girls."

"Tell them to pull their wagon out of the caravan," said the captain. "And let me know if there any more cases. And, Luke, you'll need to help Bob guard his wagon. We may have some renegade Sioux out there somewhere. They may be who's been trailing us all along."

"Is that what those soldiers said?"

The captain rubbed his shoulder. "Yeah, just something else for us to worry about."

Soda Springs was like no other place the travelers had been. The naturally carbonated water bubbled up from the ground.

At noon, Rebecca and Hannah hurried to Clara's wagon carrying two loaves of baked bread in a basket.

"Have you ever seen a bigger loaf of bread?" said Rebecca. "I used some of that water from the springs and look at it. It's double what it normally is."

Clara bent and hugged Hannah. "I guess the water's got something in it that resembles soda."

"You suppose that's why it's called Soda Springs?" said Rebecca.

"I reckon so. But you better enjoy the bread while you can. Zeb said we're pulling out first thing in the morning."

Rebecca handed the bread to Clara. "These are for you and Zeb, but I need time to bake another loaf before we leave this place."

"Then you better make haste. Zeb said the captain's in a hurry to get to Fort Hall. Supposedly it's got to do with the weather, but after all these years, I can read Zeb and there's more to it than he's telling me."

CHAPTER TWENTY-FIVE

Captain Brenner hoped Fort Hall would be in their sights within two more days. The sun set behind the mountain and the cold air settled on the wagon train. The captain and Luke stood by the chuck wagon as close to the fire as was safe. Luke warmed his hands around a hot cup of coffee.

"What do we do about the Unger's team?" Luke said. "He lost one ox before we got to Soda Springs and another one could go down anytime."

"Maybe the other two he's got can pull the load until we get to Fort Hall. If not, he may need to lighten his load some more." The captain knelt by the fire and warmed his hands. "I know Molly's not going to be happy, but we don't have any extra stock."

"And what about the Allen girls? Has the doc said how they're doing?"

"Hopefully, by the time we reach Fort Hall, we can pull them back with the other wagons."

Luke poured himself another cup of coffee. "Carl and his boys—"

From somewhere in the dark, the sound of gunshots rang out. Luke's horse jumped and pulled at his reins tied to the wagon wheel. "Whoa, boy."

The captain looked over his shoulder. "Those shots came from the back of the trail near the herd." He listened. "Do you hear that?" He scrambled to his feet. "Stampede!"

A full moon gave light to the impending danger headed toward the wagons. Jim Brewer hollered. "Get the baby." The ground rumbled underneath his feet. "It's cattle. They're headed right for us." He pulled Penelope and Mary Martha behind a mound of rocks.

Captain Brenner rode by them yelling at the cowhands. "Turn them to the north."

Dust rolled over the wagon train like a giant wave.

Crouching down, Jim hollered at Penelope. "Get behind me and stay down."

Penelope tried to soothe Mary Martha's crying.

Jim squinted from the dust caused by the cattle. Seeing someone through the cloud of dirt, Jim said, "That's Lorna Gaines."

Penelope grabbed Jim's arm. "What's she doing?"

"Lorna!" He jumped up. "She's going to be trampled." He ran toward her as she walked into the stream of stampeding cattle.

Penelope screamed. "No, Jim!"

"I have to get her." He hollered over his shoulder. "She doesn't know what she's doing?"

Lorna stood in the path of the oncoming cattle then fell underneath their pounding hooves.

Running, Jim yelled. "Lorna! No Lorna!" He hollered and waved his hands in the air. Dodging the steers, he grabbed her arm. Jim dragged her back to the mound of rocks.

Holding the baby in one arm, Penelope placed Lorna's head on the folds of her skirt. "Lorna, it's Penelope."

Jim hovered over her. "Lorna, can you hear me?" He felt her pulse then turned to Penelope. "She's dead."

Hal ran to Jim and Penelope. He fell on his knees and pulled his wife to him. "Lorna, honey." He cradled her in his arms then raised his eyes to Jim. "Why would she do this?"

Penelope held Mary Martha close to her. "Hal, she didn't do it on purpose. She hasn't been the same since Jamie died."

Hal sobbed and rocked her back and forth.

Jim put his hand on Hal's shoulder knowing there were no words to ease Hal's pain.

❧

The dust settled and by lamplight everyone gathered the items strewn during the stampede. Rebecca stood by their wagon and held her children thanking God they weren't in the direct path of the cattle.

Hannah buried her face in her mother's lap. "Mamma," she cried, "that was scary."

"I know, honey, but it's over now."

Ben held on to Rebecca. "The cattle won't do that again, will they?"

"I'm sure not. I think they were just scared by something."

She glanced over and saw Luke. Waving, she yelled. "Have you seen Jace?"

He rode over and reined in his horse. "No." He wiped the dust from his face.

"Do you know how the stampede started?"

"I just heard gunshots. Jace is supposed to be with the herd, so when we get the cattle settled down, I'm sure he'll know something. Though it may be morning before he gets back to the wagon."

Rebecca narrowed her eyes. "Who would purposely stampede the cattle through the wagon train? Unless—"

"Unless what?"

"When the prisoner was detained in the supply wagon before we reached Fort Laramie, we could see the dust from the outlaw's gang not far from the trail. I remember how that horrible man kept yelling about two men from his gang believing someone on this wagon train killed their brother, yet nothing came of it. That gang was trailing us one day, and the next day was gone."

Luke cocked his head and frowned. "So you think the stampede was started by that gang?"

She furrowed her brow. "We didn't see anything of them after the troops took the prisoner on to Fort Laramie. But Trapper Dan said he saw something. Then the stampede. Don't you think it's strange?"

He adjusted his hat. "Until we find out exactly what happened, you and the children need to be careful. Stay close to the Webster's wagon, and don't let Ben or Hannah out of your sight."

Rebecca gasped. "Jace." She stepped toward Luke and grabbed his saddle leather. "Please go find him and bring him to me."

"I'll go right now. But try not to worry. He's probably gathering strays."

"Just find him. I need to know he's okay."

The next morning, the sun was just over the horizon when Luke and Captain Brenner rode in the direction of Rebecca's wagon. She was eager to talk to them after a restless night. Rebecca met them before they got to her. "Where's Jace?" Her legs shook. "He didn't come back last night, and I see he's not with you."

Zeb and Clara walked from behind the wagon. Rebecca turned and stared at them.

She took a step backward. "It's Jace, isn't it?"

Luke and the captain dismounted. Captain Brenner removed his hat. "Mrs. Quaid...Rebecca."

"Where's Jace?" She wrung her hands but tried to stay calm.

Ben and Hannah jumped from their tailgate. Clara quickly gathered them and walked them out of earshot.

Rebecca's body trembled. Luke took Rebecca's arm and led her to the bench. She sat and stared up at the captain. "What's happened to Jace?"

The captain cleared his throat. "Ma'am, we're not sure. He's gone, along with Nate." He shifted to the other foot. "And you're going to hear soon enough—"

"Hear what?" Her eyes widened.

"It's Jim Eldridge," said Luke. "We found him lying on the backside of the trail." He paused. "He had a bullet in his back."

Rebecca put her hand to her mouth. She stared at Luke. "Jim's dead and you don't know where Jace is?"

Captain Brenner slid a stool in front of Rebecca and sat. "Ma'am, there's no sign of Jace or Nate. Their horses are gone. Tom and some of the men or out looking for them now. We're not leaving here until we have a chance to look for tracks."

Rebecca bent her head and covered her eyes. "Are you saying whoever started the stampede may have taken Jace and Nate?"

Luke knelt in front of her. "We're going to find them. They can't have gotten far."

"That's right," the captain assured her. "It's only been a few hours. We'll find them."

The captain stood, swung up into the saddle, and rode off.

Luke got a cup of water from the barrel. "Drink this."

Rebecca pushed the cup away and closed her eyes.

"I know this may seem impossible, but you have to try and not worry yourself," he added, "in your condition."

Rebecca grabbed Luke's arm. "I'm depending on you to find Jace. Find my son."

Jane and Paul Eldridge, their other three children, and Reverend Jamison gathered with the families at the gravesite of their eldest son, Jim. Another loved one left behind. Rebecca lowered her head in sorrow. Jane's grief-stricken sobs tugged at her heart. It tore open an already aching gap of loss. Clutching Ben and Hannah's hands, she tried to concentrate on Reverend Jamison's message to Jim's anguished family.

Her mind trailed off. Where is Jace? Is he in the hands of those awful men? Will I ever see him again?

Filled with worry over her son, she only heard fragments of Reverend Jamison's scripture reading. "Behold the dwelling place of God…He will wipe away every tear…death will be no more…there'll be no pain."

Millie and Bart stood close to Rebecca. Millie leaned over and whispered. "Are you all right? You look pale. Jane would understand if I took you back to your wagon where you can rest."

Rebecca gazed across the gravesite at Jane and prayed God would spare her, and Ben, and Hannah the horrendous burden of losing Jace.

She grasped her stomach when a sharp pain ran through her. "I do need to rest."

"Do I need to get Dr. Brummel?"

"No. I'm okay. Could you see if Clara would watch the children for a little while?"

Millie signaled to the Calhouns. Bart took her arm and said, "Do you need me to help you to your wagon?"

"Yes, thank you. I need to lie down."

Millie alerted Dr. Brummel and within a few minutes, he and Catherine climbed into the wagon and assessed Rebecca's situation.

"Rebecca," said Dr. Brummel, "you're under such stress that I'm afraid it could have a bearing on the health of your baby."

Catherine took Rebecca's hand. "It's vital for you and your baby that you have complete bed rest for the next twenty-four hours. Captain Brenner announced we'll be staying here while he and the others look for Jace and Nate."

Millie stood by the wagon. "Between Clara and me, you don't need to worry about the children. Please, Rebecca, listen to the doctor."

Laying on the feather mattress, Rebecca resigned. "I know I have no choice. I can't endanger the baby." She laid her arm across her forehead. "I can't do this by myself."

Millie gently patted her hand. "God knows your concerns. He loves you, Rebecca."

She sighed. "I'll do as you say. But if Luke or the captain learn anything about Jace, let me know, no matter what."

Millie assured her. "As soon as I hear anything, you'll know."

After everyone left, Luke rode up.

He called her name and she sat up. "Right here. Have you found him?"

Luke stood by the back of the wagon and peered in. "I'm sorry, no. But the captain sent Tom on ahead to Fort Hall for more scouts." He paused. "We're staying here one more day, but Captain Brenner's decided we need to get back on the trail day after tomorrow. We need supplies. But more importantly, we need to stay on schedule. After Fort Hall, we'll be going through more mountain passes. We have to beat the snows."

"What about Jace?"

"Fort Hall has scouts who know this part of the country better than anyone. Wherever Jace and Nate are, between the scouts and us, we'll find them. We have to keep trusting." He took her hand. "Promise me you'll rest."

She laid back, tears pooling on her pillow.

❧

Early the next morning, Luke and Captain Brenner rode up to Rebecca's wagon. She held a pail full of milk. Ben and Hannah sat on the tailgate of the wagon eating breakfast.

Luke and the captain got off their horses and tied the reins to the wagon wheel. Luke took the pail from her and placed it on the table by the wagon. "Dr. Brummel said you needed to rest today."

"I know, but I have to keep myself busy or I'll go crazy with worry over Jace." She swallowed. "I can see by your faces, there's no news of him."

The captain removed his hat. "No, ma'am, not yet. You might want to sit."

She froze.

Luke glance over at Captain Brenner. "The captain and I need to talk to you before we get on the trail."

She took a shallow breath. "Talk? What about?"

"Please. Rebecca, I think you need to sit," said Luke.

From the corner of her eye, she glimpsed Millie and Penelope approaching. When they stopped at the tailgate of her wagon, she knew by their faces something was going on. "Millie, Penelope? What's happening? Why are you both here?"

The captain pressed his lips together. "I've come to a decision. I thought on it long and hard." He rubbed his forehead. "There comes a time when situations that are out of our control force us to make difficult decisions. Luke and I discussed it and feel for your own good and your family you shouldn't go on with the wagon train."

She straightened her back. "But, Captain."

"Please let me finish. I'm praying we'll find Jace or he'll find his way back to us, but until that time I don't think you're able physically or otherwise to continue on."

Hot tears rose. She couldn't look at Millie or Penelope.

Millie stepped forward and knelt beside her. "Rebecca, we hate to say it, but Penelope and I agree with the captain. Without Jace and in your condition, it's not safe for you to go on."

Rebecca let out a breath. "But what do I do? What are my children going to do?" She stared up at Captain Brenner. "You can't leave us at Fort Hall."

Ben jumped from the wagon, eyes wide. Hannah put her cup of milk down and picked up Betsy.

Captain Brenner raised his hand. "No, no. There's a settlement called Winter Creek about five day's travel in a wagon southeast between Fort Hall and Fort Bridger. It's what we call a jump off. It's a place where other families decided to settle rather than go on to Oregon. It's a nice settlement with a mercantile, homes, a church; a place you and your children can rest until things get better."

"But what about Jace?" Rebecca held her breath.

"Once we find Jace, there's no way I'll allow him to leave the wagon train and make the trip to Winter Creek by himself. And I can only afford to be without Luke long enough to get you there. We're racing with time now to beat the snows through the mountain passes. It could be spring or after before Luke and I make the return trip. We'll have Jace with us."

"But what about our plans for Oregon?"

"Ma'am, if you still have your mind set on Oregon, you could meet up with the next wagon train going that way in the spring. You and Jace can decide when you see him again."

Rebecca tried to process it all. Winter Creek. She stared at her hands gripped in her lap not knowing what to do. This is all too much. She shook her head. "We don't know anyone there. And without Jace how can this be better for us? We can't leave the wagon train not knowing where he is."

Captain Brenner handed her an envelope. "This has the name of the owner of the mercantile in Winter Creek, Paul Walters, and his wife, Katy. They're fine people and will help you any way they can. I've written a letter of introduction. I've prayed about this, and for now, I believe this is the best for you and your family."

"I can't leave without knowing about Jace?"

"We still have several men out looking. And Tom should be in Fort Hall by now. I have to think this is the best."

Rebecca's eyes watered at the thought of leaving Millie and Penelope. "What am I going to do without you both? Will we ever see each other again?"

"Sure we will." Millie pulled Rebecca to her feet and hugged her. "And when Jace returns, we'll help the captain look after him." Millie let go and wiped her eyes.

Zeb walked up, spurs jingling, with Clara beside him.

Rebecca's heart stirred. How is Ben going to let his Grampa go on without him? She tried to smile when they got closer. "I suppose you've heard we're not going with you to Oregon?"

Clara smiled. "Honey, Zeb and I talked all night about your situation. And we've made a decision."

Zeb blurted. "We're going with you."

Rebecca waved her hand in the air. "I can't ask you to do that. What about Oregon?"

Zeb grabbed Ben and jostled him around. "Well, the truth is, I can't leave my Ben boy and Hannah. They're a part of us now. My heart would break to leave them behind. Anyway, Clara and I can live anywhere. And from what the captain said about Winter Creek, it sounds like the perfect place to spend some time with our grandchildren."

Ben let out a holler. "Grandpa. You can teach me how to hunt when we get there."

"I sure can, boy."

"We're trading your oxen for mules," said the captain. "They'll prove faster travel for you and the Calhouns."

Rebecca lowered her head then looked up at Captain Brenner. "This wasn't what Hank and I planned. But for now, we'll do as you say." She looked at Luke. "As long as you bring Jace back to me."

CHAPTER TWENTY-SIX

Jace struggled to pull himself out of a gray fog. Where am I? How long have I been unconscious? He lifted his head then let it drop into the dirt, tasting blood mixed with grit. What happened? The stampede flashed through his mind. Gunshots, cattle stampeding, Jim Eldridge hitting the ground. Nate.

Lying on his side next to some brush, Jace tried to move. A stabbing pain pierced his ribs. His left eye swollen shut, he peered through the slit of his right eye. The sun was going down and shadows moved around the campfire. Two men sat on a log a few yards from him.

Nate. Where is he? Jace eased his head back to look for him. Stiff from laying on the damp ground, his shoulder muscles ached. He tried to pull his hands from behind him, but the more he moved the tighter the ropes bound his wrists.

Jace focused his good eye. That's him. Nate lay not far from a clump of boulders at the foot of the rocky bluff. Jace took a shallow breath. Please be alive, Nate.

One of the men stood and walked toward Jace. Stooping, he said, "Boy." He swung something back and forth in front of him. "You ready to tell me where you got this watch?" The gold flickered from the firelight.

Jace glared into the man's face. Tobacco stains streaked his matted beard. His teeth were black and he wreaked of whiskey and sweat.

"Boy, I'm not gonna fool with you any longer. We've been at this for two days now."

"I need some water," said Jace.

The man snarled. "Sure, boy. As soon as you tell me what I want to know. I'm gonna say it again. The last time I saw my brother he was carryin' this watch." He spit. The spray splattered across Jace's face. "Whoever gave it to you killed him." He spit again. "It's a fact you didn't do it. You're still a pup. But somebody on that wagon train did." He got down in Jace's face. "For the last time, where did you get this watch?"

Nate moaned.

Thank goodness. Jace peered at him with his good eye. He's alive. He scowled at his capture. "And I'm going to tell you for the last time. I found it on the trail."

The man stood and kicked Jace hard in the chest. Jace didn't want to give him the satisfaction of hearing him groan, but the blow forced a deep cough.

"Boy, you're lyin' to me." He sneered at Jace. "You know who killed my brother."

Jace looked up at him. "Mister, I don't know anything about your brother."

"We're runnin' out of time, so maybe your friend here can tell me." He walked over and pulled Nate up by his collar and glared at Jace. "My patience is wearin' thin. If you don't tell me what you know about this watch, I'm gonna kill your friend here." He jerked Nate hard. "You hear what I said? I'm gonna kill this boy if somebody doesn't tell me where you got this watch." The outlaw pulled a gun from his holster and aimed it at Nate's head.

"Don't shoot," said Jace with a hoarse rasp.

The man let go and Nate dropped to the ground.

He walked back over to Jace. "Are you gonna cooperate now?"

"Okay, mister, I know who the watch belonged to." Jace lowered his eyes.

The outlaw stared down at Jace. "I ain't gonna wait any longer." He walked back over to Nate who was huddled by the boulder and pointed the gun at Nate's head again. He cocked the hammer.

"Okay, okay, it was my pa's."

One eyebrow raised. "What'd you say, boy?"

Through clenched teeth, Jace said, "Can't you hear? I said it was my pa's."

The man's lips curved up then he laughed out loud. "So, that was your pa who Jesse shot and left for dead."

Jace jerked on the ropes. The thought of killing that man gave him pleasure. Through his good eye, Jace counted two more men riding into camp.

The bigger one scowled from his horse. "Bill, we're not waitin' any longer. We found tracks earlier. They may be army scouts and they're gettin' close. We don't want any soldiers on our trail. We've been here too long as it is." The outlaw shifted in his saddle. "Frank said if the boy hadn't talked by now, he's not gonna. Just kill 'em both, and let's get out of here. He's waitin' for us at the pass."

Bill turned back to the man. "You can tell my brother he can just wait." He scoffed. "And, Clay, don't you be tellin' me what to do, either."

Jace tried to move when Clay jumped from his horse. In a rage, the outlaw pushed Bill away and aimed his pistol in Jace's face. Nate tried to scramble to his feet. Jace closed his eyes waiting for the gun to go off. He held his breath. His body jerked when a shot rang out. Opening his good eye, he saw Clay lying face down with a bullet through his neck, blood oozing on the ground.

A troop of cavalrymen rushed the outlaws from the dense brush surrounding the campsite. Bill and the other two outlaws pulled their guns and fired on the uniformed men. Horse hooves pounded the ground and gunfire roared in Jace's ears.

Jace hollered. "Nate!"

One last shot sounded. Bill Coulter fell on Jace then rolled to the side of him. He lay dead with the gold watch still clutched in his fist.

When the skirmish ceased, a man dressed in buckskin bent over Jace and cut the ropes from his wrists. Jace tried to sit up, but his ribs were on fire. "Did you get them all?"

"We did."

Four dead bodies littered the campsite. Bill Coulter near Jace, two lying near the campfire with bullets through their heads, and one near Nate with a bullet through his chest.

Jace grabbed the arm of the man in buckskin. "Frank Coulter's still out there. He's waiting for them at some pass. Didn't say which one."

"Don't talk, just lay still. And drink this."

Jace gulped the water

"What about Nate?"

The man pointed to the log by the campfire. "Private Young's tending to his wounds."

Jace glanced at the dead man lying beside him. "My pa's watch." He reached for it and groaned.

"Whoa," said the man. "You need to stay right where you are." He turned and called to the other soldiers. "We're camping here tonight. We'll strap the dead bodies on their horses in the morning." He leaned over, picked up the watch, and gave it to Jace.

Nate finally spoke. "How did you find us?"

"Captain Bradford sent us out, along with another scouting patrol. I'm Talbot Hawks. Most people call me Tal. We're from Fort Hall. We've been chasing a band of Sioux for days when we spotted your campfire from the top of the ridge. When we got closer we could see you were in trouble." He looked down at Jace. "You nearly met your maker today, son."

"Thanks for saving our lives."

Tal helped Jace sit up. Jace glared at Bill Coulter's dead body. "What are you going to do with those murdering thieves?"

Tal nodded toward the west. "We're taking their bodies to Fort Hall to be turned over to the territorial marshal. They all have bounties on their heads, dead or alive. Their wanted pictures are posted all over this territory."

Jace pushed his pa's watch into his pocket.

"What about the wagon train?" Nate said.

"If they're going to Oregon," said Tal, "they'll get supplies at Fort Hall. We're not that far from the fort. You can meet them there."

Jace tried to stand, but his body said otherwise.

Nate rode beside Jace on their way to Fort Hall. "Jace, what did that man mean when he said whoever had that watch killed his brother? The watch was your pa's, right?"

"Yeah." Jace turned away from Nate.

He gave Jace a side look. "I don't understand then. If they shot your pa, who killed his brother?"

"It's a long story." He was quiet again, then said, "If I'd had a gun, I'd of killed that man. I've never hated anyone like I hate those worthless murderers."

Jace felt behind his ear where blood seeped. His jaw muscles protruded. But worse was the hatred that burned from his heart.

The two-day ride to Fort Hall was long and painful. With every pound of the horse's hooves, Jace's ribs screamed at him. Tal wrapped his chest as tightly as possible with leather straps. Jace squinted through his good eye, blinded by the glare of the setting sun.

The image of the outlaws continued to run through his mind. Jace knew God's command to forgive, but relished in the rage he wallowed in. The angrier he became, the more justified he felt. He gritted his teeth through the pain of his swollen jaws. I vow I'll never be defenseless again. I know what I need, and I know how to get it.

"I can see Fort Hall." Nate hollered. "Jace, we're not far." When Jace didn't reply, Nate said, "I'm sorry you took a worse beating than me. That man would've surely killed me if you hadn't told him whose watch that was. I owe you my life, and I won't forget it."

Jace nodded but said nothing.

Corporal Halsey slowed his horse's pace and edged his way over to Jace. "As soon as we get to the fort you go straight to the infirmary. Private Smith will accompany you."

Jace smirked. "I don't need a doctor."

"It's not a request. It's an order."

CHAPTER TWENTY-SEVEN

For five days, Luke led Rebecca and the Calhouns farther from the wagon train and closer to Winter Creek. She knew the captain was right, but it didn't make leaving any easier. Jace's fate was unknown and her heart longed to stay with those she considered family.

Everyone rode in the wagons. Hannah sat by Rebecca and held Betsy close to her while Ben rode with the Calhouns. Rebecca could still see Millie and Penelope's faces as they waved their farewells. She gazed at Luke riding ahead the wagons. *Lord, how will I go on without him? I've lived through too many goodbyes. I don't know if I can stand another.*

"Mamma, will Mr. Barker stay with us in Winter Creek? And what about Jace?"

"No, honey, he'll have to return to the wagon train. Don't worry about Jace. He'll be back."

Dark clouds covered the August sun most of the day. Late in the evening, Winter Creek appeared at the base of a ridge of mountains. For the last hour a continuous rumble warned them of the late summer rain. Luke road just ahead of the wagons.

Rebecca kept looking at the sky. When she noticed Luke untie his nap sack and pull his slicker from it, she said, "Hannah, you and Betsy move inside the wagon. Looks like there's going to be rain any minute."

In seconds, thunder roared and rain poured.

Luke road back to the wagons. He pulled his hat down over his eyes, rain running off his brim. He hollered at Rebecca and Zeb. "There's plenty of tree cover, but they're too dangerous with all this lightening. Let's just keep the wagons going. The mules will help us make faster time. Winter Creek's just ahead."

The rain let up a few minutes before arriving in Winter Creek. Ben yelled from the Calhoun's wagon, "Hannah, Mamma. We're here. It's a real town."

Hannah stood up from the wagon seat. "I've never seen so many stores and houses and people."

Nearing the mercantile, Rebecca thought of the letter of introduction Captain Brenner gave her.

Luke waved his arm. "Follow me to the stables. We can dry off down there and board the animals. Rebecca, you, Clara, and the children can walk back to the mercantile. Zeb and I will meet you there when we've brushed down the animals."

Entering the store, Rebecca took in a deep breath. It reminded her of the one in Fort Laramie. Exhausted and soaked from the rain, she and Clara found a bench near the potbelly stove.

Rebecca rubbed her shoulders. "Driving mules is harder than oxen."

Ben and Hannah grinned and pulled on Rebecca's skirt. "Look, Mamma, at all the candy."

The man behind the counter lifted the lid to one of the candy jars. He walked over to the children. "How about some peppermint?" He handed Ben and Hannah the candy. "I don't believe we've met. I'm Paul Walters."

Rebecca rose from the bench. "Children, you know better than that." She looked at the shopkeeper. "I'm Rebecca Quaid and this is Ben and Hannah. I was told by Captain Brenner to give this to you." She handed him the envelope.

After reading it he said, "Oh, yes. Mrs. Quaid. Charles Brenner is an old, old friend of ours. And please let the children accept the candy. Something for them to remember on their first day in Winter Creek."

"Thank you. And this is Clara Calhoun. She and her husband accompanied us."

Luke and Zeb walked into the mercantile at the same time a woman came from the back. "Luke," Paul hollered, "good to see you. How long has it been? Oh, and Mrs. Quaid, Mrs. Calhoun, this is Katy, my wife."

Luke shook Paul's hand then introduced Zeb. "It's good to see you and Katy. It's been at least five years since I was in Winter Creek. It's growing." He smiled at Rebecca. "I guess Rebecca gave you Captain Brenner's letter."

"Yes. Charles explained everything. I'm sorry about your situation, Mrs. Quaid, however, Katy and I'll do all we can to make you and your family comfortable, as well as the Calhouns."

Katy smiled and pointed to the back. "I know you're all tired. Let me show you and the Calhouns where you can rest."

Rebecca left Luke and Paul visiting while she settled in their new surroundings.

Opening the bedroom door, Katy said, "I hope these accommodations will do." She handed her a dress. "Here is something you can change into.

Rebecca took the dress and scanned the room. "This is more than adequate." She smiled at Katy. "Thank you."

"Well, I'll leave you now to rest." She turned to Clara. "If you'll follow me, I'll show you where you and your husband can stay."

"Thank you for your hospitality." Clara put her hand on Hannah's shoulder. "Do you children want to come with me so your mother can rest?"

Rebecca smiled at Clara. "I just need to lie down for a few minutes."

Clara and the children left Rebecca standing in the middle of the room. Looking around, she thought this isn't what I wanted. She gripped the wet folds of her skirt. I need to know Jace is safe. I miss Millie, and Penelope, and sweet Mary Martha. Rebecca sighed. And tomorrow Luke will ride back to the wagon trail where I want to be. She dropped her face in her hands. Lord, help me see you in all of this.

After resigning herself to the situation, Rebecca changed into dry clothes. Her thick hair fell in damp ringlets down her back. She sat on the side of the bed trying to clear her mind when a knock sounded. She stood. "Come in."

Luke opened the door and stepped inside. He removed his hat. "I don't mean to bother you, but I need to let you know I'll be leaving before sunlight in the morning. I just wanted to make sure you're okay."

"Thank you." She smiled. "I'm so grateful to you. From the first day we joined the wagon train, you've taken care of us. We wouldn't have gotten this far if it hadn't been for you."

He stepped toward her. "I wanted to help you. And we're going to find Jace. When we do, I'm coming back for you, and Ben, and Hannah. Please remember that."

She hung her head. "I don't know if it's exhaustion," her words caught in her throat, "or my despair. I can't stop crying."

Luke pulled her into his arms. "You're weary after the long trip and frightened about Jace." His hand stroked her beautiful golden, brown curls. "I know Jace's heart is set on Oregon and you want to be with him." He took her face in his hands. "I promise, Jace and I will be back for you."

Luke stared into her beautiful hazel eyes then bent and pressed his warm lips on hers. For that moment, her troubles disappeared in his embrace. She didn't want the kiss to end. He pulled away gazing at her. "Rebecca, I know this shouldn't have happened, but I've fallen in love with you."

She closed her eyes. "With all my troubles, how can you love me?"

"All I know is I want to be with you the rest of my life."

Rebecca laid her head on his shoulder. "I didn't want this to happen for Hank's sake, but I love you too, and I need you. Please come back to me." Rebecca knew Hank would want her to be happy. She realized Luke had filled the emptiness left by Hank's death.

When Rebecca woke the next morning, she gazed through the lace covered window from her bed. Clouds hung over Winter Creek which matched the melancholy Rebecca found herself in. Hannah rushed into the room and pounced on the bed.

"Oh, Hannah, you startled me." Rebecca smiled at her daughter. "You seem happy today."

Hannah giggled. "Ms. Katy has breakfast for you. Grandma was worried you'd sleep the day away."

Rebecca stretched and asked, "What time is it?" She sat up in bed. "Oh, my, I must have been tired. I didn't hear you or Ben get up."

"Come see Ms. Katy's garden growing behind the store. There're tomatoes, and corn, and lots of stuff. She said the rain would help everything grow."

Rebecca held Hannah's chin. "How nice it will be to have fresh vegetables. Run tell Ms. Katy I'll be right there."

Hannah scurried out the door.

Rebecca looked around at what was to be her and the children's home for the next few months. Before she could put her feet on the floor, Ben bounced into the room.

"Mamma, can I go with Grandpa to the blacksmith?"

"Well, I suppose so."

His freckled face beamed. He turned to leave then twirled and ran into Rebecca's arms. "I love you, Mamma." He raced off to explore Winter Creek with Grandpa Zeb.

"Mrs. Quaid…Rebecca?" called Katy Walters from outside Rebecca's door.

"Yes, Mrs. Walters."

Katy peered around the door. "Are you hungry? You didn't eat anything last night. And please call me Katy."

She gave Katy a big smile. A flutter caused Rebecca to press her hand on her thickening waist. "I might eat a little."

After dressing, Rebecca met Katy in the kitchen. Just a few minutes with her warm laughter lightened Rebecca's mood. Pouring her a cup of coffee, Katy said, "Luke left this morning before sunlight."

"Do you know Luke well?"

"Yes. Paul and I knew him in Missouri. He and Paul grew up together in Cooper County. My best friend, Beth, and Luke married soon after we did." She sighed. "Beth and the baby died of diphtheria. That's when he started scouting for the wagon train."

Rebecca set her cup down. "Oh, I didn't know. How dreadful." She peered up at Katy. "He's been so kind to me and my family. My husband was killed right before we joined the wagon train. He took my older son, Jace, under his wing."

Katy placed the coffeepot back on the stove. "Before he left, he told us about the stampede and Jace being taken by the outlaws. Do you believe in prayer?"

"Oh, yes. I couldn't bear it if I didn't know God is protecting Jace."

Katy placed a plate of crisp bacon and hot biscuits on the table.

Rebecca smiled. "I didn't think I was hungry, but I'm suddenly starving."

After breakfast, Rebecca and Hannah ventured outside the mercantile. Clouds cast a shadow on the mud-covered streets of the busy town.

"Mamma, have you ever seen so many people?"

"No, honey, not in a long time."

"Where did they come from?"

"I guess most of them live in and around Winter Creek. It reminds me of Millbury when I was growing up. Though Millbury was much bigger."

When Rebecca and Hannah returned to the mercantile, Clara stood talking to Katy. Just seeing Clara lifted Rebecca's spirits.

With a smile, Clara greeted Rebecca and Hannah and asked how she slept last night.

"Wonderful," Rebecca said. "I'm afraid I took advantage of it and slept much too late."

Clara raised her hands in the air. "My, how nice it is to be out of that wagon and have the luxury of four walls." She glanced at Katy then back at Rebecca. "This morning the Walter's were kind enough to offer us the house normally used by Winter Creek's local teacher.

That will give you and the children the use of the back lodging in the mercantile."

Rebecca frowned. "Is there no teacher?"

"Not at this time," said Katy.

"I'm surprised. How do the children learn to read and write?"

"They don't unless their parents can teach them." Katy smiled at Clara. "And the town would rather someone live in the house than it set empty."

"It couldn't be more perfect for Zeb and me." Clara put her hand on Rebecca's arm and wrinkles covered her forehead. "Are you okay? I know you have so much on your mind."

"Just the fact that you and Zeb are here eases it. And I'm thankful Captain Brenner and Luke were able to make our transition as easy as possible. Katy, you and Paul are so kind to take us in." Rebecca gazed around at the busy mercantile. "There must be something I can do to repay you." Rebecca turned to Clara. "You wouldn't mind taking Hannah for a while, would you?" She turned back to Katy. "I'd like to help you in the mercantile if I could."

Katy raised her palm. "No, you need to rest."

"I'm fine. Please let me do something to help you." She peered around the general store. "I can measure fabric, or bag vegetables, or count out eggs. I need to be useful."

Katy tilted her head. "Okay, but I think you're overdoing it." She led her to the bench by the potbelly stove. "I'll put you right here greeting customers."

CHAPTER TWENTY-EIGHT

The weather slowed the wagons down coming from Soda Springs, which added two more days to their travel before arriving at Fort Hall. Captain Brenner didn't expect Luke to be back from Winter Creek for another week.

At noon on Wednesday, the wagon train rolled into Fort Hall. A day later, the scouts, the dead outlaws, Nate, and Jace rode in. Captain Brenner came from the stockyards and caught a glimpse of Jace entering the infirmary. Nate stood with one of the soldiers on the walkway. He called for Nate and rushed across the compound.

Nate stepped from the wooden walk. "Captain Brenner."

He shook Nate's hand. "Son, I'm relieved the scouts found you and Jace. Are you okay?"

"Yes sir, I'm fine." He waved his hand toward the infirmary. "But I'm not sure about Jace. The doc is checking him out, but it's not his wounds that worry me."

The captain pointed to the row of horses carrying the dead men. "Are those the outlaws who kidnapped you?"

"Yes, sir. Corporal Halsey and his men shot and killed them." Nate shook his head. "Through it all, I thought we were goners a couple of times. If it wasn't for Jace, I'd be dead for sure."

"I'm sorry you boys had to go through that. But the best news is you're back with us now." He put his hand on Nate's shoulder. "Are you hungry? The chuck wagon is at the west end of the fort. Pete can fix you up. I'll go check on Jace."

Nate thanked the captain and left.

Captain Brenner stepped into the infirmary. The front office was empty, but he heard voices from the next room. The door opened and Jace and Dr. Sheffield walked through.

The captain stared at Jace. He hardly recognized him. "Doc, will he be all right?"

"He has some broken ribs, and it's going to take a while for his facial contusions to heal. He needs food and lots of rest, but he'll be fine." The doctor put his hand on Jace's shoulder. "You need to be careful and let those ribs heal."

"I'll make sure he doesn't overdo it," said the captain. "We're pulling out day after tomorrow. I'll send him back over before we leave."

"That's fine." Dr. Sheffield turned to Jace. "Just put some of that salve I gave you on your cuts. In a few days, your face will look better."

The captain and Jace left the infirmary. "Am I glad to see you," said Captain Brenner. "What happened out there?"

"Nothing."

Jace and the captain walked the length of the compound in silence. Reaching the chuck wagon, Nate sat near the campfire eating the plate of food Pete gave him. Pete handed Jace a plate.

Jace took the food and said thanks. He walked over by the toolbox and sat on the ground to eat.

The captain walked over to Pete. "There's something wrong. Jace hasn't asked about his family."

"What will he do when he finds out they're not on this wagon train?"

The captain rubbed his hand over his mouth. "I don't know."

After Jace finished his meal, Captain Brenner walked back to the toolbox and broke the news of Rebecca and the children leaving the wagon train for Winter Creek. From Jace's lack of expression, he wasn't sure it sunk in completely.

He paused for a reply. When there was none, the captain said, "Your personal belongings are rolled up in your bedroll in the supply wagon. You need to take it easy for a couple of days."

"I don't need any rest."

"Son, I'm not asking you to rest, I'm telling you." The captain raised his voice. "For now, you do exactly what I tell you. Your body has to heal before you're any good to yourself or us."

Jace stood, hung his thumbs in his pockets and stared at the ground.

"I'm going to the main office. We're pulling out on Sunday. You're going to bed down here at the chuck wagon with Pete and Nate. Pete will keep you fed."

Jace walked to the supply wagon holding his ribs to help with the stabbing pain. Resigning himself that Captain Brenner was right, he knew he was useless for now. He pulled the canvas flap aside, saw his bedroll, and moaned, gritting his teeth when he reached inside the wagon.

The bedroll was heavy. When he unrolled it he could see where his mother neatly packed the few items of clothing he owned. Rolled up inside lay the whistle Ben made for him. He reached inside his pocket and pulled the smooth rock Hannah had given him. In the middle of all his things, he found an envelope with his mother's handwriting scrolled across it. Slipping the paper from the envelope he read.

My dear, dear Jace,

I know in my heart you will read this letter at some point. This is not what we planned, but Captain Brenner seems to think it will be best if we go to Winter Creek for now. Through the mercy of God, Zeb and Clara insists on going with us. The captain has friends there who can be of great help to us until we can return to the wagon train.

Jace, just know that Ben, Hannah, and I love you and pray for the day we can be reunited. Also, never forget that your pa would be so proud of you.

There are some silver coins in the pocket of your red plaid shirt.

My deepest love, Mamma

Jace folded the letter and slipped it back into the envelope. He rubbed his thumb over the rock. His head started to swim and his legs buckled. Pete stood near the wagon and caught him before he hit the ground. "Son, you need to rest. Let me get your bedroll and you crawl under the wagon and get some shut eye."

Jace didn't have the energy to argue.

Late the next afternoon, standing by a grove of trees a half mile from the fort, Jace fumbled a gun from his holster and shot.

Nate stood a few feet from him. "How can you hit a target you can't see? You only have one good eye right now."

"Just stand there and don't say anything. I need to concentrate." Again Jace shot and the bullet cleared the row of bottles.

"Jace?"

He turned to Nate. "What."

"Are you ever going to talk to Ellen? She's wearing me out asking about you."

Jace turned back to the target. "I don't have anything to say to her. Anyway, she wants to talk about Jim Eldridge."

"But, Jace—"

He turned and glared. "Either keep quiet or leave. We're not pulling out of Fort Hall until tomorrow. That gives me time to practice."

Jace squeezed the trigger. The bullet whizzed by the bottles. He reloaded the pistol.

Captain Brenner approached the boys. "What's going on?"

Nate gestured toward Jace, shook his head, and left.

The captain approached Jace with a deep furrow on his brow. "Where'd you get that gun?"

Jace glanced at Captain Brenner then focused on the target again. "It's my business." He took another shot.

"No, it's my business. Now, are you going to tell me where you got it? Because we're not leaving until you do."

Jace pressed his lips together. "If I'd owned a gun the night of the stampede, Jim might be alive today."

"You don't know that for sure. It all happened so fast. Jim got caught in the crossfire. It could have been you."

"I wish it had been me."

"Son, what's going on?"

The gun dangled from Jace's right hand.

"Where did you get the money to buy that gun? I know the gunsmith here in Fort Hall is the only place you could have bought it."

Jace put the gun in the holster and glared at Captain Brenner. "I traded my pa's watch for it."

With a frown, Captain Brenner put his hand out. "I'd like to see the gun. See what you got for your pa's watch."

Jace pulled the gun from the holster and handed it to him.

He examined the weapon. "A Colt Dragoon revolver. The gunsmith must have thought your pa's watch was worth something. It's a nice gun. Weights good. Feels natural in your hand." He handed the gun back. "What do you plan on doing with it?"

"Whatever it takes to protect myself."

The captain removed his hat and ran his fingers through his hair. "I've only known you a short time, but I've never known a young man like you before."

Jace stared at the captain with no emotion.

Captain Brenner rubbed the back of his neck. "When I got a look at you in the infirmary, I could see you've changed. From what Nate said, you both believed you were going to die at any time. And now you're carrying a gun. I know this has something to do with those dead outlaws. Corporal Halsey said one of them had a pistol at your head when they attacked the camp."

Jace stared at the ground. "Tal Hawks killed him before he could get the shot off. That's all there was to it."

The captain took a breath and exhaled. "It's getting late. Let's talk about this later. We're leaving early in the morning so you ride close to the chuck wagon tomorrow." He and Jace walked back to camp. The captain stopped and put his hand on Jace's arm. "You keep that gun in its holster."

◈

At six o'clock Sunday morning, Captain Brenner waved his hat, and Pete sounded the signal for the caravan to embark on a five hundred and thirty-mile trail deep into the Oregon Territory. This marked the last trek of their two-thousand-mile journey.

Five days out of Fort Hall, the caravan reached Raft River. The next morning, six families, along with Tom Hayes, worked to separate from the rest of the wagons and strike out for California. Dr. Brummel and Catherine were among them. Tears flowed as if it were a funeral knowing the families would probably never see each other again.

Captain Brenner motioned to Jace. "Have Dr. Brummel check your ribs one more time before they leave us."

"My ribs are fine. There's nothing he can do for them."

"Son, you keep forgetting. I'm not asking, I'm telling."

Jace shrugged and walked toward Dr. Brummel's wagon.

Pete stood by the chuck wagon packing the cook pans from lunch.

When Jace left, Captain Brenner walked over by him. "I've never seen a kid turn so bitter so fast," said the captain. "Losing his pa and being kidnapped is more than he can handle."

Pete put another pan in the wagon. "I can see where he could hate the world right now."

"Yeah, but he's too good a kid to lose."

The captain turned and from a distance saw Luke riding toward the wagon train. He smiled. "Just in time. I was wondering what I was going to do without Tom or Luke." He mounted his horse and rode out to meet him.

As soon as the captain got close enough, Luke asked, "What about Jace and Nate? Have you found them?"

"Yeah, Jace is pretty beat up. Nate's okay."

Captain Brenner told Luke about the boy's rescue and what Corporal Halsey reported about the incident.

"Jace has a pretty big chip on his shoulder right now. His pa's killers started the stampede and kidnapped him and Nate. They nearly killed them."

"What did the scouts do with the gang?"

"Corporal Halsey's waiting for the territorial marshal to pick their bodies up." He paused, "There's something else you need to know. Jace is carrying a gun."

Luke sat up in his saddle. "Where did he get a gun?"

"At the gunsmith in Fort Hall. He traded his pa's watch for it."

"He what?" Luke pulled up on his reins. "Jace would never part with that watch."

"Well, he did."

CHAPTER TWENTY-NINE

Ten days passed and Rebecca found she enjoyed the activity that went along with a small town. The mercantile helped take her mind off Jace and gave her a chance to meet the biggest part of Winter Creek's population.

Getting to know Paul and Katy was like a healing dose of medicine. Paul reminded Rebecca of Luke. He was tall with dark hair. His kind face drew people to him. She could see how Luke and Paul were such good friends.

Katy was beautiful with skin like a porcelain doll. Her red hair and green eyes accentuated her delicate beauty. But her most attractive qualities were her warm laughter and gracious hospitality.

Along with helping in the mercantile, Rebecca and Clara cooked meals and Zeb tended to Paul and Katy's vegetable garden. As they eased into a daily routine, the time quickly passed. Every day Rebecca hoped for a telegram from Luke or Captain Brenner with news of Jace. She prayed constantly.

The mercantile opened promptly at seven o'clock each morning. Around midmorning, Rebecca stood by the potbelly stove and greeted a rosy-cheeked woman carrying an empty wicker basket. "May I help you?"

"Do you have any of that checked cotton muslin left? My Henry needs a new shirt."

Rebecca led the woman to the fabric and pulled out a bolt. She examined it.

"My, that's perfect." While Rebecca measured and cut the amount needed, the woman introduced herself. "Mrs. Quaid, we haven't met but I'm Eloise Franklin. I learned from Katy you and your family just arrived in Winter Creek. I also learned you lost your husband not long ago. I'm sorry. But I hope you've settled in comfortably."

Rebecca smiled. "Winter Creek is a lovely place. Though it's unfortunate there's no school teacher."

"Our last teacher was only here a few months when she got an opportunity to go back to Boston and teach." Mrs. Franklin shook her head. "It's hard to find someone who wants to live in a small place like Winter Creek."

"It's such a shame. Winter Creek seems a nice place to raise families." Rebecca handed her the package of fabric. "Mr. Walters will help you pay out. I hope you can get a teacher soon. And it's nice to meet you. Have a good day."

"I will, dear, and thank you."

Katy came from behind the counter. "I see you met Mrs. Franklin."

"Yes, she welcomed me to Winter Creek." Rebecca moved a bolt of fabric to another stack

Katy grabbed her bonnet from behind the counter. "How would you like to walk with me down to Dr. Jones' office? I need to deliver a case of bandages and several bottles of Calomel that came in this morning."

"A walk sounds nice." Rebecca hurried to the back of the store to get her bonnet.

Katy hollered over her shoulder. "We'll be back in a few minutes, Paul."

Dr. Jones' office was not at all what Rebecca expected. From the street, it appeared to be a tiny addition to the building next door. A shingle with Dr. Jones' name swung from a wooden post.

When she entered the office the spacious front room was pristine. The floors shined. Medicine bottles and supplies sat neatly organized in the white cabinet opposite the front door. Several chairs lined the wall.

A door opened from the other side of the room, and a tall, slender woman appeared. She smiled at Katy.

"Your supplies arrived this morning." Katy motioned at Rebecca. "I wanted to bring them and introduce you to Rebecca Quaid."

Before Katy could fully introduce them, Rebecca said. "You must be Dr. Jones' nurse, and I have to compliment you on how nice you keep the office."

Katy grinned. "No, no, this isn't Dr. Jones' nurse. This is Dr. Laurel Jones. She is the doctor."

Rebecca's face flushed. "I'm…oh my, I'm sorry, but I've never met a woman doctor."

Laurel laughed. "You're not alone. And that very fact makes it hard for folks to trust my knowledge of medicine."

"It takes time for people to warm up to new and different ideas," said Katy. "But believe me, when they realize what a prize we have in Dr. Jones, they'll come around."

Laurel turned to Rebecca. "When is your baby due?"

Rebecca raised her eyebrows. "I guess it's becoming obvious. Dr. Brummel, the doctor on the wagon train, estimated sometime in December."

"Please let me know if I can help you during your pregnancy." Laurel grinned. "My practice is still quite small. Hopefully, you'll be my first delivery in Winter Creek."

Down the street from the mercantile, Zeb and Ben watched the blacksmith turn a hot piece of iron rod into a horseshoe. The black coals radiated red heat. And with each pound of the hammer against the anvil, sparks flew and the sound of hot mettle rang out.

"Grandpa, how did he know that piece of iron was going to be a horseshoe?"

"When he took the iron out of the fire, he knew exactly what he was going to make."

The blacksmith finished. "What can I do for you gentlemen?"

Zeb puffed on his pipe. "Not a thing. The boy and I were just enjoying how you've crafted your skill. Been doing it long?"

"Nearly twenty years. My pa was the blacksmith when Winter Creek first settled. I've seen lots of people come and go." He stuck out a massive hand. "I don't believe we've met."

Zeb extended his hand and introduced himself and Ben.

He shook Zeb's hand. "I'm Hank Carlson. You from a wagon train or just passing through?"

Ben blurted. "Hank was my pa's name. He died."

Hank peered down at him. "I'm sorry to hear that. But it's an honor to share your pa's name."

Ben smiled back at him.

"We were on our way to Oregon when our plans were changed," Zeb said. "That's what brought us to Winter Creek. Looks like we may be here until we can meet up with another wagon train going west. I understand it may be spring before that happens."

The men visited until Zeb glanced across the street. "Ben boy, I see your mamma and Mrs. Walters."

Hank stared at the doctor's office. "They must've been visiting that woman doctor who moved to Winter Creek not too long ago." He frowned. "I can't imagine why a woman would want to be a doctor."

Zeb nudged Ben. "We've taken up too much of this man's time. We better get back to the mercantile. I think there's weeding to be done in the garden." Zeb could see the idea of a female doctor could be a sore subject to some folks in Winter Creek.

Hank waved. "Come back anytime. I'm always looking for a reason to take a break."

During the weeks that passed, Rebecca put more hours into the store than Katy or Paul thought she should in her condition. By three o'clock one afternoon, she had finished filling the bins with fresh squash, dusting the shelves, and refolding bolts of fabric. As she worked, her mind wandered back to the wagon train and Jace.

"Excuse me."

Rebecca turned. A man she recognized from church stood with his hat in hand.

"Afternoon. Is there something I can help you with?"

He paused. "My name is Wade Morgan. We met at church last Sunday."

"Yes, Mr. Morgan. My children met your daughter, Lori." She stood waiting then said, "Can I help you find something in the mercantile?"

"No." He shook his head. "I was told you were interested in teaching children how to read and write."

"Yes. I'm surprised Winter Creek doesn't have a school teacher."

"And that's my problem. Lori needs someone to help her. She can read some, but my wife died last year, and I'm not good at things like that. I noticed last Sunday that your children could read some of the words from the hymnal."

"Mr. Morgan—"

"Please call me Wade."

She smiled. "Since you're concerned about your daughter's education, have you spoken to any of the other residents of Winter Creek about hiring a teacher?"

"Reverend Blackburn wrote several letters to schools back east hoping to interest someone into coming to Winter Creek. But no one wants to travel this far."

"Well, I'd be glad to help Lori and anyone else around here."

"Thank you, ma'am." He gave her a pleasant grin. "Just tell me when to have Lori here for her first lesson."

"I'll get back to you as soon as I can."

Katy came from the back of the store and greeted Wade.

He smiled at Katy. "My Lori may have a new teacher." As he left, he waved. "Got to go to work. You ladies have a nice afternoon."

Katy laid her hand on Rebecca's arm. "What did he mean, a new teacher? Would you really be willing to teach?"

"Yes." Rebecca laughed. "Growing up I was given the finest tutors my parents could find. When Jace turned four the teacher at Cutter Springs married and moved away. I taught until Ben came along. And you know, Katy, I think teaching is just what I need."

Katy smiled. "And a good teacher is just what Winter Creek needs."

CHAPTER THIRTY

The first week of September, the wagons rolled west heading out of what was once Fort Boise. A year before, floods plagued the area and nothing much remained now. Indian traders kept the emigrants in a few supplies.

Luke and Jace rode out after the noon break to scout the trail into Grand Ronde Valley. Since Fort Hall, three weeks passed and Jace hadn't said a lot to Luke, not even about his family. He kept to himself spending as much time as he could learning to draw his gun from his holster.

After an hour of silence on the trail, Luke said, "Jace, you ever think about your family?"

"Sometimes."

Luke wasn't sure what to do for him, but he knew Jace was pushing farther and farther away from anyone who came near him.

Luke took off his hat and wiped his forehead with his sleeve. "You figured out what you're going to do when we get to Willamette? Your mother talked about some land your uncle laid by for your pa."

At the mention of his pa, Jace stiffened and rode ahead. Luke let it pass as he had done so many times before. He prayed that God and time would start the healing process, but things were getting worse.

By mid-afternoon, they reached the edge of the valley. The Snake River ran full and swift which separated them from going directly into Grand Ronde.

"I'm not sure it's a good idea to try and cross the river here," said Luke. "I know it'll take a couple of days off the trail, but it might be better to cross on down in the valley. I don't know if the days saved are worth it."

"There'll be some who think we should cross it," said Jace.

"They may be right. Time's working against us."

That night Captain Brenner, Carl Webster, Hugh Unger, Paul El-dridge crouched around the campfire with Luke and Jace and dis-cussed the best route to take. Luke gave the men the report of what they found.

"About how deep you think the water's running?" asked Hugh.

"It could be as deep as some of the places we crossed on the North Platte River," said Luke.

"We made them fine," said Carl, smiling and looking over at Jace. "Except for one couple who decided to swim."

"Carl's right," said Paul. "It could save us time. And I'm wor-ried about crossing the Blue Mountains with a chance of an early snowstorm."

Captain Brenner stood. "You men have to take in account our livestock. They're wearing down. It'll take a lot of endurance for them to pull the wagons through that swift water. We have more oxen than mule, and they're not as sure-footed."

Hugh pointed to the west. "We need to remember they still have to get us over those mountains."

The discussion continued for close to an hour. Finally, the cap-tain said, "Sleep on it tonight. Hopefully, we'll reach the valley by late tomorrow. We'll assess the situation then and make a decision."

When the men left, Luke said to Captain Brenner, "Neither route's going to be easy."

"If we cross the river closer to the valley, there's a Shoshone trading post about half the distance along the southern side. If we cross it before then it's another fifty miles or so before the next post. Either way, we still may not make it over Blue Mountain before winter sets in."

Luke nodded his head at Jace. "You saw the river. What do you think?"

"I'm not running this wagon train. Makes me no mind." He stood, grabbed his bedroll, and headed for the supply wagon.

When Jace was out of earshot, Luke pushed his hat back. "He isn't getting any better. Last night after the camp bedded down, he snuck over to the other side of that clump of trees. I followed him. He was practicing his fast draw again."

"Did he see you?"

"No, he was too caught up in trying to get that gun out of the holster."

The captain poured himself another cup of coffee. "What do you think he's planning to do with that gun?"

"I don't know." Luke shook his head. "But I'm afraid he might point it at somebody thinking he's ready to use it." He frowned. "It's as though a deep bitterness has coiled itself inside him."

"He's got to be missing his family," said Captain Brenner. He rubbed his hand over his face. "But he's too stubborn to admit it."

"No, it's more than that." Luke buttoned his jacket. "When you told me who nearly killed him, I figure every time he pulls that gun and points, he sees the Coulter brother that got away."

"Before this gets out of hand," said the captain, "and he does something that might ruin his life, we may have to set him down and get some things straight. This sure isn't what his pa or Rebecca would want for him."

Six days out of Fort Boise, Luke and Jace rode ahead of the wagons to hunt for fresh game. Jace continued to shrug at every comment Luke made. Luke's patience wore thin, as did Captain Brenner's. Pete, Nate, and even Ellen gave up trying to talk to him, which seemed to suit Jace fine.

Not long on the trail, Jace pulled his pistol and shot at a prairie dog.

Luke frowned. "Don't waste your bullets. There're plenty of rabbits around and the shot could scare bigger game away."

Jace pointed his gun and shot at a lizard that scurried across the bare grass.

"Jace. Don't shoot at something we can't eat."

He gave Luke a sour look and shot twice into the air then placed the gun back into the holster.

"Son." Luke reined in his horse. "That's all I'm going to take from you."

"I'll shoot whatever I please, whenever I please." Jace smirked. "You're not man enough to do anything about it."

Luke shifted in his saddle. "Maybe it's time we found out."

"You won't touch me." Jace put his hand on the gun.

Luke jumped from his horse, reached up and grabbed Jace by the shirt sleeve, and threw him to the ground. Snatching Jace's gun from his holster, he said, "Let's just see what you can do without that gun in your hand." He threw it to the side.

Jace jumped up and took a swing at Luke.

Luke didn't want to hit him, but whether Jace knew it or not, he needed a good whooping.

Jace's arms thrashed but he only got a few good punches in. Luke wrestled him to the ground several times in an effort to not hit him. The battle for the upper hand continued until Luke finally decided to end it. Jace got up off the ground one more time and Luke got in two good licks. Jace went down and stayed down.

Luke stood over him. "You had enough?"

"You feel like a big man now?" Jace spit blood.

His words cut through Luke.

"No, I don't. But you've got to let go of all this anger. It's going to eat you up, and you'll be left with nothing."

Jace picked himself up and wiped his mouth on his sleeve. "It's my business if I want to be mad."

Luke sighed. "If I could change what's happened to you, I would. But I can't. And neither can you. Strapping on a gun won't fix anything."

Jace jutted his chin. Tears welled up in Jace's eyes. "It'll stop anybody from trying to hurt me or my family again." He used his sleeve again to wipe his eyes. He turned his back to Luke and took a couple of steps.

"A gun can't help you with what's going on in your mind right now. I can't see the real Jace anymore. You've built a wall to protect yourself from being hurt again. You're going to suffocate behind it if you're not careful."

Jace spun and sneered. "What do you know about hurting? My pa's dead cause of those no-good, useless animals."

Luke gritted his teeth and shifted his weight to one side. "Don't ever get the idea you know everything about me. I know what it feels like to lose those you'd give your life for." He swallowed hard. "I was married once and had a son. In fact, he'd have been about Ben's age now if he'd have lived. My wife and boy died when a diphtheria epidemic hit our town. I couldn't figure out why God took them and not me."

Jace fell to one knee and hung his head.

Luke furrowed his brow. "Son, you're fighting this battle with the wrong tool. A gun's not going to help you. The only thing that'll ever bring you any peace again is God. He's the tool that can help heal this sorrow you're carrying. It's too heavy for you. Believe me, I know."

Jace got up and paced. "None of this was supposed to happen." He hit the palm of his hand with his fist. "We planned everything, and now it's all gone. Mamma, Ben, and Hannah are gone." His shoulders slumped and his hands fell to his sides. "I...I don't know what to do." He hung his head. "I'm lost."

Luke moved closer and put his hand on his shoulder. "I don't understand why things happen. I just know God spared you from being killed by that madman, and me from that horrible disease that took my family."

Jace wiped his face and picked his hat up off the ground.

"Son, I'm a strong believer. There has to be something deeper and more to our lives than what we see." Luke smiled. "But there's one thing I do know. I promised your mother I'd bring you back to her, and Ben, and Hannah. So, once we get this wagon train to Willamette Valley and the snows thaw in the spring we'll head for Winter Creek."

"That's just it, Mr. Barker, Pa wanted us in Oregon. My uncle's waiting on us. How can I throw all that away?"

CHAPTER THIRTY-ONE

By mid-September, the autumn foliage covered Winter Creek and the mountainsides with an array of orange, red, and golden leaves. Rebecca loved the fall of the year, but her heart ached to see Jace and Luke.

Weeks passed with no news of either. And now it would be spring before she and the Calhouns could meet up with more emigrants heading for Oregon. Not knowing if Jace was dead or alive was agonizing. Though the days spent alongside Katy and teaching Lori, Ben, and Hannah seemed to fill her mind and calm her heart.

The crisp morning air drifted through the front doors of the mercantile. Katy and Rebecca restocked an empty shelf with colorful skeins of yarn.

"Mrs. Jenkins will love this shade of blue," said Katy. "She and Mrs. Franklin have an ongoing rivalry on who will win the prize for the best and most original knitted item at our annual Winter Creek celebration." She laughed. "It's gotten pretty heated some years."

Rebecca sighed. "Winter will be here soon, and I was hoping we'd be spending our first Christmas in Oregon this year. And now with Jace missing—"

"Don't, Rebecca."

"I just wish I'd hear something from Luke or Captain Brenner."

Katy pressed her hand on Rebecca's arm. "You could get a telegram any day now."

"I keep telling myself they've found him. I pray about it, but my hope lessens with each day. Why do I let myself do that?"

"Because you're human. And remember it only takes a mustard seed of faith." She peered at the front of the mercantile. "Has Reverend Blackburn been in the store this morning?"

"I'm not sure. Maybe Paul helped him."

"It's not Paul he wants to see, it's you."

Rebecca's brow crinkled. "Why would he want to see me?"

The bell on the front door rang, and the reverend walked in. He headed straight to the aisle of fabric where Rebecca and Katy stood. "Mrs. Quaid, may I have a moment of your time?"

Rebecca raised her eyebrows with scrutiny. "Why, of course."

Katy excused herself, but the reverend insisted. "Mrs. Walters, you might as well stay and hear this." When she did, the reverend continued. "Mrs. Quaid, I was informed you might be willing to act as teacher for the children of Winter Creek. I'm sure you've heard we've been unable to secure a dedicated person to take the job."

"Yes, but, what about my…situation?" Rebecca's eyes lowered. She folded her hands on her stomach. "Will it cause a problem for those in Winter Creek? There may be some who are of the opinion a woman in my condition shouldn't be teaching their children, especially since I have no husband."

The reverend shook his head. "There're always naysayers, but as I said before, we've been unable to entice anyone to fill the position. And the children are in need of a teacher. We'll make sure you'll have no problem. Will you consider our request?"

Katy grinned at Rebecca.

"If Paul and Katy can spare my being absent from the mercantile," said Rebecca, "I would love nothing better than to take the job."

Katy and Reverend Blackburn smiled. "Wonderful. I will have some of the men get the schoolhouse ready for you. We can discuss your compensation now if you'd like. And would it be possible to begin classes next week?"

Rebecca's eyes widened. "Well, I suppose so."

After a few minutes with the reverend, she was pleasantly surprised. Her wages would be adequate enough to pay the Walters for room and board and would still have some left over.

With only a week to prepare, Rebecca managed to organize the material needed to reopen the school. Never did she think she would be teaching in the quaint but lovely schoolhouse located in a meadow facing Winter Creek.

Early that morning, she gazed around the school room noticing how the sunshine flowed through the large windows opposite each other. A black potbelly stove sat near the back of the room. The scent of chalk filled the air. Several slates and well-worn history books and McGuffey readers lay stacked on her desk. Within the hour, she found herself standing at the front of a room filled with lively, eager students ready to learn…well, most of them.

"Children, quiet down." Rebecca held up her hands. "We have a lot to do today. I'm Mrs. Quaid, and I'll be your teacher for the next few months."

Ben raised his hand. "Do I have to call you Mrs. Quaid?"

"Yes, you and Hannah both while we're at school."

Ben slumped down in his seat. Hannah, however, sat on the first row and gazed at her mother as if she were the most beautiful teacher she'd ever seen.

"Mrs. Quaid." Lori raised her hand and asked, "Will we have our own books."

"Not for a while. I don't have enough for each of you now so you will have to share. Reverend Blackburn sent back east for more reading and arithmetic books."

"Awe, who wants to learn arithmetic?" scoffed Toby Gentry.

Rebecca tilted her head. "Toby, we use arithmetic every day." She stepped to the blackboard and wrote some figures. "If you were working for Mr. Carlson at the blacksmith for seventy-five cents a day and you worked thirty days, wouldn't it be nice to know how much you earned." She tallied the numbers. "He would pay you $22.50."

All the children sat up with interest, even Toby.

After the first week, Rebecca knew she was in her element. And with Zeb and Clara living behind the school, it couldn't have been more perfect. Before Rebecca and the children arrived at school each morning, Zeb had the potbelly stove warming the room. And Wade Morgan made sure an ample amount of wood was stacked on the east side of the building.

School let out at three o'clock each afternoon. On Friday, Rebecca dismissed class and began gathering books and papers to take home. She stepped out onto the porch where Wade Morgan met her.

"Let me help you," he said.

She balanced the books in her arms and smiled. "I'm fine but thank you for all the wood you cut and stacked for us."

Lori ran up to her dad. "Mrs. Quaid showed us how to find where we live on a big map hanging on the wall. And she showed us where she used to live before she, and Ben, and Hannah came to Winter Creek."

"That's wonderful, sweetheart."

"Can I play with Ben and Hannah for a while?"

"Yes, you go play." He looked at Rebecca. "And I'll help Mrs. Quaid carry these books. That's the least I can do since she agreed to be Winter Creek's teacher." He took the stack of books from her.

"Oh, but I enjoy teaching. I forgot what a pleasure it is to watch their eyes light up when they learn something new."

While the children played in the meadow, Rebecca and Wade strolled to the mercantile.

"What is it you do for a living around here?" said Rebecca.

"I own a timber mill a few miles north of Winter Creek. My uncle owned it until his death five years ago. My late wife and I moved here and kept it going. We supply all the timber to the surrounding settlements in this area."

"That's interesting. My father owns a timber mill in Massachusetts."

"You don't say. So you have some idea of the timber business."

"No, not really. I left Massachusetts when I was eighteen, and I've never been back." Before he could reply, she stepped up onto the wooden walk. "Here we are at the mercantile."

He followed her into the store and put the books on the counter. "When you find Lori," said Rebecca, "would you send Ben and Hannah home? And thanks for carrying the books."

He grinned. "Maybe I can carry them again sometime."

CHAPTER THIRTY-TWO

Autumn weather added to the breathtaking beauty of Grand Ronde Valley. The Blue Mountains surrounded the lush pastures that contrasted the dry prairie trail the travelers had known. After finding a more manageable part of the Snake River to cross, Luke, Jace, and the captain led the caravan down into the thirty-five-mile-long valley. By sundown, the campsites flickered and the animals grazed on green grass.

After supper, Luke and Jace sat at the captain's campsite. Captain Brenner and Luke studied a map by lamplight. Luke poured himself some coffee. He took a sip then said, "Jace, go ask Pete for another blanket for your bedroll. The temperature's dropping, and it may get below freezing tonight."

Captain Brenner moved closer to the fire and said to Luke. "When Trapper Dan left the wagon train at Fort Hall, he said we could be seeing snow once we get through this valley." He followed the trail on the map with his finger. "We've reached Grand Ronde Valley two weeks later than usual. The weather could slow us down even more."

"The colder the weather, the harder it is to find fresh game." Luke rubbed his knees. "Most of the families are running low on supplies, and Dalles is another twenty days down the trail."

"Tell the families not to waste anything." Captain Brenner lowered his head. "This trail gets harder every time I make it." He confided. "When we get to Oregon City this may be my last trip. Willamette Valley might be a good place to finally plant roots." He warmed his hands over the fire. "How is Jace doing?"

"Still hanging on to that gun. But more like his old self." Luke put some wood on the fire. "He needs more time. His anger over Frank Coulter still boils up every once in a while."

"I know it's hard, but he's going to have to put it down if he's going to have any peace. What about when we get to Willamette Valley? He still planning on putting down stakes?"

"I'm not sure. He doesn't say much about his family, but I can't imagine him settling there without them. I'm hoping by spring things will look better for him."

"Some situations change your life forever. But I've watched him and he knows what's right." The captain warmed his hands by the fire. "Speaking of Willamette, what are your plans when we finish the trail?"

Luke took a deep breath. "I'm not sure. It all depends on—"

Jace returned carrying a blanket and some broken reins. "I guess I let these get too dry." He handed the reins to Luke. "Can these be fixed?"

Luke ran a hand over the leather. "Doesn't look like it. They're too brittle. Even if you oiled them, they might not hold up when you needed them." He tossed the cracked reins into the fire and pointed toward the supply wagon. "I've got another set in the tack box."

Jace started for the supply wagon. He stopped and turned around. "Thanks, Mr. Barker."

Luke waved his hand.

When Jace walked out of earshot, the captain said, "He's going to be fine." He stirred the fire with a stick. "About your plans. They depend on what?"

"Rebecca."

Climbing out of Grand Ronde Valley and reaching Blue Mountain, the wagon train faced a new challenge. Since Luke's trip through the mountain pass a year ago a wooded growth covered the trail. Tall lodgepole pines and fir trees sprung up through the snow-covered path. Older fallen trees crisscrossed along the route creating a barrier. Luke, Captain Brenner, and the other men began the backbreaking toil of clearing a large enough swath for the wagons to climb the ridge of the mountain. The continuous days of snowfall hampered their progress.

Luke put his ax down, fastened the top button his coat, and pulled his collar up around his ears. He walked to the fire pit built for the women and children to warm themselves while the men cleared the trees.

Molly Unger handed him a cup of coffee. "How much more can any of you stand before you completely give out?"

"I know it's slow, but we're making headway." Luke edged his way to the fire.

"I'm scared Hugh's going to get pneumonia before we get over these mountains." Molly pulled the quilt tighter around her shoulders and exhaled a white billow of air. "I've never been so cold."

A loud boom echoed against the mountain. Luke swung to see a group of men rejoicing over a fallen elk.

Carl Webster hollered. "I got him. Look at the size of his antlers."

"One shot took him down." Bert Ingles yelled, "And it's the biggest elk I've ever laid eyes on. Hope he's not too tough to eat."

Luke and the captain helped the men drag the elk to the wagons. He savored the thought of elk meat. Would be a nice change after weeks of pork belly and jerky.

Clearing the path and crossing the Blue Mountains took all of the strength and tenacity the emigrants could pull together. When their animals died from sheer fatigue they would drag them to the side of the trail.

Captain Brenner huddled by the fire at his wagon, along with Luke and Jace. Studying the frayed map, the captain edged closer to the fire. "Tomorrow we should be nearing Columbia Plateau. Hopefully, there'll be enough Indian trading posts to keep us in supplies until we get to Dalles."

Luke blew warm breath into his gloved hands. "Once we get to Dalles and cross the Cascade Mountains, it's still another hundred miles to Willamette Valley. Most of our animals are walking on cracked hooves and some breathing like it may be their last."

The captain pulled the collar of his coat up around his ears. "We're going to be forced to take longer rest periods at noon each day. We can't push them any harder than they can stand. That goes for everybody on this wagon train."

"What about the snows going over the Cascades?" Jace crouched by the fire. "How are we going to make it over them?"

"With God's help, "said the captain. "This is the tenth wagon train I've led, and it's here the trail tests every soul. Our energy's sapped and rations are low, but somehow we always make it."

"When we get on the other side of Dalles, taking Barlow Road, on the south side of Mount Hood, is safer than floating down the Columbia River," said Luke. "Neither route is easy, but I've seen too many wagons float down the river on their sides. Barlow Road will get us over the Cascades."

Captain Brenner stoked the fire. "Then Willamette Valley will hopefully be in our sights. If nothing holds us up, we should be in the valley by the middle of November."

Jace looked over at Luke. "And then what?"

"I don't know. Have you thought about your ma, and Ben, and Hannah?"

"Most every day."

Luke leaned closer to the fire. "When I left Winter Creek, I promised your ma I'd bring you back to her in the spring. But you're old enough now to make up your own mind." He rubbed his legs to warm them. "What about your pa's brother?"

"Four years ago he wrote Pa and told him if he could reach Willamette Valley there would be plenty of land to settle."

"Jace," interjected the captain, "do you know how many emigrants have flooded into that valley in the last four years?"

"No, sir, but until we get there, I'm going to believe there's land enough for all of us."

"That's a good way to look at it," said Luke. "We never know about anything until we face it."

Captain Brenner checked his saddle and mounted his horse. "I'm going to take the first watch tonight. I saw a pack of wolves hovering around earlier."

Luke untied his bedroll. "We can't afford to lose any more of our stock. We only have fifteen head of cattle left."

The captain tied his neckerchief around his ears. He pulled his hat low on his head. "Jace, before you bed down, check on the stake line. Make sure those horses are tethered tight just in case they get jumpy. And, Luke, I've got enough men for the night watch, so try and get some sleep tonight."

Early morning broke crisp and sunny. Everyone relished the slight warmth it brought. Though now they and their oxen bogged through the icy, half-melted snow. The sunlight bounced off the water filled ruts.

Ellen Jacob concentrated to keep upright. The mud was slippery and the trail uneven. "This hideous mud," she grumbled. Her shoes pressed into the deep mire. With each step, the mud threated to suck them off her feet. She shaded her eyes from the glare of sunlight. "Why couldn't we have settled in the Grand Ronde Valley? Then we wouldn't be trudging through this mess, and my dress wouldn't be ruined."

"Do you always talk to yourself?"

She pulled her hand from her face to see Jace riding alongside her on his horse. "Jace Quaid. How dare you tease me." She flailed her arms to help balance herself on the slimy ground. "Especially since you've ignored me all these weeks."

He kept up with her slow pace. "I wasn't ignoring you."

"Yes, you were."

"Well, maybe a little." He shook his head. "But I didn't mean to hurt your feelings."

She glared up at him. "I was worried sick over you when you disappeared."

"I'm sorry. I can't explain what I was thinking." He got off his horse. "I didn't want to talk to anybody. I didn't want to be around anybody."

She frowned. "I noticed you're wearing that gun all the time. You never did that before."

"I never thought I needed it before." He put his hand on the gun handle. "Things are different now."

"You're the same person you were before."

"No, I'm not." His voice had an icy tone.

She stepped away from him and stared.

He reached out for her. "I'm sorry. I didn't mean to—"

She jerked back. "You're right. You're not the same person I knew before. It may be better if we don't spend time together."

"Ellen, please forgive me." He sighed. "Until I straighten some things out in my mind, you're probably right for now." He mounted his horse. "You were right about something else too."

She furrowed her brow. "About what?"

"Jim Eldridge."

The days were somewhat warmer, but the night air was frosty. Luke rode to the east side of the wagon train to check the herd and the night guards. He scrunched his head deep into the collar of his wool coat and pulled his hat down as far as it would go. He rubbed his horse's neck. "It's a cold one tonight, isn't it Bay?" He pushed his gloved hand down into his pocket. Checking the herd on cold, lonely nights gave him time to think about Rebecca. He missed her and longed for the day he would see her again.

Cody Jacob reined his horse beside Luke. "Sounds like a pack of wolves about two hundred yards back in those mountain crevices. They're getting closer."

"Keep your gun ready. They can take a steer down before you know it." The howling and yelping started up again, but this time in the opposite direction.

"If I didn't know better," said Cody, "I'd think they're trying to surround us."

"Ride through the herd as calmly as you can," said Luke. "We don't want them stirred up. I'll ride around the other way and see what it looks like."

At the campsite, Jace, Nate, and Pete bedded down as close to the fire as they dared. Jace laid listening to the commotion the wolves made. They gave out another stream of yelps. "Nate, are you awake? Sounds like those wolves are getting closer."

Nate hollered and sat up when a wolf jumped from the dark and bit down on his leg. "Jace! Pete!" He swung his arm across its body. "Help!"

Jace flung off his bedroll and grabbed his gun. Trying to get a good shot without hitting Nate, he moved closer.

Nate screamed and thrashed.

The wild animal yanked and growled as his teeth clinched Nate's bedroll.

Jace aimed and took a shot.

The animal let go of Nate, lurched back, and fell to the ground.

Pete ran to Nate.

Jace peered down at the wolf. He picked up a stick and nudged it to make sure the animal was dead.

Luke raced up and jumped from his horse. "What happened?"

Captain Brenner was right behind him. "Is everybody okay?"

"A wolf," said Jace, stepping back from the dead animal. "Looks like it may have been rabid. There's foam coming from its mouth."

"Everybody stand back. Don't get close," said the captain.

Pete pulled back Nate's bedroll. "Where'd he bite you?" He quickly began to strip off Nate's pants and socks.

Nate stammered. "I…I don't feel anything."

Jace, the captain, and Luke stood around Nate.

Pete examined his legs then smiled up at them. "By gum, this boy just beat the odds. There's not a scratch on him." He looked a Nate. "You have any idea what an animal with hydrophobia can do to a person? It's not pretty. Your bedroll saved your life."

Nate shook his head. "Jace saved my life…again."

Captain Brenner glanced over at the dead wolf. "We've got to bury that animal now. Don't anybody touch it. I'll get the shovels."

CHAPTER THIRTY-THREE

Rebecca stood at the counter of the telegraph office. "Mr. Peterson, is there a telegram for me today?"

"No, I'm sorry, Mrs. Quaid, I don't have a thing for you this morning."

Rebecca smiled and thanked him. She bundled up and walked out onto the wooden walkway. The morning breeze was cold.

Katy caught up with her in front of Mueller's Shoe Shop. "I can tell by your face you didn't get anything from Jace or Luke."

"No, and it's been nearly two months now. I'm afraid something's happened to Jace. It's getting harder to hold on to hope."

"I've known Luke for a long time. He'd never say anything he didn't mean, and he said they would both be back."

"But what if Jace is—

"Don't say that. Until we know for sure, Jace is fine." They walked toward the mercantile. "Now, let's talk about the school play. Winter Creeks' annual celebration is only three weeks away. Have the children learned their lines yet?"

"All but Toby Gentry. He's one of the smartest boys in the class, but you'd never know it by the way he slouches and clowns around."

"Does he have many lines?"

"Yes, and so far he's fumbled most of them. But if I know him, he'll have them learned by the evening of the play. He knows enough not to embarrass himself in front of the whole town."

Rebecca moaned and held her stomach.

"Are you okay?" Katy grabbed her arm. "Is it the baby?"

"I'm fine." Rebecca took a deep breath. "It's nothing. It comes and goes."

"Have you seen Dr. Jones?"

"No, there's no need until time comes for this baby to be born. I still have two more months before my due date." She grinned. "Remember, I've done this a few times before."

"I know you have, but it wouldn't hurt for her to know about these pains you're having."

Rebecca took Katy's arm and continued down the street. "You're worse than Clara. If both of you had your way, I'd be in bed until time to deliver. Now, let's get back to the celebration. What exactly does this entail?"

"Oh my." Katy's face brightened. "There's baking and canning contests. The ladies contend for the best knitted items." She chuckled. "Mrs. Jenkins and Mrs. Franklin go toe to toe when it comes to that contest. We have a drawing at our store, and Hank Carlson teaches the boys how to make ropes. The church choir gives a short concert after the school play."

"This reminds me of when I was growing up in Millbury," Rebecca said. "Where's the celebration held?"

"In Hank Carlson's barn behind the blacksmith. It takes a couple of days and a lot of work, but the men clear it out. Then the ladies start in on the decorations."

Passing the barbershop, Katy snapped her fingers. "Oh, I nearly forgot. That evening we have a dance to top it off. I think you'll be surprised at the talented musicians we have here in Winter Creek."

"I'm sure I won't attend the dance." She placed her hands on her swollen stomach. "Not like this."

"And what has that got to do with anything? If you can teach our children, you certainly can attend a dance. Anyway, there's not a soul in Winter Creek who won't be there."

"I'll think about it."

"Rebecca Quaid," Katy teased her, "you better do more than think about it." Both rushed into the mercantile to get out of the cold wind.

Paying no attention as to where they were walking, they ran into Wade Morgan. "Whoa, you ladies look like you're discussing something serious."

"I'm trying to talk Rebecca into attending the dance at Winter Creeks' celebration."

Wade frowned at Rebecca. "You can't miss the biggest gathering of the year."

"I'll give it some thought." Her face flushed.

"Lori would be disappointed if Ben and Hannah weren't there. I hope you change your mind and join us." He pulled his collar up. "You ladies have a good day." Then continued out the door.

"He's always so pleasant," said Katy. "He's such a fine man." She gave Rebecca a side glance. "Don't you think?"

"Now, Katy," Rebecca protested, "don't you start that again. I agree. He is a fine man."

Rebecca remembered Luke's words the night they arrived in Winter Creek. Though her fear that he and Jace would never return haunted her, her love for Luke hadn't changed.

Zeb pulled the wagon up to the school yard that afternoon. Rebecca and the children stepped from the schoolhouse door. "How about a ride home?" He hopped from the wagon seat and relieved Rebecca of her heavy satchel. Ben and Hannah jumped into the back of the wagon.

Rebecca hugged Zeb. "You're a wonderful sight after a long day with so many restless children. Winter Creek's celebration is all they can think or talk about."

He laughed. "I'm excited about it myself. It's been a while since we've enjoyed a good get together with friends. I miss those from the wagon train."

"I wonder about all the people we left when we came to Winter Creek. I try to visualize them getting closer to Oregon." She stared out across the meadow. "I know Millie's taking care of Jace for me, if they found him."

"Honey, I picture him riding alongside Luke scouting the trail for Captain Brenner." He patted her hand. "We're going to see him and Luke again one of these days."

He pulled the reins to slow the wagon when they neared the mercantile.

Paul stepped from the store. "Zeb, how's everything going?" Then he helped Rebecca from the wagon.

"Fine. Clara's home making a list of pies she's planning on bringing to the celebration." Zeb tussled Ben's hair before he jumped from the wagon.

Paul took Rebecca's satchel. "Katy's waiting in the kitchen with some hot tea for you both." Rebecca smiled and hurried in while Zeb and Paul resumed their visit.

Entering the kitchen, she got a whiff of the strong tea. Katy set a plate of freshly baked cookies on the table. Ben and Hannah rushed to the kitchen when they smelled the cookies. They each took one, thanked Katy, and ran to play before starting their homework.

Rebecca gave a heavy sigh and sat at the table. "How did you know what I needed?"

"After a long day, we both deserve it." Katy sat and blew on her tea to cool it.

Before they could relax, Paul came to the door. "Rebecca, I think you need to come to the front."

"Is it one of the children?"

"No. You just need to come quick."

Katy helped Rebecca from her chair and they rushed to the front. Approaching the counter, Rebecca saw a soldier resembling the ones Captain Brenner met with on the trail.

"This is Corporal Jennings," said Paul. "He and his men are here for supplies, but, Rebecca, he's from Fort Hall."

Rebecca came from behind the counter. "Corporal Jennings, do you know if the wagon train led by Captain Charles Brenner has made it to Fort Hall?"

"It came through the first week of August."

She stepped closer. "Was there a young man with them? He's tall and has auburn hair. A gang of outlaws captured him and another young man. Captain Brenner sent a rescue party to find them."

"Are you Mrs. Quaid?"

She grabbed his arm. "Yes, did they find my son?"

He nodded. "Corporal Halsey and his men found the two boys. Your son went with the wagon train on to Oregon."

"Thank God." She turned to Katy. "He's alive."

Rebecca clenched her fist. "What about the men who kidnapped my son?"

Katy put her arm around Rebecca to steady her.

"All but one was killed in the rescue attempt. That's why we're patrolling this territory. Frank Coulter, the last of the brothers, managed to get away. We've tracked him as far as Soda Springs, but it looks like he turned south."

"Is there any way to get word to Captain Brenner about my son?"

"Not after the wagon train left Fort Hall. There's no place between there and Dalles in the Oregon territory to send a telegram. I'm sorry, ma'am."

Paul filled the list of supplies for the Corporal and brought them to the counter. The soldier handed Paul the money, grabbed the tow sack of supplies, and turned to leave.

Katy led Rebecca to the bench and eased her down onto it.

Before walking out, the Corporal cautioned. "Frank Coulter's dangerous. If you see him, he's wanted dead or alive."

The second week of October brought the first freezing weather to Winter Creak. Rebecca sent Ben and Hannah to the kitchen after school to do their homework. She and Katy sat on the bench near the potbelly stove and listened to Paul and Zeb discuss the possibility of a stage line running through Winter Creek.

Paul stoked the stove. "Reverend Blackburn said when he was in Fort Bridger last there was talk of a stage line called the Overland Stage. Said they were looking for men to take charge of relay stations that'll be located about ten to fifteen miles apart."

"The commerce a stage line could bring to Winter Creek would certainly boost the economy." Zeb leaned against the counter and puffed on his pipe. "And we'd be able to have regular mail service."

Rebecca enjoyed hearing Paul and Zeb get excited about the community's possible prosperity. It confirmed her yearning even more to make her and her family's home in Winter Creek.

"There's plenty of places between here and Fort Hall and even Fort Bridger to build relay stations," said Paul. "If people traveling to Oregon or California could see what this part of the territory offered them, they might decide to settle right here. We have the finest timber, plenty of water, and the best land for growing wheat south of the Rocky Mountains."

Zeb stepped closer to the stove. "I know stage lines are used to deliver government mail out west now. So it's only a matter of time before they'll be coming our way. A stage line would make all the difference."

"Winter Creek has a telegraph line, businesses, a school, and even a doctor now." Paul pointed his finger in the air. "People coming from the east could thrive in Winter Creek."

Rebecca knew Jace believed their destiny depended on reaching Oregon. However, listening to Paul and Zeb made her heart quicken thinking Jace might never want to make Winter Creek his home.

Only a few more days before the Winter Creek annual celebration, and Ben stood at the counter in the mercantile staring at the jar of gumballs.

"Ben? Can I help you with something?" said Paul carrying a box of canned goods from the storeroom to the front counter.

Without looking, Ben answered. "No, Mr. Walters. I'm just counting these gumballs."

A large jar filled with colored gumballs sat on the counter just at Ben's eye level. Beside it, a sign read: "GUESS THE NUMBER AND WIN THE BUCKSKIN SCABBARD."

"Trying to win the scabbard, are you?"

"I'm going to win that scabbard. Grandpa and I've studied this jar." Ben had never seen a finer looking scabbard. And the fact that Mr. Carlson made it deepened his desire to own it.

"Have you picked your number yet?"

"Not yet." Ben scratched his head. "We're waiting until closer to the celebration."

"Well, I wish you luck. That's a nice scabbard Mr. Carlson donated."

Rebecca called from the back of the store. "Ben, Mr. Walters is trying to close the store. You can look at the jar tomorrow. And by the way, I think you've got homework waiting on you."

"Awe, Mamma."

CHAPTER THIRTY-FOUR

The third week in October, Winter Creek woke to their first snow of the season.

"Mamma, come see." Hannah's nose pressed against the kitchen windowpane. "It's like a fairyland." She turned from the window. "Come look, Ben."

He hurried from the table and peered out. "They won't call off the big party tomorrow night because of the snow, will they? I'm going to win that buckskin scabbard Mr. Carlson made. Blake Peterson says he is, but he's not."

"How do you know you're going to win it?" said Hannah.

"Because I know how many gumballs are in that jar."

"How do you know how many gumballs are in it?"

"I'm not telling you."

"You both need to get ready for school." Rebecca gathered their coats. "The snow may slow us down some this morning. Thanks to Grandpa, he'll have the school nice and warm for us."

Rebecca could hardly believe they were more than halfway into October. Each morning she counted the days to spring. If Jace didn't return until the flowers bloomed, her baby would be months old before he joined them.

In spite of the weather, most of her students arrived on time. Keeping them on task took most of her energy. The annual celebration consumed their interest.

Lori held up her hand. "Mrs. Quaid, have you seen Mr. Carlson's barn? Pa said all the ladies decorated it with pine boughs and red bunting."

"It's all going to be beautiful, but we need to finish our history lesson, and then we can talk about the party."

Ben waved his hand in the air. "Grandma said she's bringing three apple cobblers and—"

"Ben, no more about the party." Rebecca tapped the ruler in her hand. "If we don't finish our lessons you'll all have homework for Monday. Would you rather have homework or go to the party?"

Her students chorused. "Go to the party."

"Well, then let's get to work."

If it weren't for her students who filled her time and mind, Rebecca would be at a loss. Several times a day she caught herself daydreaming about the wagon train and Willamette Valley. She was glad Hank didn't know how his plans for his family detoured in so many different directions.

She presumed the wagon train must be getting close to their destination. Until Rebecca and the children reunited with Jace, she knew Hank's brother, Robert, and his family would take Jace in. But for her, waiting for spring to arrive might as well be an eternity. She ached to hold Jace in her arms again...and Luke.

Rebecca, Ben, Hannah, and the Calhouns walked from the mercantile down the wooden walkway toward Hank Carlson's barn. The snow added to the joy of the celebration.

From the outside, Hank's barn appeared the same as any other. However, stepping inside was like entering a wonderland filled with glowing lanterns and colorful trimmings. Everything from apple strudel to pickled peaches adorned the checkered, cloth-covered tables lining the east wall. Beautiful quilts of all patterns and colors hung on the north end of the barn.

Zeb felt Ben tug at his hand. "Let's go, Grandpa. I see the gumballs." Ben pulled him across the floor to the table holding the jar alongside the scabbard displayed on a mounted board.

"Grandpa, I can't wait till I win that scabbard."

"Ben boy, don't get your hopes up too high." Zeb tussled his air. "We made a good guess, but until they announce the exact number we won't know. Have you got your number?"

Ben took the ragged piece of paper from his pocket. "One hundred and seventy-three." He showed it to Zeb and took his hand. "This is the number, Grandpa. I just got to win it."

Paul stepped up to the table. "Attention everyone. If I could have your attention, please." A smile spread over Ben's face which made Zeb smile. Paul picked up the scabbard and held it high for everyone to see.

Ben mumbled. "Tell us the number."

"And the winning number is…one hundred and seventy-five."

Toby Gentry hollered. "Yahoo! I have the number!"

The crowd separated to make a path for Toby to retrieve the scabbard.

Ben's hand dropped from Zeb's.

Zeb rubbed Ben's head. "You weren't that far off. You just missed it by two numbers."

Ben raised his eyes at Zeb. Tears welled up. His lower lip quivered. "I just knew I was going to win that scabbard, Grandpa."

Zeb's heart ached for Ben. He gently steered him away from the crowd and got a glimpse of Rebecca and Clara. Rebecca rose but sat back down when Clara took her hand and whispered something in her ear.

"Let's go get some fruit punch," said Zeb. "And I see a piece of Grandma's pie waiting on you."

Ben lowered his head and walked alongside Zeb. Halfway across the floor, he said, "I'm not hungry."

"Disappointment can surely take your appetite. Why don't we sit over here for a while?"

Zeb found a bench in the corner away from the crowd. They sat down. "Things don't always work out the way we'd like them to."

Ben sniffed and wiped his eyes.

"We have to learn some hard lessons as we go along. Disappointment's one of the big ones. It happens to us no matter how old we are or how much we know."

Zeb pulled a clean handkerchief from his pocket and handed it to Ben. "Wipe your face and blow your nose."

He eyed Clara and Rebecca. "I think I see Grandma and your mamma waving at us. Looks like Grandma saved you a big plate of apple pie. Now we don't want to hurt her feelings, so we better get over there."

Ben blew his nose, crumpled the used handkerchief, and gave it back to Zeb. Before they got up, Ben said, "Grandpa, I just knew I was going to win." He sighed. "But if I can't have the scabbard, I'm glad Toby got it."

Zeb's heart wanted to burst. He loved Ben more than he could ever tell him.

Throughout the evening, Rebecca enjoyed the judging of the contests. Mrs. Franklin could have used some wise words from Zeb after losing the first-place ribbon to Mrs. Jenkins for the knitting contest. Rebecca overheard her words snap with sarcasm when she congratulated Mrs. Jenkins on the fair job she did on her project.

The musicians warmed up while the men stoked the fire and the women gathered empty plates. Rebecca's mind traveled back to Ash Hollow. She remembered the music while Luke held her in his arms. She loved Winter Creek but missed the wagon train, as difficult as the days were. Her heart ached to see those who became like family to her. She closed her eyes trying to picture Jace's face…and Luke's.

"Rebecca?" She opened her eyes to see Wade Morgan. "I'm glad you decided to stay for the dance." He held out his hand. "Would you do me the honor?"

Rebecca's face flushed and she shook her head. "I really shouldn't."

"Please, Rebecca. Just one dance?"

Reluctantly, Rebecca took his hand and he led her to the dance floor. After a few steps, he smiled down at her. "You dance well."

"Thank you. You're a very good dancer yourself."

As hesitant as Rebecca was about being there, no one seemed to notice or be concerned with her situation. She and Wade laughed and danced as though they were old friends.

CHAPTER THIRTY-FIVE

The third week of October brought the wagon train within a few miles of Dalles. This was where the wagon wheel ruts stopped. Captain Brenner knew from this point there were two options the emigrants could take to get to Oregon City in the Willamette Valley. His job was to convince the families to take Barlow Road rather than raft their wagons down the Columbia River.

After supper, Captain Brenner called the families together at his wagon. "We should reach Dalles sometime tomorrow afternoon. You're going to find it to be a thriving city because of the Columbia River. Wagons wait for days, even weeks, and pay overpriced fees for the ferry boats to take them down the river to Oregon City. The Columbia River is treacherous at best. The chances of wagons capsizing and floating sideways occur more times than not."

Carl motioned toward the captain. "But will it save us some time?"

"It will, but you could be risking you and your family drowning in its swift current. If we take the Barlow Road around the southern portion of Mt. Hood it will get us over the Cascades and into the valley. When we reach the Barlow Pass at the summit of the Cascades, Oregon City will be in our sights."

The captain knew both routes and each carried serious hazards. The emigrants would face their greatest hardships on this last trek of the trail.

Arriving in Dalles, the wagon train gathered not far from the group of wagons waiting for the next ferry boat.

Millie, Penelope, and Molly made their way to the mercantile and numerous shops that lined the main street. Passing a dress shop, Penelope stopped and gazed through the window. "Have you ever seen a more beautiful dress?" She jostled Mary Martha in her arms.

"No. and look at the bonnets and hats." Millie looked down at her dress and sighed. "The dusty trail has ruined every dress I own." She could hardly remember what it was like to have a new dress.

"I wish I could talk Hugh into staying in Dalles," said Molly, "rather than climbing those mountains to get to Oregon City. I'm ready to stay in one place and never see another covered wagon again."

"I think every woman on the wagon train feels the same way." Millie laughed. "If most women made the choice of moving west, Oregon would probably still be unsettled."

Millie peered at all the businesses and homes that made up Dalles. A white, clapboard church sat at the end of the street. "I'm praying Willamette Valley will meet all our expectations."

First thing after arriving in Dalles, Luke searched out the telegraph office knowing Rebecca's concern over Jace. At noon, he, Captain Brenner, Jace, Nate, and Pete ate by the chuck wagon. Luke sat on a bench beside the wagon wheel. He said to Jace, "I'm sure your mother will be relieved to know you're okay. The telegrapher didn't know when she would receive my telegram. He sent it to Fort Hall. They'll send it on to Winter Creek."

Jace nodded. "Thanks for taking care of that."

"I reminded her I'd be back her way sometime in the spring." He waited for Jace to respond. When he didn't, Luke said, "If you decide to settle in Oregon, there's always wagon trains headed this way. You could meet up with your ma and the Calhouns at Fort Hall."

Captain Brenner stood and put on his gloves. "With what we're facing before we reach Willamette Valley, you may wish you were with your mother in Winter Creek." He glanced at Luke. "Bob Allen and Joseph Jenkins have decided to risk taking the Columbia River. They're staying in Dalles until they can secure a ferry boat."

"Did you let the rest of the caravan know there's a five-dollar fee for each wagon traveling Barlow Road? Plus ten cents for each head of livestock."

"Yeah, but it's still cheaper than the ferries and a lot safer."

Captain Brenner gave everyone the afternoon to restock their wagons. The next morning he ordered the caravan to line up and push forward continuing on the trail to Willamette Valley.

Scaling the snow-capped Cascade by way of Barlow Road proved the most demanding of the trail. The wagon train encountered steep inclines and heart-stopping descents. By the first of November, the caravan reached Barlow Pass which crested the Cascade Mountains.

From the summit, Luke and Jace surveyed the vast landscape. "There it is." Luke shielded his face from the cold wind with his bandana. "Oregon City. You're looking at Willamette Valley."

"I wish Pa was here to see this." Jace gazed at the land he dreamed of settling.

"Even though we can see Oregon City," said Luke, "there could be some animals that aren't going to make it. Our supplies are nearly gone and with the snow and wind we haven't seen any fresh game in days."

Luke knew these people were tough and determined, but the two-thousand-mile journey had them ragged and hungry.

"Carl's down to one ox." Jace pulled his hat brim down.

"We have about two more weeks before we reach Oregon City." Luke reined his horse around. "The captain wants to slow our pace going down the mountain. We can't push the animals any harder or we won't have enough to get us to the valley."

In mid-November, the wagon train followed Captain Brenner into a wide, creek-fed meadow near the Willamette Valley. After months of dry, dusty prairies, difficult mountain passes, and unbearable exhaustion, civilization awaited them. The excitement of reaching their final destination buzzed throughout the campsites. Though Jace could sense an air of mixed emotions knowing the possibility they would never see each other again. Some of these people were as much family to him as his mother and siblings, especially Luke.

For the last time, Pete sounded the bugle to circle up for the night camp. Captain Brenner called to Jace. "You and Nate water the oxen before gathering them inside the formation." He motioned to Luke. "Let everybody know this'll be our last night together as a wagon train. Oh, and Luke, I'll settle up with you and Pete's wages after supper tonight."

Jace and Nate walked the animals to the creek with very little conversation. After a spell, Nate said, "You got plans now that we made it to Oregon?"

"Pa talked a blue streak about moving here to be near his brother. I haven't seen Uncle Rob since I was about ten. He wouldn't know Ben and Hannah if he saw them now."

"You haven't talked this much in a long time," said Nate.

Jace shook his head. "It's a funny thing. For a while now, I haven't had much to say. I've been trying to sort things out." He stopped and turned to Nate. "I want you to know you're a good friend. Through all of this, you've stuck by my side, and I know there have been times I treated you bad. I hope you can forgive me."

Nate's eyes widened. "How could I not be your friend? You've saved my life twice. I wouldn't be here if it weren't for you." Nate paused. "Have you talked to Ellen?"

Jace frowned. "Yeah."

"Yeah what? For weeks she hounded me about you. Now that you've talked is everything normal again?"

"Not really. Anyway, when the wagon train breaks up, we'll probably never see each other again."

Captain Brenner stood at the chuck wagon that evening handing out wages to the cowhands, Pete, Nate, and Luke. The cold wind caused the wagon canvas to flap. Jace huddled near the campfire working on a bridle bit.

"Jace," called the captain.

He got up and walked over to Captain Brenner. When the captain handed him his wages, he shook his head. "I can't take this." Jace handed it back to him. "You fed me and kept me on so I could get to Oregon."

"Son, you worked right alongside the other hands. You work, you get paid." The captain pulled something from his pocket and handed it to Jace. "Here, this is yours."

Jace stared at it and swallowed hard. "Pa's watch. I traded it in Fort Hall. How—"

"It doesn't make any difference how. That watch belongs to you."

"But I don't deserve it."

"Deserving doesn't have anything to do with it. If that was the case none of us would be worthy of a thing."

Jace offered his hand. "Thank you. And, Captain, I'm sorry about—"

He put his hand up. "Everybody has to figure out how to deal with their troubles. Sometimes it takes a while to get over things. But I'm here to tell you, God has a way of easing our pain if we'll let Him."

"Mamma taught me that as far back as I can remember. Pa was a forgiving man too."

"You thought about what you're going to do?"

Jace shook his head. "Not really. I need to find Uncle Rob. His land is near Oregon City. It shouldn't be hard to find him."

Jace, Luke, and the captain moved closer to the fire. Pouring himself a cup of coffee, Luke shivered. "That north wind cuts to the bone."

"Mr. Barker," said Jace, "are you going back to Missouri with the captain?"

"I'm not sure. I noticed a lot of good grassland around Winter Creek. I've managed to save up a little money. I could see where cattle could thrive on that land."

"My pa always talked about raising cattle on good wheat ground."

Luke warmed his hands near the fire. "There's plenty of land in this country. A person could make a good life for himself building a ranch and home."

CHAPTER THIRTY-SIX

November rolled into the first day of December and Rebecca found teaching to be a joyful part of her life while preparing for her new arrival. Each day her normal chores took a little more time and effort. However, receiving Luke's telegram of Jace's rescue gave her even more to be grateful for. Though spring seemed so far off.

She peered out the store front window that morning to see Winter Creek with a new layer of snow. She and the children bundled up and waited just inside the mercantile for Zeb to pick them up for school. But instead, Wade and Lori pulled up in their two-seater buckboard and waved for them to come out. Lori sat in the rear seat wrapped in a lap blanket.

Rebecca and the children hurried out the door. Rebecca stopped at the hitching post. She grabbed on to it with one hand and with the other hand she held her satchel. Ben and Hannah ran and hopped into the rear seat with Lori. Rebecca called to them. "Grandpa's picking us up this morning."

Wade jumped from the buckboard and went around to the hitching post to help Rebecca. "I told Zeb I would be glad to come fetch you and the children."

"You didn't have to do that," Rebecca said. She tightened her lips. "It's out of your way to come into town."

"Not at all. I wanted to make sure you got to school safely."

With her due date not far off, she struggled to step up onto the wagon seat with Wade's help. He took the lap blanket and covered Rebecca before circling back around the wagon. "You need to be especially careful now."

"Thank you," she worked to be gracious, "but I'm fine."

"You look fine. In fact, you look beautiful this morning."

Rebecca blushed. "I don't know how you can say that." She took a deep breath and laughed. "I'm barely able to squeeze through the aisles at the mercantile and I still have three more weeks."

"By that time, it will be Christmas."

Approaching the schoolhouse, Wade reined in the horse. Smoke rose from the chimney as evidence Zeb had been there. Wade hurried to the other side of the wagon and took Rebecca's hand. Before she stepped from the wagon, she jerked and grabbed her stomach.

"Wade." She grabbed his arm and moaned. "Get me to Zeb and Clara's." She gripped the side of the wagon seat. Her face twisted with pain.

"Go on into the schoolhouse, children," said Wade. "I'll send Mr. Calhoun to stay with you."

Hannah cried. "But Mamma."

"Do as he says." Rebecca tried to smile. "I'm fine. Now go on to school."

Wade jumped back into the wagon. "Is it the baby?"

"Yes, but there's something wrong."

He slapped the reins and hurried to the Calhoun's house.

Late that evening, Dr. Jones walked from the bedroom where Rebecca writhed. She joined Zeb, Clara, and Wade in the kitchen. "Clara, can you stay with Rebecca for a few minutes?"

Wade stood. "It's been hours. Are she and the baby going to be all right?"

Dr. Jones sat at the table, and Zeb brought her a cup of coffee. As he set it down, he asked, "Doc, can you tell us what's wrong?"

She stared at her cup. "She's not due for another three weeks at least, but her contractions are getting worse. The baby's breech. A natural delivery is too dangerous on Rebecca and the baby at this point. They both could die."

Wade pulled a chair in front of the doctor, turned it around, and straddled it. "There has to be something you can do. You must have learned something in medical school that could help her."

"Yes, I did." Dr. Jones stood and walked to the window. "But there are risks to the procedure."

"Tell us. What is it?" Wade stood.

She stared at him. "It's called a cesarean and is basically a surgical procedure."

"I've never heard of it," said Zeb.

"It's done in larger hospitals and not that common here."

"Can you do it?" said Wade. "Because if you don't she could die."

Dr. Jones headed toward the bedroom. "Wade, can you get her to my office?"

Wade followed her into the bedroom. Clara and Dr. Jones wrapped Rebecca in a blanket. Wade scooped her up into his arms. She cried out with pain and moaned when he laid her in the bed of the wagon.

Besides risking the lives of Rebecca and her baby, the doctor knew if she was unsuccessful she would lose any trust she had gained in Winter Creek. She could lose her practice.

The procedure was a success. Zeb and Clara couldn't take their eyes off of Hank Matthew Quaid. "Rebecca, honey, he's beautiful," said Clara. Tears glistened her eyes. "Zeb and I never imagined ourselves with grandchildren and now you've given us another. Are you going to call him Hank after his pa?"

Rebecca studied her son's face. "I thought about it, but I think we'll call him Matthew." She lightly rubbed his cheek. "You were supposed to be born in Oregon." She grinned. "We didn't quite make it, did we?" Rebecca turned to Clara. "And you were right all along. He is a precious gift. I just wish Hank was here to see him... and Jace and Luke."

The cold weather hung on not wanting to succumb to spring. Nevertheless, with April came crocuses pushing up through the ground all over town, and the early rains caused the grass to flourish. Winter Creek came alive with colorful wildflowers. But the beauty of the landscape, along with baby Matthew, couldn't throw off the gloom that plagued Rebecca.

Early one spring morning as Rebecca rushed out of the mercantile, she met Wade coming in. He hugged and greeted her.

"You're in a hurry this morning. And it's awfully early for you to be out. School doesn't start for another hour."

She sighed. "I know, but I couldn't sleep. I wake every morning thinking this is the day Luke will bring Jace back to me."

Wade's expression softened. "Waiting can get mighty burdensome. I know you miss your son. I certainly would if it were my Lori."

Rebecca couldn't help but be drawn to his warm smile. She waved her hand as if to brush away her gloom. "I have to keep reminding myself that God's timing is perfect. I trust they'll be riding into Winter Creek soon."

"Could I brighten your day by asking you and the children to have supper with Lori and me? I promised her she wouldn't have to eat my cooking tonight. We were going to eat at the café."

"I'm sorry. We're having supper with Clara and Zeb." She smiled. "But I'm sure she'd have plenty if you and Lori wanted to join us. She cooks as if she's expecting a bunch of ranch hands."

"You're sure it's okay?"

She smiled. "I'm sure. I'll see her—"

A man on horseback rode by and caught Rebecca's attention.

"Rebecca, what is it? Your face is pale."

She pointed down the street. "Do you know that man?"

He stared in the direction of the rider. "No, I've never seen him before. Why?"

"I must have mistaken him for someone else." She forced a smile. "I need to get to school."

Heading down the walk, Rebecca's mind reeled. Him. He's back. The wanted picture burned in her mind. The rider had to be one of the Coulter brothers. She called for the children and they hurried through the meadow to the schoolhouse.

When they got near the school, Clara hollered from across the way. "Ben, Hannah. I have sweet rolls for you this morning."

Rebecca smiled at her children. "Go ahead. Just don't be late for school." Rebecca stepped inside the warm schoolhouse.

Zeb stoked the fire in the potbelly stove. "Morning," he said. "There's still a chill in the air. Thought you might need a little heat."

Rebecca put her things on her desk and turned to the blackboard. She worked to erase the previous day's arithmetic problems. "What would I do without you and Clara? And speaking of Clara, do you think she would mind if Wade and Lori join us for supper tonight?"

"Why, my goodness no. You know Clara. She loves to show off her cooking." He hesitated, then said, "Rebecca, honey, have you noticed Wade's getting sweet on you."

She stopped erasing and turned to him. "I know. His intentions are so pure and he's so kind."

He hesitated then spoke. "Forgive me if I'm sticking my nose where it's not wanted, but Clara and I see how you shine when Luke's name is mentioned."

She put the eraser in the tray. "Oh, Zeb. Luke told me he'd be back in the spring. He and Jace are on my mind continually."

"One of these days we'll look up and they'll be riding up. Faith, honey, that's what we hang on to."

She gave Zeb a hug and dabbed at her eyes. "Tell Clara I'll bring an apple cobbler I baked last night. And I'll tell Wade as kindly as I can how I feel about Luke."

Zeb's eyes sparkled. "Say, where's little Matthew this morning?"

"Katy wanted to babysit him today. I don't know how I've been so lucky to have Katy and Clara to help watch him while I'm at school." She sighed. "As much as I love teaching, I miss him during the day."

"Clara loves that child."

She grinned. "The truth is, my children think you belong to them."

Zeb picked up the wood pail and went out the back door of the school while Rebecca headed for the front doors to ring the morning bell. The rest of the day she worked at pushing the rider out of her mind.

CHAPTER THIRTY-SEVEN

Spring gave way to summer and Rebecca forgot about the stranger she saw in Winter Creek several weeks earlier. Though, she continued to wake each morning with the hope Jace and Luke would soon return to her.

However, the big news for Winter Creek was the stage line. Mr. Peterson, at the telegraph office, received news of the Overland Stage line's decision to open a run through Winter Creek starting within the month. The company established several relay stations between Fort Hall, Winter Creek, and Fort Bridger.

Zeb and Ben walked into the mercantile, and Zeb gave Paul a friendly slap on the back. "The stage line is the beginning of big things for Winter Creek. Mrs. Owens may need to add on to her boardinghouse."

"Having regular mail and newspaper deliveries," said Paul, "could sure keep us up on what's happening in the east. The last time I was in Fort Hall, I heard there might be a railroad stretching from the Nebraska territory all the way to the Pacific."

Zeb puffed on his pipe. "Times are changing, and Winter Creek needs to be ready."

"The stage line is a sure sign of commerce," said Paul. "With so many people coming west, businesses could boom. This could mean statehood. Texas has been a state since '47. We could certainly be next."

School dismissed for the summer and the warm mornings felt good to Rebecca after such a frosty winter. She and Katy stood near the front window of the mercantile counting bolts of fabric just delivered from the east. Rebecca ran her hand over the cloth. "I can see Hannah in a dress and bonnet out of this pattern."

"It is beautiful, isn't it? But if you want it, you better get it now. You know how fast things fly out of the store. Paul can't keep up with the orders."

Rebecca looked up from her receipt book. "What a nice problem to ..." She glanced across the merchandise and glimpsed a man staring at her.

Katy frowned. "Rebecca, what is it?"

Before she could reply, Toby Gentry hurried into the store calling. "Mrs. Quaid, Mrs. Quaid. Mr. Peterson said to deliver this to you." He handed her a telegram.

Rebecca took the piece of paper, but not before she noticed the man look straight at her then leave the store. "Thank you, Toby." She ripped opened the telegram.

"What is it?" Katy said. "What does it say? Is it from Jace or Luke?"

Rebecca read the address. "It's from Oregon City. No, wait. The original telegram was sent from Millbury, Massachusetts." Her expression got sullen. "It says my mother and father were killed when another horse-drawn buggy collided with theirs." She examined the signature. "It's signed by Anthony Bassett, Attorney at Law."

"Rebecca, I'm so sorry."

She continued to read. "It happened over a year ago." She studied the telegram trying to make sense of it. "That was just after we left Cutter Springs."

"How did Mr. Bassett know to send it to Winter Creek?"

Rebecca kept reading. "He hired someone from a detective agency, a Mr. Drake. Somehow he learned I was with a wagon train led by Captain Charles Brenner." She paused. "The captain must have sent this from Oregon City. That means Luke and Jace should have been here by now."

Katy grabbed Rebecca by the shoulders. "Rebecca, don't read something into this that's not there. Now read the telegram. Is there any more?"

Rebecca took a breath and focused. "There's something about a will." Her forehead wrinkled. "A will? Katy, I don't understand. When I married Hank they disinherited me. They made it clear I was no longer a part of their family."

"Well, evidently, they had a change of heart."

"It says Mr. Bassett needs me to telegraph him as soon as possible."

Katy walked Rebecca over to a bench. When they sat, Rebecca caught a glimpse of the man peering at her again through the front windows of the store.

The summer months gave Rebecca more time to be with Ben, Hannah, and Matthew. In the evenings when the heat cooled from the breeze floating down from the mountains, she enjoyed sitting on Zeb and Clara's front porch watching Ben and Hannah play. Rebecca and Clara sat in rocking chairs and took turns holding the baby. The three of them would spend hours reminiscing about the families left back on the wagon train.

Crickets chirped while Clara hummed a lullaby and rocked Matthew.

Rebecca leaned forward in her chair. "Would you like for me to take him for a while?"

"Oh, no child. There's nothing more comforting than holding a sleeping baby." She smiled down at his sweet face. "I see Ben and Hannah when I look at him."

"He has Hank and Jace's eyes." Rebecca sat back and rested her head on the back of the chair. "Isn't it strange how our lives take odd turns?"

"Honey, when we're born into this world there are very few things we're in control of. The Lord makes our way for His purpose."

"I know Hank was set on settling in Willamette Valley, but I find myself being so grateful living here in Winter Creek with you and Zeb. The children are happy, and I so enjoy teaching." Rebecca laughed. "I'll never forget our first night in Winter Creek. The very thought of living in the rooms behind the mercantile was so disheartening. I knew Hank wouldn't want that for his family. But Katy and Paul managed to create a home for us, a home that's perfect for now."

"Look Mamma." Hannah yelled, gazing into the sky. "A falling star."

"Did you make a wish, Hannah?" hollered Ben.

She thought for a second. "Yes. I wished for Jace to come home."

Rebecca squeezed her eyes to push the tears back. Clara reached over and took her hand.

Ben and Hannah ran up the steps of the porch. He held up a jar. "Look Grandpa. I caught ten fireflies. I got more than Hannah."

"Why, Ben boy, that's a bunch."

Rebecca stood. "I think it's time we started home."

Zeb rose to get the buckboard. "Let me give you a ride."

"No, you don't need to hitch up the horse. As bright as the moon is tonight, it'll light our way across the meadow." She bent down and took little Matthew in her arms. "Ben, Hannah, say good night."

Zeb took his pipe from his mouth. He looked down at little Matthew. "God gave us a family we never thought we'd have."

CHAPTER THIRTY-EIGHT

The first of August marked a year since Rebecca and the children moved to Winter Creek. Memories of the difficult challenges she and her family lived through on the wagon train lessened. Her belief that Jace and Luke would return diminished as well.

She found teaching deepened her sense of belonging in Winter Creek. Taking advantage of some free time, Rebecca walked to the schoolhouse during the warm afternoon to start preparations for the new school year. After an hour of organizing her lesson plans, she gazed out the window at the meadow resembling a canvas covered with beautiful yellow wildflowers.

At her desk, Rebecca bowed her head. "Lord, you've placed us where we can thrive. Thank you for your gift of salvation. Reverend Blackburn reminds us each week of your unconditional love. Thank you for my children and Zeb and Clara. And, Lord, I know you're with Jace and Luke. You know how much I miss and love them. Please bring them back to me. Amen."

She raised her head to see Wade Morgan standing by the stove. He took his hat off. "I'm sorry. I didn't mean to eavesdrop on your prayer."

"No, don't apologize. I didn't hear you come in." She stood and slid her lesson plans into her satchel. "I'm finished for today." She came from behind the desk.

Wade strode toward her. "Rebecca, I'm going to speak honestly with you."

She put her hand up. "Please, Wade."

"No, I need to say these words to you. From what Zeb told me," he fidgeted with his hat, "and from your prayer, there's someone from the wagon train you care for." Moving a step closer, he continued, "I can't go up against someone I've never met. But he's not here and I am. And I care for you. Rebecca, I've fallen in love with you."

Rebecca gripped her satchel. "Wade." Her mind scrambled to find the right words. "You're one of the kindest men I've ever known. You have a warm and generous heart. But—"

"How long are you going to wait for this man to come back to you? I can give you and your children a fine home and a good life."

Her heart pounded. "I know you can, but I can't do that to you or Lori. As fond as I am of you, I don't love you." His anguished look caused her heart to ache. "I have no idea if I'll ever see Luke again, but I could never marry anyone feeling the way I do about him. Please understand. I don't want to hurt you."

Wade's eyes pleaded to at least consider his proposal. Rebecca stood silent. He exhaled and stepped back. "I'm sorry if I put you in an awkward situation. But I had to tell you how I felt about you."

"Oh, Wade, I wish things were different, I really do."

"I hope I haven't hurt our friendship." He stood in the middle of the schoolroom, then put his hat on. "You know if you ever need anything, I'm here for you."

"I know. And your friendship means so much to me."

"I only want the best for you." He turned and slowly walked out.

Rebecca sat back down. Her heart was heavy. *He's right. I may never see Luke or Jace again.* She covered her face with her hands.

Three weeks into August, the Overland Stage line ran through Winter Creek twice a week. Hank Carlson offered the use of his blacksmith and barns as a place to keep fresh horses. The stage line compensated Hank for feed and keeping the horses shod. Zeb became Hank's right-hand man for the scheduled arrivals each Tuesday and Thursday.

Ben tugged on Zeb's arm. "Grandpa, can I help the next time the stage comes in? I can feed and water the horses."

"If it's okay with your mamma and Mr. Carlson, I could sure use your help."

Ben ran as fast as he could across the meadow to the schoolhouse to ask his mother. He rushed into the school and scrambled between the rows of desk. Rebecca sat writing arithmetic exercises for the coming school year. He gasped for air and leaned across her desk.

"Mamma." He took a breath. The words tumbled out. "Grandpa said I could help him with the stage line next time they come through if it's okay with you, oh, and Mr. Carlson."

"Whoa, Ben, slow down."

He took a couple of breaths. "Grandpa needs me to help him with the horses. He said he'd ask Mr. Carlson if it would be okay." He wiped his forehead.

"Well…"

"Please, Mamma, Grandpa really needs me." The more he begged, the more he fidgeted.

"I'll need to talk with Grandpa and Mr. Carlson to make sure it's okay."

Ben toyed with a ruler lying on Rebecca's desk. "Can you talk to them now before the stage gets here?"

She placed her hand over his. "Honey, this is Friday and the stage isn't due until Tuesday. I think I'll have plenty of time to discuss it with them. Now, you need to go clean the chicken coop." Rebecca took the ruler and put it in a drawer.

He frowned. "Now? But I need to go back to the blacksmith."

"Yes, now. Tell Hannah to help you."

He turned and drug his heels across the wood floor toward the front door.

From the window on her right, Rebecca caught a glimpse of a rider approaching the front of the school. When she recognized him, she dropped her pen and knocked over her ink bottle.

Frank Coulter. He dismounted and headed for the front steps.

The ink soaked into the papers on her desk.

She stood and hollered at Ben. "Go out the back door and run get Sheriff Waters."

"But what about the chick—"

"Now Ben. Run as fast as you can. Now."

He ran out of the back door at the same time Frank Coulter walked in the front. Rebecca's heart pounded in her chest. Lord, help me. His eyes glinted at her just as his brother's did over a year ago.

He ambled toward her. When he reached her desk, he asked, "Your last name Quaid?"

Rebecca trembled but tried to stay calm. "Yes, I'm Mrs. Quaid."

A smile spread across his face. He pressed his hands on the desk and leaned toward her. "You're the one." He straightened. "I never thought it would be a woman who killed my brother." Smirking, he said, "You're better looking than the picture in the watch."

Rebecca's body stiffened when she saw his two fingers missing. "The sher—"

"Shut up! I'm the only one talkin' here." He reached across the desk and grabbed her arm. "Lady, you're gonna pay. I've been wantin' to do this for a long time. And if it hadn't been for those soldiers traipsin' after me you'd been dead long ago. You're gonna get just what you gave my brother."

Rebecca tried to scream.

He yanked her arm toward him and grabbed her neck with his other hand. Then taking both hands, he tightened his grip, lifting her off the floor.

He sneered. Spittle drooled from his mouth. "You're gonna wish you'd never laid eyes on my brother."

Rebecca scratched his hands trying to loosen his grasp and struggled for air.

He squeezed harder and pulled her across the desk, the black ink soaking into her dress.

She grabbed a pair of scissors, aimed at him, and stabbed his shoulder.

His eyes widened, and he yelled in pain. He let go of her, pulled the scissors from the wound, and threw them across the room. He slapped Rebecca with the back of his hand.

She fell to the floor. Rebecca shook her head then jumped to her feet. She ran for the back door, but he grabbed a handful of her hair. She screamed, but his hands wrapped around her throat again. He lifted her up by the neck, her feet thrashing. She couldn't breathe. Her ears rang, and her head pounded with each heartbeat.

He slung her around until her body fell limp. With her brain starved for oxygen, a wave of peace flowed through her as if she were floating under water.

A gunshot rang out. Footsteps. She struggled to open her eyes then fell to the floor. A heavy object landed on top of her. The man's grip loosened, and she tried to breathe. Couldn't. Too much weight on top of her.

The heavy object rolled off of her. She gulped in air. Her throat throbbed. The smell of gunpowder permeated the air. She opened her eyes and worked to focus. The room swirled.

"Rebecca, Rebecca. Breathe. Open your eyes and breathe. Rebecca. You're going to be okay."

That voice. She should know that voice. She opened her eyes. "Luke." She reached up and touched his face. "Luke, it's really you."

He cradled her in his arms. They held on to each other until finally finding the courage she asked, "Where's Jace?"

Ben, Jace, and Sheriff Waters rushed through the front door. The sheriff bent over the dead man lying on the floor. "That's Frank Coulter all right. And he's dead." He turned to Rebecca. "Are you okay? Don't move till we get Doc Jones."

Ben and Jace gathered over Rebecca. "Mamma. Mamma. Look, it's Jace. Jace came home."

Jace gazed into his mother's eyes. "I'm home, Mamma." He glanced at the dead body. "We don't have to worry about the Coulter brother's anymore." He took Rebecca's hand. "I've missed you, and Ben, and Hannah."

Ben laughed. "And Matthew. You don't know him yet."

Pulling Rebecca toward him, Luke peered into her eyes. "We're all home." Then turned to Jace and Ben. "And with your children's consent," he smiled down at Rebecca, "will you marry me? I love you Rebecca Quaid and your family."

Tears glistened her eyes. "Luke Barker, I love you. Yes, I'll marry you."

EPILOGUE

Winter Creek 1891

Ellen Quaid surveyed the expansion of acres surrounding their large, two-story house. As far as she could see, wheat and grassland spread west. The Snake River cut through the valley leaving numerous tributaries. Seven thousand head of cattle grazed the hundred-thousand-acre ranch.

A sign bearing 'LJ RANCH' hung over the gate at the entrance. Numerous corrals and cattle pens dotted the acreage, along with a bunkhouse, a red barn, a stable, and a smokehouse. Lying peacefully in the family cemetery under the large oak tree were Luke, Rebecca, Zeb, Clara, Hannah, among others.

Annie, the long-time housekeeper, walked out onto the large porch that stretched across the front of the house. "Ma'am, how many chickens you want us to fry for the party?"

"I think ten at least," Ellen said. "You know how those grandchildren love fried chicken."

A fiftieth birthday celebration for her husband, Jace, was eagerly anticipated by all their children and grandchildren.

"Yes, ma'am." Annie laughed. "I've never seen children eat as much as those little babies can." She pointed to the barn. "The beef is roasting in the pit. The cowhands will bring it to the kitchen when it's ready."

"Thank you. Oh and, Annie, I'll help you ice the cake. We need to have everything ready by five o'clock. Though, it wouldn't surprise me if everyone started showing up before then."

Nana, as Ellen's grandchildren called her, felt the morning heat rising. She mopped her forehead with a lace handkerchief. "It's June all right. Lord, can you bless us with a cool mountain breeze this evening? I'd sure appreciate it."

The list of chores still waiting for her attention ran through her mind. She stuffed her handkerchief in her pocket and rushed to the kitchen.

The clock in the entry struck five times. Upstairs, Jace and Ellen heard Annie calling, "They're here."

"Papa, did you hear Annie? Are you ready to go downstairs?" Ellen grinned. "The grandbabies are as excited about your birthday as if it were theirs."

He smiled. But before they started downstairs, he pulled her close. "Nothing could make me happier on my birthday than you." He kissed her as though they were young sweethearts.

Her heart fluttered remembering the first time that happened. "Papa, you've made me so happy all these years."

Jace and Ellen descended from the staircase and stepped onto the porch. The children and grandchildren deluged them with hugs and laughter.

"Papa," said six-year-old Ben, "it's your birthday. Nana baked you a cake."

"It is my birthday, Ben. And I can't wait to taste Nana's cake."

After devouring the fried chicken and birthday cake, the children played in the yard while the grown-ups relaxed in rocking chairs on the front porch and enjoyed the mild evening breeze.

Before too long, all the children gathered on the porch around their Papa.

Little Ben put a hand on his arm. "Will you tell us the story again?"

"Well, Ben, I've told it so many times, I bet you could tell it to me." Jace tussled Ben's hair and grinned.

"Please tell us again," said Betsy, Ellen and Jace's oldest grand-daughter. "We want to hear how you and Nana met."

Ben stood by his Papa. "Can we see the watch again?"

Jace reached in and pulled the gold watch from his pocket. Handing it to his oldest grandson, Jace said, "Daniel, can you read it?"

Daniel turned it over and read: "Hank Matthew Quaid, September 1852." He opened it, and each grandchild got to look at the picture inside. When Ben saw it, he said, "This is your mamma when she was young, right, Papa?"

"Yes, her name was Rebecca Quaid Barker. She helped settle this country."

"Oh, please, tell us the story," said Betsy hopping up and down.

Jace glanced at Ellen. She reached over and put her hand on his. Then he started. "When I was fifteen years old, my family and I left Cutter Springs in the Kansas territory. We headed north to meet a wagon train going west, known as the Oregon Trail."

THE END

Made in the USA
Monee, IL
20 February 2021